THE WORMHOLE SCREAMED . . .

Kira sensed rather than heard it, as though the spine inside her shivered at the same mute pitch. A living thing—its pain struck her once more.

Watching from the outside, Kira saw that there was no light—the wormhole drew darkness into itself, a writhing contraction of space itself.

Kira leaned over the viewscreen. *Bashir is in there.* The thoughts inside her head had contracted to one alone. *Inside . . . somewhere . . .*

Look for these titles in the
STAR TREK: DEEP SPACE NINE series
from Pocket Books

#1   Emissary
#2   The Siege
#3   Bloodletter

coming soon:

#4   The Big Game

STAR TREK®
DEEP SPACE NINE™

BLOODLETTER

K.W. JETER

POCKET BOOKS

New York   London   Toronto   Sydney   Tokyo   Singapore

First published in Great Britain by Pocket Books, 1993
An imprint of Simon & Schuster Ltd
A Paramount Communications Company

Simon & Schuster Ltd
West Garden Place
Kendal Street
London W2 2AQ

A CIP catalogue record for this book is available from the
British Library.

ISBN 0–671–85238–8

Printed in Great Britain by
Harper*Collins* Manufacturing, Glasgow

To Chris and Lynn Hoth,
with thanks

Historian's Note

This adventure takes place before the STAR
TREK: DEEP SPACE NINE episode "Battle
Lines."

PART
ONE

CHAPTER
1

A CRY RANG through the engineering bay.

"Lousy piece of Cardassian *crap!*"

More words followed, in a vocabulary colorful enough to draw expressions of distaste from a Bajoran work crew nearby. Dressed in the drab gray of one of their planet's more puritanical sects, they hadn't yet become used to the rougher edges of station life.

Chief Engineer Miles O'Brien, still cursing, emerged from a thrust-device compartment's access port. Blood threaded from the corner of his brow, gashed on one of the gantry chains running taut to the vessel's exposed innards. It was only slightly redder than his sweating face.

"Is there some difficulty you have encountered?" O'Brien's Cardassian counterpart inquired with mock solicitude. Behind him, curved panels of ship's armor hung in the bay's depths like brutalist stage scenery.

"If you will recall, I warned you that working on our equipment was a matter best left to experts—"

"No difficulty; nothing that I can't handle, that is." He looked at the blood smeared on the rag he'd taken from his pocket. The wound was minor enough; a typical machine-shop accident that he could safely ignore for the time being. It was much harder to ignore the thin smile on the Cardassian engineer's face. *If lizards could grin*—a major effort of self-control was required to keep from decking this one. "I just need the right tools." He turned and headed toward the bay's heavy equipment locker, ducking beneath the power cables looping overhead.

A satisfying expression of alarm showed in the Cardassian engineer's eyes when O'Brien came back. "What . . . what do you think you're doing . . ."

It was his turn to smile. He pressed the joystick on the control box in his hands; behind him, the ponderous articulated device that had followed him out of the locker clumped forward, the steel deck clanging at each step. "I've been here long enough to be plenty familiar with the quality of Cardassian construction." He deliberately steered the jacksledge so that the uplifted striking weight clipped one of the bay's structural girders; the resulting shock wave came close to knocking the Cardassian off his feet. "And if there's one thing I've learned, it's that your stuff responds to an old Earthly engineering principle—*If it doesn't fit, use a bigger hammer.*"

"You've gone mad—" The Cardassian scrambled out of the way as the device swung toward the drydocked vessel. "This . . . this is impossible. . . ."

Hammers didn't come any bigger than the jacksledge. O'Brien and the rest of the DS9 tech crew had cobbled it together for smashing through whatever interior sections of the station had collapsed so badly that only brute force could clear a path. The striking weight was loaded with enough depleted fission material to punch a humanoid-sized hole between one deck and the next. Now, it followed O'Brien like a puppy on a leash as he clambered inside the open thrust-device compartment. The jacksledge's servo-mechs allowed it to delicately pick its way into the space, the massive legs settling between the thrust chamber and the surrounding bulkhead.

The Cardassian engineer's face appeared at the rim of the access port. He had recovered enough to begin blustering. "The use of this device is totally uncalled-for—" His voice echoed off the chamber's wall towering above O'Brien's head. "This is a complete violation of the operational protocols agreed to by the administration of this station . . . it cannot be done—"

"Bet me." O'Brien thumbed the trigger button on the control box, and the striking weight swung through an arc close enough that he heard the rush through the air. The last he heard was the jacksledge hitting the bulkhead like the clapper of a monstrous bell. When the diaphragms inside his protective ear inserts opened up again, he could hear the ringing of the dented metal, and cutting through that, the ululating wail of the vessel's security alarms going off.

He eyeballed the effect the hammer blow had made upon the bulkhead. If anything, the freight hauler wasn't crap, but rather, overengineered for the research purposes to which it had been converted. It would take another dozen blows, at least, to bend the metal for enough clearance; then the buffer shields could finally be lowered into place.

The alarms didn't shut off, but grew louder instead, shrieking from the violated core of the vessel. Before readying the jacksledge for another swing, O'Brien glanced out the access port and saw the Cardassian engineer running for the loading doors—whether from terror or to summon help, he couldn't tell. The Bajorans looked up from the eyepieces of the assembly bench. They weren't so puritanical, he noted, as to be able to resist smiling at the Cardassian's discomfiture.

"Let's get a few more in." He patted the closest of the jacksledge's legs. "Before anybody comes to stop us."

After the DS9 security team had taken away the chief engineer—the head of security himself had snapped the hand restraints on—the Bajorans glanced around at each other. Events did not usually get so dramatic in the engineering bay.

"He seems a decent enough man." One laid down the delicate tools and flexed his cramped fingers. "This O'Brien—he has not been ungracious toward us."

A few of the others nodded in agreement. They had all expected the chief engineer to have greeted them with hostility, to have impeded their being made part of the station's construction and retrofitting operations; O'Brien had been forced to take them on as part of an agreement hammered out between the station's commander and the government authorities down on the surface of Bajor. But if O'Brien had not been exactly overjoyed by their arrival, he had at least been fair to them since.

Another of the crew pushed aside his magnifying optic. "I will admit that, when the great time comes, I may even miss him. A bit . . ."

The sympathetic comments were more than the group's leader could take. None but the other Bajorans knew that he was in charge of their spiritual and moral welfare, charged with shielding them from the temptations to be found among the heathens. He bore no mark that would have indicated his hidden rank to the Starfleet officers. It was just one more thing of which they were unenlightened.

"Perhaps," he said coldly, "in your devotions you could strive to remember why we're here; the purpose behind our coming to this place." The leader cast a stern gaze around the assembly bench.

The others, suitably chastened, looked down at the glittering components of their labors.

"I only meant—" The first who had spoken, the youngest of the group, now made an attempt to defend himself. "Just that there's surely no harm in being on good terms with the man. That's all."

"Ah . . . *harm.*" The leader nodded, making a show of mulling over the word. "As if our people hadn't suffered enough of that, already. From just such creatures as this chief engineer of whom you seem so fond." His own words lashed out, before the other could protest. "It doesn't matter that he's not a Cardassian. He, as well as all the rest of them, is still an outsider. They are not Bajoran."

Silence wrapped itself around the group. None of them could raise his eyes to meet the harsh gaze of the leader.

"From now on—" He spoke softly, having vanquished all opposition. "Keep company only with your brethren, and you will be shielded from falling into error."

No one spoke. One by one, they picked up their delicate tools and resumed their work.

He could hear them coming up the corridor outside his office—even with the door closed. For Benjamin Sisko, that was one of the unforeseen advantages of the Deep Space Nine station's ramshackle state of construction. Aboard the *Enterprise*, or any of the other Starfleet vessels, acoustic isolation between one sector and another, between the public spaces and the private compartments, was total; you didn't know who might be at your door until they announced their presence. Here, however, the ringing of footsteps on bare metal, the echoing of raised voices against the walls—all came clearly to him. Which gave him time, if only a few seconds, to put on his game face, the mask of calm authority that everyone expected from the station's commander.

". . . sabotage . . . *blatant* sabotage. On my world, that is a capital offense. . . ." One voice had the grating tones of a Cardassian officer, the combination of overweening arrogance and innate hostility, without which all of them seemed unable to even order a drink in one of the station's lounges. From the sound of it, this one seemed to have been pushed from mere annoyance to vibrating rage. "We shall see what kind of justice can be expected from your Federation superiors. . . ."

Another voice muttered something in reply, too low

for Sisko to make out the words, though he recognized his chief engineer's accent. He had a vague idea of what this was all about; the station's head of security had been able to give him a rushed comm call, with an indication of the mess that was about to land on his desk.

The desk . . . that was the other advantage of a bit of warning. These days, any interruption seemed to come while he was chin-deep in the intricacies of Bajoran diplomacy. Spread before him were things not meant for the prying, advantage-seeking eyes of a Cardassian officer. As the voices and footsteps approached, Sisko blanked the computer screen.

"Enter." He settled back in his chair, expression composed so as not to show that he'd just painfully nicked his shin on the drawer's corner. Every damned thing the Cardassians had built seemed to have sharp edges sticking out of it, waiting to draw blood; that seemed the way they liked things to be.

Worse luck—there were *two* Cardassian officers. One he recognized as the chief engineer for the vessel currently being retrofitted in the drydock bay; the other—he suppressed a sigh of aggrieved annoyance —was Gul Tahgla, the vessel's captain. Tahgla, in his brief time aboard DS9, had already proved himself to be an apt pupil in the arts of obstruction and connivance practiced by his crony and superior, Gul Dukat. Sisko sometimes wondered if Dukat had sharpened the metal edges before vacating the desk at which he now sat; he wouldn't put it past him.

"For the love of—" Behind the Cardassians, Chief Engineer O'Brien whispered to Odo, loud enough for Sisko to hear, then grimaced as he held up the restraints binding his wrists. "Did you have to put 'em on so tight? If you're just trying to show these jokers you're serious—"

The security chief glared back at him. "I do nothing for show."

The Cardassian captain nodded stiffly toward Sisko. "I believe we have a small . . . *problem,* Commander." A relishing smile lurked on his face as he spoke the word. "Or perhaps not so small. A certain matter of deliberate and unprovoked sabotage on the part of one of your senior crew members—"

"Bull." O'Brien snorted in disgust. "I've been plenty provoked, thank you."

Sisko listened to the Cardassian engineer's account of what had happened in drydock. Now, he had to work to suppress his own smile; he would have liked to have been there when O'Brien had fired off the jacksledge, just to have seen the Cardassian scurry for the bay's exit.

"I'm sure the commander will appreciate the ramifications of this incident." Gul Tahgla's voice grew more icily formal. "The agreement with the Federation, by which your technicians are given access to some of the most crucial areas of our ships, was accepted by our council under duress. In your guise of protectors of the hapless Bajorans, you have obtained control of the stable wormhole, access to which is permitted only to those who meet *your* conditions." The formal tone was displaced by a sneer. "Odd, isn't it, how such deep altruism just *happens* to give the Federation the keys to the entire Gamma Quadrant."

"Please. There's no call to—"

"Hear me out, Commander." The Cardassian leaned threateningly over the desk. "It has been long suspected by our council that the Federation's requirements for travel through the wormhole are a pretext by which spies could be given free run of our vessels, in the guise of workmen installing these ridiculous, nonfunctioning devices—"

"Believe me, if they were nonfunctioning, they wouldn't be so expensive." The Cardassian had hit a sore point with Sisko. A major portion of the station's budget, the Federation resources devoted to keeping DS9 up and running, had gone into the on-site construction of the impulse energy buffers. Although no vessel, Federation or Cardassian or any other, would be allowed into the wormhole without the buffers in place, the reimbursement schedule that Starfleet had mandated covered only a fraction of their actual cost—at least until the next appropriations review.

In the meantime, DS9's operations were being squeezed tight by the need to get craft such as the Cardassian research vessel ready for *intra*wormhole travel. It had been less than twenty-four hours ago that Major Kira had stormed into this office with the figures of the expected shortfall, rows of numbers on the screen of her data padd, as much as demanding that he immediately order a halt to any further retrofit work. *Why should we go in the hole for the sake of Cardassians?*—those had been her words. Kira had little experience with the subtleties of the Federation bureaucracy; he'd had a difficult time convincing her that running a deficit was the best way of persuading Starfleet to increase their budget.

As for doing things for the sake of Cardassians . . . he had his reasons for that, as well. And, for the time being, he was telling no one.

"—and *you'd* better get it straight, nothing leaves that drydock till *I* say so! You can be a friggin' admiral for all I care—"

The sound of his chief engineer's shouting brought Sisko up from the deep workings of his thoughts. "Please, gentlemen." He held up a hand for quiet, then gestured to Odo. "You can go ahead and take the restraints off. I hardly think they're necessary."

Tahgla's expression soured even further. "Sabotage is treated so lightly by you?"

"I very much doubt that there was any criminal intent here; perhaps just a simple misunderstanding, that's all. Mister O'Brien, if you could give us your interpretation?"

The engineer left off glaring at Odo and rubbing his chafed wrists. "It's simple enough, Commander. We've gone back and forth with this bunch. We must've had twenty communiqués, at least—I could call up the archive from the data bank and show you—concerning the dimensions of the impulse energy buffers that were going to be installed on their vessel." Teeth-gritting frustration showed in O'Brien's face. "It's just a matter of how much clearance they'd have to leave us so we could fit the damn things in around their engines. We finally get it worked out—or so I thought—and then they show up in our drydock, and their engine compartments are almost a meter too narrow." He shrugged. "So I fired up the jacksledge and went to make myself a little working room."

"The dimensions of those chambers are *exactly* as you stipulated." Tahgla jabbed a finger at O'Brien. "Our technicians are not given to the sort of errors you seem to expect from your own—"

Sisko angled the computer panel toward his chief engineer. "Let's just take a look, shall we?"

An interlocking display of construction diagrams appeared, with the words SECURITY—ACCESS RESTRICTED blinking in red at the top of the screen. O'Brien lifted his hands from the keyboard and pointed to the specifications. "There—that's what they're supposed to be."

His counterpart leaned past him, the sharp ridge of his finger tapping the Cardassian numerals. "And that's what they *are.*" He glared as fiercely as Gul Tahgla, like an attack dog straining against its leash. "Just as you specified!"

Before Sisko could say anything, his security chief interrupted. "Excuse me; I don't wish to parade my own expertise here—" Standing behind the quarreling engineers, Odo had craned his neck to see what was on the computer panel. "But I think I may be able to clear this up for everyone." He glanced toward Sisko. "You see, Commander, I've lived among the Cardassians; so I'm a little more conscious of the stratifications in their society. The various sectors have different systems of mathematical notation—the numbers are the same, but the bases used for dividing and multiplying into units of measurement are not." His fingertip drew a line across the numerals as he turned his level gaze toward the Cardassian engineer. "I believe that if you recalculate and use *damur,* the mercantile base, the results will come closer to what our chief engineer wanted."

Sisko leaned back in his chair, watching the others assembled around his desk. He could see a smile tugging at the corners of O'Brien's mouth as the

Cardassian engineer squinted at the panel, a furious computation almost visible behind his scaly brow.

Though less emotion showed on the other Cardassian's face, Sisko kept a closer eye on him. Gul Tahgla had watched Odo the whole time the security chief had been giving his short lecture, as though waiting for some particular word or phrase to come out of Odo's mouth. Evidently, it hadn't; Tahgla had kept his own silence, the suspicion that had narrowed his gaze finally dissipating.

"Well, yes . . ." The Cardassian engineer straightened up, his voice stiff with sullen anger and embarrassment. He managed a nod toward Odo. "Your point is well taken. Perhaps . . . perhaps the confusion arose during your chief engineer's initial communications with us. . . ."

A snort of disgust came from O'Brien.

Sisko went on observing. Especially Odo; the shapeshifter's usual expressionless mask had betrayed no inner emotions. But he had picked up an unintended sign, anyway: a slight curling of Odo's fingers, as though he were grasping, seizing hold of something. A clue, something that explained or revealed . . .

"It is not important to assign blame now." Tahgla knew when he had been beaten. "Our own technicians will make the necessary adjustments, and then the installation of the impulse buffers can proceed as originally agreed upon." The tone of insinuating politeness colored his words again. "I trust our scheduled departure date will still be met?"

"I'm sure Mister O'Brien will make every effort. In fact, that's an order."

"Glad to." The words *sooner the better* didn't need

14

to be spoken. As O'Brien turned away, he leaned close to Odo's ear. "And next time, not so damn tight!"

Odo stayed behind when all the rest had left. "I wouldn't like to be in the shoes of Tahgla's chief engineer right now." He gazed down the corridor before palming the office's door closed. "A Cardassian *gul* doesn't enjoy being caught out in an underling's mistake."

"Rather an interesting mistake, actually." The diagram and specs were still on Sisko's computer panel. "I remember learning at the Academy that the Cardassians had these differing math systems. But—" He smiled. "I don't recall much more than that. Was there something else you wanted to tell me about them?"

"Just this, Commander." Odo looked behind himself, a show of habitual, if needless, caution. "The Cardassian numerical bases have their origin in the various economic classes; the *damur* that's used for scientific computations comes from the base devised by their ancient merchants and traders; the unit of linear measurement is based upon the size of a seed grain common on their home planet, I understand. The *umur* notation—" He pointed to the numbers on the screen. "That's the numbering base that originated with the warrior caste."

"Ah." Sisko knew what Odo was about to tell him.

"Somewhere along the line, the Cardassians translated the specifications sent by O'Brien, but into *umur* rather than *damur.*" Odo's hand clenched tight. "That's not an unarmed research vessel sitting in drydock. It's a Cardassian military ship in disguise."

CHAPTER
2

HE WALKED right into the ambush. He should have
known that she would be looking for him. *Gunning for
me,* thought Sisko, ruefully. *That'd be the right expression.*

"I've been doing some more thinking." Major Kira
swung into stride next to him, almost as soon as he
had entered the station's main corridor. "About our
previous conversation."

She had come straight toward him, the crowd
parting before her, as much due to her well-known
temper as her rank. Plowing through them with a
head-lowered determination, she was like an icebreak-
er navigating the frozen seas of some intemperate
planet.

What he needed right now—after a long shift of
studying classified Federation position papers and
transcripts of the bickering provisional government

down on the surface of Bajor—was dinner and a talk with his son Jake about the boy's schoolwork. Followed by a hot bath and a spinal adjustment, and a seat along Wrigley Field's first-base line, where he could contemplate the holosuite's re-creation of a solid home run going in a perfect heart-lifting arc over the left-field wall. He didn't need Major Kira bending his ear any further than it already had been.

Sisko kept on walking, not even looking around at her. "I don't suppose it would make any difference," he said, "if I told you the matter was closed." He kept his voice low, to avoid being overheard too easily. Faces, familiar and unrecognized, permanent and transient, humanoid and otherwise, thronged the corridor.

"You know me better than that." Kira made a joke of it—or nonjoke, similar to the thin nonsmile that marked her grudging tolerance of all fools that she hadn't been empowered to toss out of the station's airlock. At least, not yet. "I don't give up very easily."

"Indeed." At the mouth to one of the corridor's unused branches, a Gameran peddler had set up his quick-folding table, and was doing a brisk business in what appeared to be mildly stimulative transdermal patches. Though it would have been faster to take a turbolift from his office to his living quarters, he'd made it his habit to physically walk some sector of the station every shift, to see for himself what might be going on in this strange, small world he supposedly commanded. He made a mental note to have Odo move the patch peddler on, then just as quickly canceled it; for all he knew, the Gameran was part of the security chief's network of snoops and petty informants.

"I feel it's imperative to remind you that—"

"Major Kira." He stopped and turned toward her. The soft bulk of a Buhlmeri cargo-tech bumped against his shoulder, muttered an apology, then went on. The standing population had increased markedly over the last several shifts; when he'd first been posted here, the station's public areas had been sparsely occupied ruins. "I'll be frank with you: I'm tired. I've been working hard the last few shifts, and I'm not in the mood to rehash a subject that I've made abundantly clear to you is no longer open for discussion. Now, if you'll excuse me—"

"But that's exactly my *point.*" Kira spoke through gritted teeth, her eyes flashing twin laser-points of anger. "And you're only fooling yourself if you think it's something recent. You're swamped up to your eyeballs in diplomatic affairs, enough to fill every second of *every* watch, and you're still trying to manage all the particulars of DS Nine's operations—"

"You forget, Major; that's my duty. My first duty."

"Wrong. Your duty is to see that it *gets* done." She made no attempt to keep her voice down; faces along the corridor turned their way. "It's not going to do you or the station any good for you to keel over in your tracks from exhaustion. As long as the Federation expects you to oversee negotiations with the planetside government, you're going to have to learn to delegate some of these things."

Sisko felt a blood vessel at the corner of his brow begin to throb. Kira was far out of line. It would have been difficult enough for him to check his own temper, on receiving a warning like that from a superior officer; to hear it from his nominal second-in-command was aggravating beyond endurance.

"I've delegated quite enough, Major." He started walking again, to burn off the adrenaline that had welled up inside him. "Especially to you." He swung a narrowed glance at her. "Perhaps more than I would have, if your position here had been a matter of choice for me."

She ignored the last comment, as she matched his stride. "Oh, you've certainly delegated." Sarcasm seeped between her words. "Minutiae, the smallest things, those you think anyone else is capable of handling." She grabbed his arm to halt him. "I'm talking about policy decisions, Commander. This station is Bajoran property—in actuality, not just as some technical legalism. The time is coming when all of DS Nine's operations are to be turned over to my people. That's by your own Federation's edict. And your commission here includes preparing for that time. As the senior Bajoran officer aboard, I should be given the greatest possible authority to—"

"My commission, Major, is to *suitably* prepare for the transfer of DS Nine's control. To Bajorans who are ready to assume the responsibilities for it."

Kira's lowered voice spoke of anger hotter than any shouting could express. "And what exactly do you mean by that?"

He glanced along the corridor. The other pedestrians had slowed down, trying as subtly as possible to stay within earshot. "Come with me."

They were only steps away from Quark's number-one lounge. Inside, Sisko signaled over the heads of the patrons stacked up at the bar. "Give us a private booth. And if you switch on any of your bugs, you'll wind up eating them."

The Ferengi displayed his sharp-toothed smile. "Commander, I would *never . . .*" In fact, he probably wouldn't; such discretion was part of the understanding by which Quark was allowed to keep his various enterprises running.

With the booth sealed shut, Sisko and Major Kira were encased in a soundproof bubble. He leaned across the narrow table. "Perhaps I didn't make myself clear before. Or perhaps you think I've forgotten about some of the decisions you have been allowed to make—and their consequences."

"If this is about that group of Redemptorists I let come aboard—"

He cut her off. "What else would it be about? Correction: it's not just about whether you showed a lack of judgment in granting them entry to the station. It's a question of the underlying sympathies that might have prompted that decision."

The Redemptorists, a team of six microassembly specialists currently assigned to O'Brien's drydock bay, had been brought up from Bajor enough shifts ago that the issues raised by the group's presence should have begun to lose some of their sharp edges. Major Kira had been in charge of their security clearance—she still was, for any other Bajorans that might come aboard in the future; he hadn't relieved her of the assignment—and she had personally signed their entry and residence chits. All of which Sisko had been able to verify for himself when Odo had first told him of the irregularities in the new workers' backgrounds.

Odo's worries were justified, given the reputation of the Redemptorists as one of the most intractable elements in the overheated stew of Bajoran politics. They were more of a religious movement, a fundamentalist group opposed to the conciliatory mainstream faith headed by Kai Opaka. Fanaticism had inevitably progressed, as it seemed to on any world, to violence; several Redemptorists had been involved in terrorist activities directed against other Bajorans who didn't follow their particular annihilating creed. In the murderous infighting that characterized the Bajoran splinter groups—the ever-shifting coalitions and temporary alliances and eventual drawing of daggers—the Redemptorists were notable for the ruthlessness by which they dealt with long-standing enemies and onetime friends alike.

"Those men are not murderers, Commander. They're all followers of the Redemptorists' political defense wing. Their group even has members sitting in the Bajoran parliament—"

"I'm well aware of the fine shadings that afflict Bajoran politics. As you noted, I seem to spend a great deal of my time lately on precisely that. I'm also aware—perhaps more than you are, Major—of the difficulties that the Redemptorist movement has presented to the provisional government. In fact, your government has contacted me directly, to see if there's anything that can be done from aboard the station to jam the pirate broadcasts by which the Redemptorists recruit other Bajorans to their cause."

"That doesn't alter the status of the ones I allowed on board. They're *legal*—"

He and Kira had gone over this before. " 'Legal'

21

seems to be a very flexible concept with you, Major. I don't make quite the same distinction that you do between those who murder and those who *condone* murder. And what the Bajoran government needs to do—the elements it has to bring inside itself to stay alive—is not going to be the guideline for how this station is operated."

"This *Bajoran* station, Commander." Kira's anger leapt another notch. "You keep forgetting that this is Bajoran property—"

"Currently administered by Starfleet—and that responsibility is *mine.*" He spread his hands flat on the table. "And it will be that way as long as the situation on Bajor's surface remains the mess that it is right now."

"But how is that ever going to change?" The words took on a desperate edge. "Those groups have to be brought into the center of things. They have tremendous energy and capabilities—"

"Oh yes, they've demonstrated *that,* all right."

She pushed past his sarcasm. "If the Redemptorists and the others are left out on the fringe, unable to achieve any measure of legitimate power, what other choice are they going to have?"

"Besides violence?" Sisko shook his head before replying. "How about patience?"

"After what the Cardassians did to us, Commander, *patience* is not a word of which the Bajorans are very fond."

"It may not be a word that's to your liking, Major. But it's one you're going to learn the meaning of. There was a time not too long ago when I felt assured of your loyalty to this station; that it was of at least equal weight with your devotion to your people. But now, I've begun to wonder. This incident, combined with other things you've said and done, raises grave concerns in my mind as to whether an underlying sympathy with the aims of these terrorist groups— and your own impatience—has gained the upper hand in your thoughts. Until I'm convinced once more that the survival of DS Nine is your top priority, the question of your being given greater authority here is, as I said before, not open for discussion." He stood up and reached for the door control, then stopped and looked back at Kira. "I'm disappointed, Major. I would have thought that you of all people, with your own experiences back on Bajor, would remember what damage these people can do." He saw that the reference to the incidents in her past, before she had been posted as military attaché to the station, was equivalent to a slap across her face. She glared back at him in silence.

The booth's door slid open, revealing Quark right outside. "Refreshments?" He smiled and raised a tray with two synthales. "On the house."

Sisko got past him without mishap, but Kira didn't. Quark looked at the major's back as she pushed her way out into the crowded corridor, then glanced down at the puddle and overturned mugs at his feet. "I guess not. . . ."

"When you say 'liquid state,' what do you mean? How much—a liter? Ten liters?" A malicious grin sliced across the Cardassian security officer's face. "A pint?"

Odo looked away from him in annoyance. "I find

your interest in my bodily functions to be distasteful.
You can be confident that I have no interest in yours."

He continued walking, his visual scan moving
across the maze of pipes and exposed wiring that lined
the station's lower decks. These areas were little
trafficked—at least by anyone who had a legitimate
reason for being here—and were far down on the list
for eventual upgrading and being brought back into
service. The deep shadows—some sectors were almost completely unlit—and even deeper niches were
consequently perfect for all those with illegitimate
reasons. By his own calculations, he estimated that he
had discovered and confiscated perhaps only 10 percent of the contraband moving on, through, and off
DS9; the damage that the Cardassians had wrought
upon the station's exosystems had left it a smuggler's
paradise. Until the new security perimeters were
phased in, all his vigilance was needed to keep the
station from becoming an open thoroughfare for illicit
goods.

By contrast, his counterpart from the Cardassian
research vessel sitting in drydock—inside his head,
he put quotation marks around the word *research*—
kept his gaze locked on Odo. That annoyed him, as
well. Of course, he knew that was the reason for the
Cardassian's constant presence: to keep an eye on
him—the watcher watched.

"Isn't it pretty close to that time for you?" Gri
Rafod peered at him in amusement. "I'd hate for you
to melt into a puddle just because you were giving me
the grand tour."

"I'm not giving you anything." Odo clipped the
words short. "You wished to accompany me on my

rounds; you do so against my wishes. However, I am bound by the terms of the agreement worked out between your superiors and Commander Sisko. You persist in this fiction that you are preparing a report to the Cardassian council on recent improvements to the station's security; fine. As you wish." He stopped and turned his severest gaze on the other. "But you're not fooling me."

"How your harsh speech wounds me." The Cardassian should have been an actor; he laid a hand dramatically upon his chest. "When I spoke to Gul Dukat, he told me that you were given to such groundless suspicions of others' motives. I didn't want to believe it, but . . ." He shook his head. "I suppose it's an inevitable result of the jobs you and I have been given. We see the worst sides of sentient creatures, don't we?"

Odo kept silent. He had already lied to the Cardassian, a small but necessary violation of his own inner code. He wasn't bound by any ludicrous agreement; if the maintenance of the station's security required actions that weren't officially approved of, the commander didn't need to know of them—or could at least pretend not to know. Unfortunately, if he were to elude this Gri Rafod's obnoxious surveillance—easy enough for a shapeshifter to do— it would play right into the hands of the Cardassian security officer's superiors. The Cardassians were looking for any excuse to break the hard-negotiated pact by which all vessels, including their own, were brought into the DS9 drydock to have the impulse energy buffers mounted around their engines before being allowed access to the stable wormhole. The fact that the buffers enabled vessels to pass through the wormhole without harming its inhabitants seemed to bear no weight with the Cardassians. They cared little enough for the welfare of creatures that they could actually observe and touch, let alone the seemingly nonmaterial ones inside the wormhole.

If he were to slip away from the Cardassian security officer, then Gul Tahgla, the vessel's captain, would immediately cry that the duplicitous Starfleet officers manning the station had unleashed their resident shapeshifter to spy out all the secrets and classified information that might be aboard the ship. The Cardassian council would howl that the installation of buffers was just a ruse to get their vessels into Starfleet's prying hands. The proverbial hell would break loose, the pact between the Federation and the Cardassians would collapse, the Cardassians would press for whatever advantage they could derive from the resulting chaos.

Of course, none of that altered the fact that Odo had already decided to leave Gri Rafod hanging, and sneak undetected into the vessel sitting in drydock. He had determined his course of action even before the Cardassians' unconscious error had revealed the vessel's military nature.

"I hope you don't feel that this time we're sharing together is wasted." Rafod smiled as he strolled beside Odo. "I assure you that I'm learning a great deal from you."

More than you realize, thought Odo. If his own face had been capable of it, he would have smiled back. The Cardassian wouldn't even realize how much he'd learned, until it was too late.

26

Their route led them to the active—officially so—
sectors of the station. To the drydock itself. Odo
detected Gri Rafod's attention going up a notch, a
tensing of the spine into full alertness. As they walked
through a shower of sparks from a bank of welding
torches, the dull gray shape of the Cardassian vessel
loomed before them, its flanks crossed with scaffold-
ing and the heavy cables of the overhead cranes.

Chief Engineer O'Brien stood before a shop computer panel, head lowered as he punched up progressively more detailed layers of schematics on the
screen. "Some kind of problem, gents?"

"No, of course not. Merely routine." Odo stood
with hands clasped behind his back, gazing across the
drydock's bustling activity. Shouting voices and the
clash of metal against metal assaulted his senses.
While in the empty spaces belowdecks, he had tuned
his hearing for maximum sensitivity, to pick up the
slightest sound; now, he simply flowed an extra layer
of molecules across the tympanum inside each ear, to
block the loudest noises hammering through the air.
"Busy, I take it?"

Gri Rafod wasn't as fortunate; without filter plugs
such as those O'Brien and his crew wore, the
drydock's noise level made it difficult for him to
follow even a shouted conversation. Still, it was wise
to remain cautious in front of him; Odo could see the
Cardassian watching from the corner of his eye, as
though an attempt to penetrate the vessel's mysteries
might happen at any moment.

"We're about back up to speed." O'Brien shrugged.
"Now that we got that little, uh, *miscommunication*
sorted out." The chief engineer had left the jacksledge

sitting in the middle of the drydock, a squat and silent totem of power and a warning to the Cardassians against any further interference.

"Have you had a chance to work on anything else around the station? I know that there was a small plumbing problem the commander was concerned about—"

A sheet of meter-thick plate slipped and fell, its edge striking the drydock's floor with an impact that Odo could feel through the soles of his boots. Beside him, Gri Rafod winced in pain.

The accident had distracted O'Brien's attention; when he turned back after looking to see that no one had been injured, his expression was puzzled. "What plumbing problem?"

He'd been keeping his speech gruff, as though to indicate he was still annoyed at having been arrested and taken in hand restraints to Sisko's office. Odo glanced quickly at Gri Rafod, to see if the Cardassian had picked up on this lapse.

Before Odo could say anything, O'Brien caught himself. "Oh, you mean the hydraulics system." The security chief nodded. "That was no problem. You can tell the commander it's all been taken care of. Ready to go."

"Fine. I'll tell him when I see him." He turned to Rafod. "I'm afraid I'll have to cut our little tour short. As you so considerately observed a while ago—it's about that time for me."

As they headed for the station's Promenade and the security office, Gri Rafod shook his head, as though his auditory organs were still ringing. "It's a pleasure to be out of that place."

Odo said nothing, but gazed with satisfaction at him. The Cardassian didn't suspect a thing.

She almost didn't see him until she bumped right into him. Preoccupied with her thoughts, the deep brooding in which the commander had left her, Major Kira stepped into her quarters as the door slid open. She looked up and saw the station's head medical officer standing there, holding a book in his hands.

"What are you doing in here?" The invasion of privacy would have offended her, even if she had been in a better mood.

Julian Bashir smiled as ingratiatingly as possible under the circumstances and placed the book back on the shelf. "Don't you remember? You coded me one-time access, so I could give you the results of your medical tests." He picked up his data padd from the corner of the desk set into the bulkhead and turned its small screen toward her. "I think you might recall that you wanted to keep it, um . . . *private.*"

"Right." She rubbed her forehead. "Okay, I'm sorry—I didn't mean to tear your head off." Kira sat down heavily on the corner of the bed. "So, what's the verdict?"

It had taken some resolve on her part to ask a favor of Bashir. For some time now, she had found him, of all the DS9 crew members, to be the most personally irritating—completely at odds with her style of doing things, her notions of how to conduct oneself. She had long ago bolted herself into the direct approach, to put her foot down and pile right into any problem, any confrontation with another person. That was so she could endure, and even admire, Benjamin Sisko, even when she was 180 degrees opposed to him; she was never in doubt as to what the commander's feelings were. But Bashir relied too much on charm—or at least what he must've thought was charm—and an easy, flattering manner, none of which she trusted. *Stop trying to be friends with the universe,* she wanted to tell him. *And get on with your job.*

"Nothing." Bashir shrugged and tossed the data padd back onto the desk. "There's nothing at all wrong with you. All the test results are within normal ranges. Perhaps a little elevated on some of the electrolytes, but nothing I'd worry about. You're probably just tired." His would-be ingratiating smile appeared again. "From overwork."

She didn't know if she was relieved or not. She'd asked him to run the tests and draw a blood sample after-hours, when the only medical unit staff on duty would all have been over in the emergency facilities. He'd assured her of confidentiality, that no one else—particularly Commander Sisko—would know that she'd been there; that was part of his duty as a physician. So now, if she didn't need to be concerned about that, and the tests had all come out clear, then she only had to worry about what had prompted her request in the first place.

"It's no secret how hard you push yourself." Bashir gazed up at the ceiling as he musingly rubbed his chin. "Now, if I were your *personal* physician—if you'd put yourself under my care exclusively—I'd prescribe a long course of relaxation. A rest shift with no thoughts of duty or work . . . a fine dinner, a bottle of wine, pleasant company . . ." He brightened. "Say, with *me.* How does that sound?"

Kira groaned inside herself. That was another reason she had taken a dislike to him. The same thing about which she had commiserated with Dax and every other humanoid female aboard the station. You couldn't say hello to him without it leading to a come-on—a serious overestimation of his own appeal.

"It sounds like a bad idea." She laid her head back against the pillow, not even caring what ideas might be zipping through Bashir's head now. "As you said, I'm probably tired. Too tired." He didn't seem to get the message. Or did, but chose to ignore it. He went on scanning across the items on her shelves, the few books, the various little remembrance-enhancers of her past—there weren't many of those, either. That was a result of her own war on whatever scraps of sentimentality might still be left inside her, and the fact that a childhood spent in refugee camps didn't give one much to fondly look back on.

"Really, Kira, you can do better than this." Bashir's voice became mock-chiding as he examined the small, portable chip-player sitting between its minuscule speakers. He shook his head. "This is *pathetic*— barely adequate."

"It works; that's all I care about. And I got a good price on it from Quark—something about it having fallen off the back of an interstellar transport." Her problem was getting into moral debt with Bashir— he'd done her a favor, having run her tests at a time when he knew that she knew he was already swamped with getting the station's quarantine module up and running. So now, she supposed she had to have a semblance of conversation with him, when all she really wanted to do was boot him out of her quarters. "I suppose you think I should have something totally modern and up-to-date."

"Oh no; by no means. You should have something *classic.*" He didn't appear to be joking around. His face lit with enthusiasm. "Right now, I'm restoring a vintage Earthside music-playback system. Talk about old-fashioned: you wouldn't *believe* the size of the media it uses. The discs are nearly the size of your *hand.*" He held up his own to demonstrate. "But the Theta decoding algorithms are just pure gold—the last great Sinclair-Moffett design breakthrough. They were supposedly up for some kind of Nobel prize before they died. . . ."

"I had no idea." She gazed up at the ceiling, struggling to conceal her boredom.

"When I've got it up and running, it's magic. The walls just fall away, and you're in the *Concertgebouw* in old Amsterdam, or the pre-restoration Carnegie. Better than a holosuite—at least as long as you keep your eyes closed." His voice dropped a few tones in pitch. "You should come by my quarters sometime and listen to it."

Another come-on. The man was relentless. Now, she could put him out the door with no guilt feelings. She was about to tell him so when she heard another voice speaking. It took her a moment to realize that Bashir had pushed the start button on the chip-player.

She was off the bed and had shoved her way past him before he knew what was happening. She punched EJECT and pulled the chip out of the machine.

"What's wrong?" Bashir stared at her in puzzlement.

"Nothing—" She grasped the chip firmly in her hand. "But you don't want to hear this. It's just some, uh, Bajoran folk music. Really monotonous." That had been a screwup on her part, leaving the chip where anyone could come across it; she'd have to be more careful in the future.

"Oh, I wouldn't mind. I have very . . . *wide-ranging* tastes."

Yeah, I bet. "Some other time. Right now, I think I'm getting a headache." The old lines were still the best ones.

After he had left—finally—and she was alone, Kira pulled the bed's mattress away from the bulkhead, enough to reveal the small hiding place she had created. She pried up the corner of the wall panel, and was about to drop the recorded chip in with the others, when she stayed her hand. She squeezed her eyes shut, breathing deep, and trying to control the pounding of her heart.

Maybe Bashir was right. Maybe she needed a rest, a long one, during which she could somehow find a way to stop thinking about the things that shouted inside her head. Stop thinking, and stop remembering . . .

Or perhaps it was Commander Sisko who was right. It was something different that caused her errors in judgment; she couldn't even decide if it had been a mistake to approve letting the Redemptorists come aboard the station. Not fatigue, but something much more fundamental, the division that cleaved her soul. Between what she was trying to become, was pretending to be . . . and what she could never stop being.

She drew her hand back, still holding the chip. She got up and put it back in the machine, then hit the PLAY button. She turned down the volume so there wasn't the slightest chance of anyone outside the door overhearing, then lay back down on the bed.

Eyes closed, she listened to the stern, compelling voice. It was the same as that on all the other chips in the hiding place, recordings of the illicit broadcasts of the Redemptorist leader on Bajor.

The man's voice spoke of blood and fire, the need for the great cleansing of their planet, the driving away of all intruders from beyond the stars. In shame, mingled with a fierce, irrational pride, Major Kira Nerys clenched her teeth and listened. A single tear welled up and traced a line across her cheek.

CHAPTER
3

THE HIDING PLACE had been changed several times already; to prevent the station's security chief from finding it and exposing the unauthorized guest it held—the most important person to the future of Bajor. He was aboard DS9, and only a select few knew of his presence. The youngest of the Redemptorist microassembly crew hurried through the darkened passageway, head ducked to avoid the pipes above. He kept the parcel in his arms clutched tight to his chest, mindful of the awesome responsibilities he bore.

"Unauthorized" was—as he had been instructed and as he had to keep telling himself—a relative term. At the end of the passage, he stealthily raised a little-used access hatch and began clambering down a set of metal rungs to the even darker level below. If he felt uncomfortable about breaking the regulations of the station's administrators—these strangers who, from Chief Engineer O'Brien on up, had treated him and the rest of the devout with unexpected fairness—then he had to remind himself that their laws were as nothing compared to the dawning of Bajor's glory and liberation. To remember that at all times was a test of his own faith.

He came to the last rung, his next step dangling into unlit space. This sector was one of the most heavily damaged aboard the station, the narrow passages and shafts torn apart by the fire set by the departing Cardassians. The station's autonomic defenses had managed to extinguish the blaze, but only after the local power grid and sensors had been charred to a nonfunctioning state. The smell of blackened filaments lodged tight in his throat.

Drawing in as much of the stifling air as he could, he forced the hand clutching one of the rungs to let go. The drop into darkness was less than two meters, just enough for a spark of panic to flare inside his chest, the fear that he would go on falling forever.

He rolled off a mound of singed insulation material and got to his knees. The impact had jarred the parcel loose from his grasp, and he fumbled about for it with a growing desperation. At last he found it, right on top of the wire marking the rest of the way to the hiding place. He crawled forward, holding the parcel even closer to himself.

"Arten . . . how good to see you." In the dim light, a smile rose on the face of the most important man on Bajor—or off the planet, since he had been smuggled aboard DS9. "I thought perhaps you had forgotten about me."

Though the words were obviously said in jest, they

still made Arten's gut feel hollow. "Of course not—" His own words rushed out. "How . . . how could . . ."

"Never mind." Hören Rygis, the leader of the Redemptorist movement, unwrapped the parcel that had been set before him. "Of course, your services are greatly appreciated. By all the faithful."

Still on his knees—the hiding place was too small for anyone to stand upright—Arten turned and made sure that the flexible panel had sealed shut behind him, preventing any light or sound from leaking out. Though Hören spoke in a low, even soothing, voice in this enclosed space, Arten couldn't help hearing that other voice, the one from the broadcasts that went out to the Redemptorists scattered across the surface of Bajor. It must be a miracle, a sign of their cause's righteousness, that the source of those hammering, apocalyptic sermons, with their calls to revolution and a burning purity, hadn't yet been detected here in the bowels of the station.

Hören set aside the flasks of water and the food containers. At the bottom of the parcel were its most important contents. He held up the blank recording chips, turning them between his thumb and forefinger so they sparkled in the portable lantern's glow.

"Through such simple things," he mused aloud. "Thus is that day hastened, that all true Bajorans will rejoice to see. By virtue of the simple . . ." He turned a sharp glance toward Arten. "You would do well to remember that."

"Yes . . ." He nodded, wondering just what Hören had meant. Some words of wisdom seemed to be no more than those that he already knew, homilies with which even the nonbelievers would have agreed. Others, he had realized bit by bit . . . the other words could mean things much deeper. And darker . . .

"In truth, however, you needn't have worried about me." Hören opened a flask and took a drink. "I had a visit last cycle from one of your companions." He spoke casually, as though of a neighbor he had welcomed into a sunlit house.

Arten felt his spine stiffen. "Oh?" It was his appointed task to carry supplies to the hiding place, to bring the blank recording chips, and to carry away those with the fiery words locked inside. "Who was that?" He had wanted to ask *why*, but had held his tongue.

"Your group's leader. Deyreth Elt. He brought me a few things." Hören pointed to the items on a ledge that had been improvised on the space's rounded wall. "Nothing much."

"And was that . . ." He couldn't restrain his growing anxiety. "Was that the only reason he came to see you?"

"By no means." Hören picked through an opened container, looking for a choice morsel. His long-fingered, almost delicate hands were at odds with the broad-shouldered bulk that seemed to push against the hiding place's confines. Arten felt, as he had before in the man's presence, that all the available space was somehow being absorbed, leaving only a thin margin in which to exist, bringing the harsh angles of that face right up against his own. Hören licked a dab of sauce from a fingertip. "Deyreth and I had a most intriguing conversation." The angles sorted themselves into what might have been a kindly smile on another's face. "About *you*, as a matter of fact."

His heart stopped for a moment, then raced to catch up with the shallow breathing he tried to conceal. He couldn't speak.

"Calm yourself. You have nothing to be afraid of." Hören's voice lowered even further from that on the recording chips. "Self-doubt is not a characteristic of those wearing the armor of faith." The smile vanished. "Do you doubt yourself, Arten?"

"I . . . I don't think so . . ."

Hören sighed. "You'll have to work on that. In the meantime, bear in mind that Deyreth is one of the oldest Redemptorists, one of the first to have accepted the revelation of struggle, back when we were a ragged band hunted by the Cardassian oppressors and Bajoran collaborators alike. Deyreth is worthy of your respect, a man of great devoutness, confirmed in the truth of his beliefs. Perhaps a little *too* confirmed—do you follow what I'm trying to tell you?"

A small light appeared, that didn't come from the lantern. "Perhaps . . ."

"It would be wrong to expect someone like Deyreth, as virtuous as he is, to adapt his ways to changing conditions, to the new opportunities that even I have been slow to recognize. The new rulers of this station, these representatives of the Federation—they're different from the Cardassians, aren't they? In many ways."

Arten nodded. "That's what I was trying to tell Deyreth and the others."

"Ah. So, what Deyreth came here to report to me—the remarks you are said to have made, expressing some admiration for this Chief Engineer O'Brien who supervises your work—those things are all true? You *did* say them?"

He hesitated, his pulse lodged high in his throat.

"Come, come; you can speak openly with me." Hören lowered his head, to bring his gaze level with Arten's. "As I have tried to teach you: the simplest, the least among us, can be of the most value. You see things differently from Deyreth; that is to be expected. But you dared to speak to him the truth you perceived in your heart—that is commendable."

A stone seemed to dissolve inside Arten's chest. An influx of breath dizzied him. "It is true." How much easier to say that, than to carry the weight of shame through these dark corridors! His words tumbled forth now. "The chief engineer—and the ones above him—they know what we are; they have no reason to treat us as well as they have. But they *are* different, they're—"

Hören laid his hand on Arten's forearm. "There is no need to explain. I understand." He drew back, his gaze turning inward. "I understand . . . everything. . . ."

No need to say any more. Arten closed his eyes, feeling the knots of his spine loosen. Everything would be fine now. Now, they would all—Deyreth and the others—they would all see how different things were here.

In darkness, buried in the station's hidden recesses, the voice of blood and fire spoke, in a slow whisper. "I understand . . . just what needs to be done. . . ."

"Well, this certainly looks comfortable." Gri Rafod looked over the edge of the basin. His reflection wavered up from the depths of the polished brass. "That is, comfortable for some people."

Odo found the Cardassian's presence no less irksome, and the attempts at banter no more clever, than before. "It serves its purpose." He didn't look up, but continued sorting through the arrest reports on his data padd. He'd retreated to his private quarters, from the outer security office. With the door sealed, the glare and noise of the Promenade beyond were shut away. "It doesn't need to do any more than that."

"I suppose not." Rafod stretched his legs out from the chair, looking bored and impatient. "Is it going to be much longer? Before it . . . happens?"

He glanced up. "My actions are bound by the agreement between your superiors and Commander Sisko." He kept his voice level, to avoid giving Rafod the pleasure of knowing how irritated he'd become. "But my statements are not. You see fit to invade my privacy for no good reason—fine. I obey my orders. But I would like to point out to you that what 'happens,' as you put it, is simply a matter of my physiology. I must periodically revert to and remain in a liquid state; it's as simple as that. It's not a sideshow act for your amusement."

"Yes, yes; of course. Whatever you say." Gri Rafod looked around at the cluttered walls. "Though it's rather a pity . . ."

Odo sighed wearily. *"What* is?"

"That it's not a sideshow act. I imagine it would be rather a good one. Perhaps you should talk to your friend Quark, see what he could set up for you."

More loudly than he'd intended to, Odo dropped the data padd into his desk drawer and slammed it shut. The display device's security codes were unbreakable, but on general principle he didn't want the Cardassian handling it while he waited here.

He stood up and came round to the front of the

desk. "If it will make you any happier—or perhaps more pleasant to be with—you should know that the time is at last here. Your unseemly interest in other creatures' biological functions will be satisfied." He stepped into the basin. "For a while, at least."

Rafod ignored the dig. "Rather like getting into a bathtub, isn't it?" He leaned forward to watch.

"I had thought that might be a novelty for you and your people. Now, my suspicions have been confirmed."

"Very amusing." The Cardassian smiled sourly. He nodded. "Yes, very much like an old-fashioned bathtub . . . though, of course, without any plumbing attached."

Odo rested his hands on the basin's edge. "I hope you've brought something with which to amuse yourself for the next couple of hours. As fascinating as our conversations have been, I will have neither the capability nor the inclination to indulge in them."

"I anticipated that." Rafod unfastened one of his uniform's pockets and extracted a folded pouch and a small implement of hand-carved wood. "Speaking of Quark . . . he sold me all this, at what I'm sure was an extortionate price."

The sharp scent of the pouch's contents caught at Odo's nostrils. "That's tobacco."

"Yes. Quark told me it'd come all the way from Earth. Seems to have rather a mild narcotic effect. Pleasant, but not soporific."

"I would prefer that you not indulge while you are here in my quarters."

Rafod busily fussed with the paraphernalia of lighter and tamping tool. "Yes, well, we'll talk about that when you get back. To your proper form, that is." He started filling the pipe with the shredded organic matter.

There was nothing Odo could do about it now. Or that he wanted to; if Rafod was preoccupied with this new toy, it would help to keep him from noticing anything going amiss, right beneath his scaly nose. "Then, if you'll excuse me . . ."

The Cardassian had managed to get the pipe lit. He leaned back in the chair, exhaling a cloud of smoke. "It strikes me that you're well advised to keep your doors so tightly locked here. With the number of enemies that a chief of security garners aboard a station such as this, or even just those bent on mischief and petty vandalism . . ." Rafod suppressed a cough, then nodded. "If someone like that managed to get in here, while you were in your, ah, *defenseless* liquid state . . ." He shook his head. "Someone could dump just anything into the receptacle there with you. Trash, old scrap metal . . ." He smiled around the pipe. "Ashes, perhaps."

Odo had been on the verge of letting himself sink into the basin, letting the individual atoms of his existence loosen from the constraints of solid matter. He stopped and drew himself erect.

"If *someone* were to do that, it would be very foolish of *someone.*" Odo leaned over the basin's edge and through the tobacco fumes. "Let me tell you a little story, Gri Rafod. First, you have to understand that while I'm in my liquid state, I may be defenseless, but I'm not unconscious; in that sense, this periodic claim that my nature makes upon me is not exactly similar to the sleep that most other creatures require. I am awake, and aware of everything that happens around me.

"Now, here's the story: once, someone did come in here, and he did just as you said; he tossed something into the basin while I was in my liquid state. And I was very, very annoyed by that."

Rafod looked uneasy, as though realizing that he had pushed the shapeshifter too far.

"And when I came back from my little rest, I tracked that someone down. And do you know what I did to him?"

The Cardassian shook his head.

"Without his seeing, I turned myself into a morsel of food upon his plate, something so small that he would gulp it down without even chewing—the way I've seen you and your people eat. And then, once I was inside him, I stopped being quite so small, and I reached up through his throat, all the way into his head, and pushed his eyeballs out from the inside." Odo wished he had mastered forming an unpleasant smile; it would have been perfect now. "It must have been quite an unsettling experience. I understand that even after having artificial optics grafted into his sockets, this someone remains under heavy sedation in a psychiatric ward on his home planet."

Rafod took the pipe from his mouth. "You never did any such thing. It would be against the law."

"You're right," said Odo. "I didn't do that—because I just now thought of it. But I would *love* to do it sometime." He moved back to the center of the basin. "Do we understand each other now, Gri Rafod? Good. Enjoy yourself."

After he had become liquid, with his level below the rim of the basin, he formed a light-sensitive patch and rudimentary lens at his surface. Just enough to watch the Cardassian security officer, without him noticing.

Rafod scowled and muttered something to himself as he poked at the smoldering contents of his pipe, but he made no move away from his chair.

Good, thought Odo. *The fool suspects nothing.* He let the primitive eye dissolve and set himself to the tasks before him.

The temptation to remain a simple liquid was strong—the time when that change would become necessary was close at hand, and he could feel the ease it would bring to every particle of his being. But he could put it off a while longer, despite what he had told Rafod. There would be just enough time to do what was needed.

At the bottom of the basin, he emitted a discharge of ions sufficient to trigger the microelectronic switch the clever O'Brien had finished installing. The metallic membrane covering the basin's floor contracted slightly, revealing the tiny slits around the edge. Even if Gri Rafod had closely examined the basin, he wouldn't have been able to detect the openings.

Distilled water, colored with a slight gold tint to match that of Odo's liquid state, seeped into the basin. He carefully adjusted his own specific gravity, so that the water floated above him as he let his matter slowly drain into the receptacle chamber hidden below his quarters. The exchange had been carefully timed, so that not even the slightest ripple showed at the surface of the basin.

When the last of his atoms had flowed through the drainage tube, Odo solidified a finger and reached up to press the switch at the top of the receptacle. The membrane expanded again, sealing the basin. O'Brien's "hydraulic system" had worked perfectly.

In a corridor of the access level beneath the Promenade and the security office, Odo glanced around to make sure no one had spotted him. Having slipped away from Gri Rafod's constant surveillance, he would just as soon continue about his business in secret. He gave himself the face and uniform of an engineering crew member, and hurried toward the drydock sector.

A few minutes later, Chief Engineer O'Brien stepped into a storage locker and found a reel of single-filament comm line out of place. He smiled, picked up the reel, and carried it out to where the Cardassian research vessel was being worked on.

Odo appreciated the personal touch, that O'Brien had kept all their confidential arrangements to himself.

The next thing he knew, O'Brien had dropped the reel onto the hard metal flooring. The impact jarred Odo's thoughts from their tracks.

"Sorry," whispered O'Brien as he bent down to scoop up the reel. "I guess my hands are still a little, uh, *numb* from those restraints. . . ."

Odo supposed that he and O'Brien were even now. Or at least, he hoped they were.

In the vessel's engine compartment, after O'Brien and the rest of the work crew had left, a length of comm line slid, snakelike, off the reel and twined itself into the other wires and cables running along the bulkheads. Unnoticed beneath the bored gaze of the Cardassian guards, the line vanished into the heart of the ship and its secrets.

When Arten had retraced his way to the torn access shaft, he saw a glimmer of light, no bigger than the palm of his hand, playing against the fire-scorched metal. He looked over his shoulder, down the length of the narrow spaces through which he had just crawled, and saw the source of the glow. In the distance, the flexible panel that concealed the hiding place of Hören Rygis had caught one of its corners on a sharp-edged scrap peeled away from the bulkhead. Just enough to let the faint glow from the portable lantern leak out. Just enough to give away the hiding place to any nonbeliever who might come snooping through this sector.

He inched back toward the hiding place, even more carefully and quietly than before. After the revelation that Hören had come to see things his way, that the Starfleet officers aboard the DS9 station could be honorable and accommodating, it would be a shame to endanger that new level of understanding by his own carelessness. To have Hören discovered by the security chief before the time was right for him to step forward, or to have Hören himself find the gap in the hiding place's camouflage . . . either would be tragic. As comforting as Hören had sounded when talking to him, Arten had still been aware that the flashing force of the great man's wrath lay just beneath the surface.

As he came within arm's reach of the panel and the chink of telltale light, he thought of how much was at stake. Not just his own relationship with Hören and the others but the whole future of the Redemptorist movement. Perhaps this was the turning point, a change of heart in the man who represented the essence of their faith. If Hören could see a non-Bajoran as someone worthy of respect, perhaps even friendship . . . then, the day might not be far off when all the Redemptorists might step into that greater light, reconciled with the Bajorans who followed the teachings of the Kai Opaka. It could happen . . . and, in his own simple way, Arten might have helped bring it about.

He reached for the corner of the panel, to set it as it should have been left. As he did so, he heard the voice.

Hören's voice—not the low, soothing one with which he had spoken to Arten. But the old one, the voice of fire and blood, the voice that lashed both apostates and the strangers who had come from beyond the stars. A voice of dire prophecy that could make a planet tremble, riven to its dark, molten core . . .

Arten realized what was happening. On the blank chips that he had brought, Hören had already begun recording another broadcast, which like the others before it, would be smuggled down to the surface of Bajor and scattered to the waiting ears of the faithful. Those who also believed in the sanctity of fire and blood.

He felt his heart tremble inside his chest. It would have been too much to expect all the change to happen in a matter of moments. There was still much left to be done. . . .

It dismayed him to hear that voice speak of the Bajorans whose deaths would be required to purify their sullied world. Heretics, collaborators, traitors . . . all those who by word or deed had offended the righteous.

The list seemed to get longer with each recording. Hören repeated one of the names, and then again, slowly, as though he were already savoring the satisfaction that he would receive from that particular assassination.

". . . she with the blood of the faithful upon her

hands . . . Kira Nerys . . . she knows not, how soon justice will embrace her . . . and crush the life from her foul body . . ."

Arten's heart fell—into a darkness greater than that which surrounded him.

"Kira . . ."

He set the corner of the panel into position, turned, and hurried away from the hiding place.

CHAPTER
4

THE PROOF WAS on the computer screen. Everything he had suspected, felt deep in his bones . . . every time Gul Tahgla or any of the other Cardassians had opened a mouth to speak, as though for creatures such as they, the simple ritual of greeting was only the prelude to another scheming lie. . . .

"Is there any point that requires elaboration, Commander?" On the other side of the desk, Security Chief Odo stood waiting.

"No—" Sisko shook his head. "It's all pretty much as I thought it would be." He sat forward in the chair, his chin propped against his fist. The bleak feeling that the ancients of Earth might have termed *melancholia* had overtaken him for a moment, as he had read through Odo's report on the Cardassians' so-called research vessel. *They lie to us,* he thought, *and in turn we send a spy into their midst.* It demonstrated how deception led to deception, turnabout and turn again, a snake with its own tail grasped in its jaws.

He found it even less cheering to ponder that the cycle of deception had only just started. His own lies—or, if he felt inclined to be charitable with himself, the concealing of the truth—would go on. He'd already decided as much. All that remained was to order his security chief to stay silent about what he'd discovered.

"This report"—Sisko reached out and tapped the computer screen—"is to be placed under *total* access restriction. For the time being, no one is to see it but me. Understood?"

"As you wish, Commander."

" 'No one' includes my first officer, Major Kira, on down—got it? And I'll have a word with Chief Engineer O'Brien myself. I don't want it even talked about that you entered the Cardassian vessel."

Odo drew himself to his humanoid form's full height. "You can rely upon my discretion, Commander." His tone indicated that his professional pride had been nicked.

"Yes, of course; I didn't mean to imply otherwise." With a few taps on the keyboard, Sisko blanked the screen, sending the report to a local memory node rather than to the station's main data banks. "I merely wished to stress the gravity of the situation."

"I understand." Odo seemed mollified—though, as always, it was hard to tell. "That's why I took the initiative of ordering the disembarkation procedures for the Cardassian vessel to be put on indefinite hold. The exit crews have been so instructed."

"What—" Sisko sat bolt upright. "That's not within your authority!"

"But, Commander—" Odo had been taken aback by the other's reaction. "I thought it the prudent thing to do, given the fact that the installation of the impulse buffers has been completed; the vessel has already been transferred from the engineering bay to one of the docking pylons. Its scheduled departure time was within the next hour—"

Sisko ignored the security chief's explanation, as he quickly punched through a priority comm line to the pylon. "This is Commander Sisko. The hold order on the Cardassian vessel is hereby countermanded. Recommence all appropriate departure procedures. The vessel's original schedule is to be complied with."

No sooner had he gotten a confirmation of his order and had disconnected, than another call came through. Gul Tahgla's face appeared on the viewscreen.

"Commander Sisko." Tahgla's image nodded to him. "Is there a problem? Your exit crew informs me—"

"It's been taken care of," replied Sisko. "I trust you'll accept our apologies for any delay. Please bear in mind that yours is one of the first non-Federation ships to be cleared for travel through the wormhole. We're still fine-tuning our procedures."

"Nothing more than that?" The Cardassian *gul*'s eyes peered out from the screen. "I was concerned that there might be some second thoughts on your part. About letting us proceed on our mission. Perhaps you never anticipated that we would cooperate as fully as we did with your invasive technical requirements."

"My only concern, Gul Tahgla, was for the safety of the wormhole's inhabitants. We have an agreement with them, as well. Now that the impulse buffers are in place around your engines, you're free to go."

"Thank you. As I've mentioned before, I find your concern for these immaterial creatures to be . . . amusing." He reached for the comm switch on the panel before him. "It might be some time before I return this way. Perhaps we can resume our conversation then. That is, if you're still here." The screen went blank.

"Are there any further instructions, Commander?" During the exchange with Tahgla, Odo had stayed discreetly out of range of the comm lens.

"No . . ." Sisko shook his head. He knew that Odo was wondering, after the report he'd received about the true nature of the Cardassian research vessel, whether he had lost his mind; whether the nonstop pressure and mounting responsibilities of both running the station and overseeing the Federation's diplomatic relations with Bajor had deranged his rational faculties. The time would come—and soon, he hoped—when he would be able to explain to Odo and the others the reasons for the decisions he'd made. The gamble he'd taken. But until then . . . "Proceed as I've indicated. Until further notice."

When he was alone again in the office, he set the viewscreen to a remote scanner on the station's exterior, opposite the currently engaged docking pylon. Gul Tahgla's vessel was in the process of casting off, the arcs of the securing mandibles and the transfer umbilical cord slowly retracting from the ungainly Cardassian shape. The quick, bright flares of the maneuvering jets turned the vessel's main thruster ports away from the station. The screen darkened against the engines' sudden pulse. In only a few more minutes, the vessel had disappeared beyond the scanner's highest magnification.

From the position of DS9 in the Bajoran system's asteroid belt, there would be no visual check of the Cardassian vessel's entry into the wormhole. Other, more sensitive tracking devices would record that moment. And as to what happened after that, on the other side . . .

Commander Sisko gazed at the blank screen, as though it could show him his own brooding thoughts.

"Any luck?"

Bashir looked over his shoulder at the voice that had come from behind him. Framed by dangling wires and the thicker cables of atmospheric life-support systems, Chief Engineer O'Brien stood in the quarantine module's doorway.

For a moment, he wasn't sure what O'Brien was asking about. Over synthales in Quark's establishment on the Promenade—perhaps a few too many synthales—he had divulged some of his more personal plans to the engineer. Most of them—all, actually —had dealt with getting closer to some of the station's female crew members. O'Brien had listened to the various schemes and machinations with the tolerant nostalgia of the happily married. *Easy enough for him to take that attitude,* Bashir had thought glumly. *He goes back to his quarters with Keiko at the end of every shift.*

"Pardon me—"

"I mean, with that diagnostic contraption you've been wrestling." O'Brien pointed to the blood analysis unit perched precariously at the limits of Bashir's outstretched fingertips; the device threatened to come crashing to the module's floor at any moment. "Need a hand?"

"Well, yes, actually." As with every other working and living space aboard DS9, the quarantine module was a hodgepodge of components finessed or brute-forced into working together. Or hopefully so; the QM was still a long way from going on line. As confusing as the interior layout was, its improvised nature was even more readily apparent from the outside, as it rested in one of O'Brien's largest engineering bays. A heavy-ore transport that the Cardassians had abandoned now formed the linear spine of the QM; a turbolift would have been handy to get from one end to the other, though Bashir knew there was no chance of an equipment request like that being granted. Along the transport's windowless sides, O'Brien had mounted every sealable living and working space that he could scrounge from DS9's innards, linking them with a branching network of corridors; the ungainly result looked like a cubist grape cluster, rendered on a gigantic scale. Something sleeker would have better suited Bashir's aesthetic preferences, but for the moment he was only concerned about not dropping the blood analyzer onto his head. "It should fit in here all right, but . . ."

O'Brien stood on tiptoe and peered into the overhead niche in which the unit was wedged partway. "Looks like your clearance is just a smidgen too tight. Tell you what—down in the drydock bay, I've got a jacksledge that'll clear this problem up in no time." He smiled. "I've had a lot of success with it lately."

"So I've heard." The account of the chief engineer's run-in with the Cardassians and its eventual outcome had already circulated around the station, adding considerably to the stock of anecdotes about O'Brien's creative temper displays. "The difference here is, however, that this piece of equipment belongs to *us*. So I'm a little more concerned about keeping it in one piece."

"Suit yourself."

Between the two of them, they managed to get the unit in place, after O'Brien had stripped away some of the casing insulation that he judged to be superfluous. Bashir sat with his back against the module's bulkhead and tried to regain his breath, as he watched O'Brien wrench down the retaining bolts.

"There, that should hold it." O'Brien tossed the wrench in with the rest of the tools that had accumulated in one corner. "I'll get the shop to dummy up a face panel so it doesn't look quite so ragged."

"I take it you have more time for this project now?" Bashir had been working single-handed on the quarantine module for the last several shifts. "The Cardassians must have finally left—"

"Sure enough. And I was never so glad to see the backs of anyone as I was that lot." O'Brien shook his head. "Sneaky bastards, too."

"What do you mean by that?" The comment, and the vehemence with which it had been spoken, took Bashir by surprise. The crew of the Cardassian research vessel had been unusually unobtrusive by their standards, confining themselves to either their shipboard quarters or the DS9 guest area that had been set aside for them. Generally, when Cardassians were aboard the station, a standing order went into effect, based upon the ancient Earth military slogan "Loose lips sink ships." It hadn't seemed to be necessary this time.

"Never mind." O'Brien's expression darkened. "You'll probably find out about it soon enough." He looked into the farther reaches of the QM, unlit except for the temporary work lanterns secured to the ceiling. "So, what've we got left to do here? I don't want to spend the rest of my life fiddling with this setup."

The quarantine module had been the chief engineer's main project before the arrival of the Cardassian research vessel. And a high-priority project, as well, given the limited resources with which they had to contend. O'Brien and his technicians were proving themselves masters at the art of improvisation, converting the station's odds and ends into functioning medical equipment.

Pressure to complete the QM was mounting. Before DS9 could be considered an operational transit point, capable of handling the amount of anticipated traffic for the stable wormhole, the means of handling shipborne contagions would have to be in place. It was a problem as old as the art of navigation itself; in pursuit of a specialization in interstellar medicine, Bashir had studied the old practices of seaports on several ocean-dominated planets, Earth included. Plague carried ashore by the fleas on a rat climbing down a wharf line could decimate a population with no immunity to foreign diseases; a feverish sailor coughing up red-tinged phlegm in a waterfront tavern could infect the crews of every ship tied up in the harbor. Diagnostic procedures and treatment had improved since the days of towing a plague ship out to open water and setting it afire, but in an uncharted universe, the dangers were still close to infinite—even more so, now that the wormhole had opened up the entire Gamma Quadrant for exploration. That was the reason Bashir had pushed for this assignment; this was the edge of medicine, a place where careers and reputations were forged.

Now, he responded to O'Brien, "Most of the environment chambers still need to be sealed." He kept a running checklist inside his head, on what still needed to be done. "I'll have to be able to maintain hyperbaric atmosphere pressures with some gases that are fairly tricky to work with." The QM was designed to treat nonoxygen breathers, as well as the range of humanoid life-forms. "There are the rest of the monitors, of course—I should be getting a cargo shipment from Procurement any time now." Bashir started ticking off the items on his fingers. "Alarm systems, comm lines . . ."

"Small stuff," said O'Brien. "We'll be able to knock all that out pretty quick. The hard part's going to be getting the extrusion gantry working. Any time you go poking things out beyond the perimeter shields, you start running into problems."

Bashir knew how much work the chief engineer had already put into the QM's positioning abilities. The necessity for the module to be able to move outside the station had dictated its placement near one of the main cargo bays, so it could access the massive airlock doors opening onto empty space. In the event of a disease outbreak aboard a vessel approaching DS9, depending upon the nature of the infection, the stricken individuals could be brought aboard the station in hermetic-containment gurneys and placed directly into the QM; if the virus or other pathogenic agent was considered too dangerous, however, the QM with its medical team aboard could be extruded through the cargo bay doors on its segmented gantry arm. The only contact with the plague ship would be through the trailing umbilical cord providing an outward flow of life-support systems to the QM and the vessel to which it had attached itself. Until the crisis had passed, the sufferers had been treated, the infection banished . . .

Or not.

"I got the clearance from the ordnance master." O'Brien's voice lowered; he was aware that there were some details of a quarantine module's construction that a chief medical officer wouldn't want a casual passerby to hear of. "The explosive charges are being constructed in the station armory right now. Soon as they're ready, I'll set 'em in place myself, and then we can get the last of the bulkhead panels finished up. You'll have to go down and code the fuses."

Bashir nodded. It was a secret shared between him and the chief engineer, and otherwise known only by the station's highest officers; the final necessary element of the module's construction. An image from a med school lecture came unbidden to his mind, of an ancient sailing ship set afire in open water. He could imagine how it would have looked, the flames leaping up through the rigging, the billowing black smoke clouds woven with sparks, the faces of the pale dead, the dying consumed by an even greater fever. . . .

Some diseases couldn't be cured. They could only be stopped; the infection kept from spreading any further. A cleansing fire, and then the vacuum as cold and final as the first uncharted depths that man had sailed upon.

That was what the explosive charges were for; why they would be buried right in the fabric of the quarantine module. Better that, to annihilate the QM and the diseased ship, and the medics and crew together, than risk the spread of an untreatable contagion. The few would be sacrificed for the many. That was sound medical practice, a decision a doctor would have to make.

And that was why the coding for the fuses, the explosives' trigger commands, would be known only to the station's chief medical officer. Bashir felt his blood temperature drop a notch as he thought about it, as he had so many times already. A situation unique in Starfleet regulations, a destruct sequence that could not be initiated or countermanded by any other officer, including the station's commander—in this and any other deep space posting, the quarantine module was the inviolable territory of medicine, with its fate and the lives of its crew solely in the hands of the doctor in charge. On DS9, that would be Bashir; he had already decided—as other chief medical officers before him had—that if the moment should come, he would be aboard the QM when the explosives were triggered. It was an unwritten regulation that ensured the destruct sequence would be undertaken only in the gravest of circumstances.

As Bashir stood in the center of the uncompleted module, it was as though he were finally seeing the reality of his ambitions gathering around him—everything that had brought him to DS9. *This is what you wanted,* he told himself; the edge of medicine, a place where reputations could be made . . . even if the cost was his own life.

"Ah, cheer up." O'Brien had read his dark thoughts. He clapped Bashir on the shoulder. "How often does a man get a chance to blow himself up in such style? Kind of a shame, actually, that it hardly ever happens. Tell you what, though—I'll see if I can get the charges doubled in strength, so if you have to, at least you'll go out with a proper, fine show."

Bashir laughed. "Thanks. I appreciate your concern."

Though later, after O'Brien had left him alone once more in the module, he had to admire the chief engineer's poker face. As he walked through the area, switching off the work lights, he realized that he couldn't be sure whether O'Brien had been joking or not.

He crawled forward in darkness, as he had before, until he reached the hiding place. Arten turned the panel aside and entered the glow of the portable lantern. As dim as it was, he still had to squint and blink until his eyes had adjusted.

"How good of you to come once more." The voice spoke from the blurred silhouette in front of him. Hören's voice. "So much is made possible by the labor of the faithful."

"I was told it was important." He had brought nothing with him; the supplies he'd carried last time were sufficient for several days more. "I came as soon as I could get away."

With his shoulders scraping the close metal struts, he watched as Hören rummaged through the objects spread along the wall. The Redemptorist leader's muscled bulk turned awkwardly in the space, like a plowbeast caught in a pen too small for it. The longing in Arten's breast grew sharper—the day when this man would stand upright in the open, an equal with other spokesmen for the Bajorans, couldn't arrive too soon.

"Take this." Hören set a pair of recording chips in Arten's hand. "They must be smuggled down to Bajor as soon as possible. A message to all believers . . . our future . . ."

His heart leapt. Perhaps these were the words, the treasure hidden in the black, square objects barely larger than his thumbnail, that would bring about the dawn. "Yes . . . of course. . . ." Arten hurriedly tucked them inside his jacket. "A freight shipment is scheduled to leave at the end of the shift. These will be at their destination tomorrow. . . ."

"Good." Before Arten could back toward the hiding place's exit, Hören leaned forward and clasped an arm around his shoulder. "You have done much already. For this you will be rewarded."

The other's face was so close to Arten's that their breaths mingled. He felt his soul mirrored in the eyes, fierce yet also inexpressibly sad. "There . . . there's no need. . . ."

"But you will have your reward," said Hören. "In this world—and the next." He gathered Arten toward him, as though to bestow a kiss of peace upon the younger member of the brethren's forehead.

Arten saw then, at the limit of his vision, a flash of bright metal as the other drew his hand from inside his jacket. Suddenly, the air seemed to rush from Arten's lungs, leaving him unable even to gasp, as a widening circle of pain radiated from his gut.

Hören let go of him, and he was unable to keep his balance, collapsing onto the hiding place's floor. His hands scrabbled futilely at the dagger that had torn open his abdomen.

"That is the reward you have earned. . . ."

The voice came out of the darkness that had engulfed the close space.

"By the treachery of your heart . . . that would love your people's enemies. . . ."

He could barely hear the last few words. In the widening pool of his blood, he curled around the metal that had become the gravitational center of a collapsing universe. He managed to raise his head and could just make out Hören gazing down at him, and beyond, the figure of Deyreth Elt emerging from the shadows, a look of triumph on his narrow, wizened face.

That was the last he saw. Except inside himself, where he fell toward a dawn whose light erased every world and pain.

CHAPTER
5

"PEOPLE, WE HAVE a small problem before us." Sisko leaned forward, hands clasped atop his desk. In a semicircle before him sat his chiefs of security and engineering, his first officer, and his chief medical officer. "It's also an opportunity for us."

None of the others spoke. The low, somber tone of his voice indicated the gravity of the situation he was about to present to them.

"You will recall that some ten shifts ago, we were hosts once more to our old friends the Cardassians." He spread his hands apart. "Whether we like it or not, that's the nature of our job here. DS Nine's function as a transit point, the doorway to the Gamma Quadrant, is just beginning; we're going to be seeing a lot more traffic coming and going at our docking pylons. We need to prepare for that—"

"Commander." In one of the center chairs, Major

Kira stirred restlessly. "You're not telling us anything we don't know already. If this is just some sort of pep talk, there are a lot of other, more important things back at Ops I should be taking care of."

Sisko turned his unsmiling gaze straight toward her. "I can assure you that I'm not wasting your time. As you will see." He leaned back in his own chair. "The point I'm trying to make to you all is that, at the present time, under the orders we have received from the Starfleet high command, we are not at liberty to pick and choose among those seeking to travel through the wormhole. The Federation wishes to achieve a greater *rapprochement* with the Cardassian empire; allowing them access to the wormhole, and to the Gamma Quadrant beyond it, is seen as the primary means of accomplishing that. Of course, this is the age-old conflict between diplomatic intentions at headquarters and security concerns on the line. There are undoubtedly some things we would do differently here if we had a completely free hand."

Chief Engineer O'Brien smiled wryly. "Like telling the Cardassians to take the long way around if they want to get to the Gamma Quadrant?"

"More or less. Frankly, I share the opinion of some of you, that if the Cardassians were never to set foot aboard this station again, it would be too soon. But that's not the case—at least for now."

Kira's expression had become progressively more irritated. "Commander . . . please. As you've said before, there's a lot we still have to get ready here. So, if you could just . . ." She made a rolling, speed-it-up gesture.

Instilling patience in his second-in-command was

going to be a long process, he knew; losing his own patience with her wouldn't help. "I bring these points up for a reason, Major. I want it understood that I consider the present situation—the reason for our meeting now—to have been unavoidable. There should be no guilt feelings or pointing of fingers at other officers. Do I make myself clear?"

She had provoked him into speaking more forcefully than when he had begun; he could see in her eyes that she had started wondering just what the problem could be. Behind Kira's back, Odo and O'Brien exchanged glances; they had the advantage of having been in on it from the early stages.

"Take a look at this." From the desk drawer, Sisko extracted his data padd. "Our security chief managed to find a way aboard the Cardassian vessel before it left the station. Here's his report on what he found." Sisko watched as Kira scanned through the display, O'Brien and Dr. Bashir looking over her shoulders. "As you'll recall, the vessel in question was represented to us as being for the purposes of scientific research—the Cardassians supposedly were initiating a sectorwide survey of the Gamma Quadrant, with an orientation toward joint commercial development with the Federation. That's the main reason why their application for access to the wormhole was granted so quickly. When their vessel arrived here at the station, we certainly had no reason to doubt their stated intentions—"

"True enough," said O'Brien, nodding. "We've seen the same sort of craft before—basically nothing more than converted long-haul freight carriers—in a lot of the other systems that the Cardassians have trading protocols with. They strip out all the light armament and substitute a bunch of different sensor arrays. If they're going into a sector where hostilities could be expected, they'll convoy with a cruiser or two and some advance scouts." A shrug. "And that's certainly what this one looked like from the outside."

"We certainly had little way of knowing otherwise. The agreement between the Federation and the Cardassians stipulated that no search of the vessel would be permitted while it was being worked on here. Technically, we're already in violation of that agreement—"

"What does that matter?" Kira struck the back of her hand across the data padd with mounting anger. "'Research vessel'—they were lying to us from the beginning! It's stuffed with weaponry—"

"I've read Odo's report," said Sisko dryly. "I'm aware of what he found inside the vessel."

Odo leaned toward her. "If you'll look at the last few screens, you'll see the details of the shielding with which they had surrounded the arms. Even if we had done a scan of the vessel, we probably wouldn't have been able to detect what they had aboard."

"And now, they're on the other side of the wormhole." Kira shook her head in disgust. "Gul Tahgla and the rest are probably laughing themselves sick, over how they sneaked this right past us. Just before they head off to attack some defenseless system in the Gamma Quadrant—"

"There's very little chance of that, actually." Odo pointed to the data padd. "My analysis of the vessel's armament—and I believe the commander concurs with me on this—is that it is essentially defensive in nature. The vessel lacks the speed and maneuverability with which to mount an offensive campaign; whereas its perimeter shields are several times more powerful than those of a regulation Cardassian cruiser." He was enjoying the display of his expertise. "The other significant finding I made is the degree to which the vessel has been modified for long-term stasis under deep space conditions. The crew quarters, the life-support systems, food and atmosphere replication—everything has been set up so that the vessel can operate indefinitely without the need for planetfall."

Kira scowled in puzzlement. "What's the point of that?"

"Isn't it obvious?" O'Brien had looked up from the report. "Wherever they're going, they're planning on a long stay. And they're prepared to fight off anybody who tries to move them."

Bashir had stayed silent through the discussion, but now spoke up. "Do we have any idea of where that's going to be?"

"That is the problem, people." Sisko looked across their faces. "Now that the Cardassian vessel is on the other side of the wormhole, we've been able to trace its position with our remote monitoring devices—plus, unknown to them, and thanks to the efforts of our chief engineer and security officer, they're carrying aboard a couple of miniaturized activity trackers. We not only know where they are, but also have a pretty good idea of what they're up to. At this moment, the engines of Gul Tahgla's vessel have been placed in standby mode; it's no longer in motion—after having been traveling continuously since it exited into the Gamma Quadrant. It now has apparently rendezvoused with a group of other Cardassian vessels that had previously gone through the wormhole. Our sensors indicate that a large volume of equipment

and supplies is being transferred to Gul Tahgla's vessel, as well as additional crew members; there's some pretty extensive structural work being done, too. They obviously wanted to do all their retrofitting at what they thought would be a distance sufficient to keep their activities from being detected by us. The probability is high that the vessel is in the process of being converted to operational efficiency as a self-sufficient outpost base. Once the Cardassians are done, though—and that shouldn't be too much longer—by our best estimates of the vessel's engine capacities, it would take them at least ten shifts to return to the vicinity of the wormhole."

"Wait a minute." Kira set the data padd down on the corner of the desk, and reached across to turn the computer screen toward her. She called up a navigation chart. "There's nothing out there—that's totally empty space."

"Precisely. So we have to assume that the intentions of Gul Tahgla and his crew, once they've completed the modifications to the vessel, are to return to the zone surrounding the wormhole's exit point. That's the only thing of value in which the Cardassian empire could be interested."

"But sovereignty over the wormhole has already been established—it belongs to Bajor—"

"Correction, Major. Sovereignty over *this end* of the wormhole has been established. As this is the first stable wormhole to have been discovered, there are points of interstellar law regarding it that have yet to be determined—and the Cardassians appear to be placing themselves in a compelling legal position. There's an old Earth maxim that possession is nine points of the law—that's undoubtedly what the

Cardassians will argue, as well. DS Nine was moved to its current orbital position to validate Bajor's claim on the wormhole and to fend off any attempt by the Cardassians to seize control of it. But the wormhole's exit point in the Gamma Quadrant is light-years away from any inhabited system. There's no intelligent species on the other side for whom a similar claim of sovereignty could be made." Sisko swiveled his chair, turning back toward the others. "Now, the Cardassians have seized this opportunity, to gain back at least some of what they inadvertently let go when they abandoned Bajor and this station."

"It is," said Odo, "the sort of thing they might've been expected to do. As a species—and I state this from experience—they are addicted to legal maneuvers, exploitation of loopholes, and the like. For all their military swaggering, they are at their heart a race of lawyers." He shrugged. "That may account for their persistent . . . *public relations* problems."

Bashir nodded thoughtfully, as though having been presented with a particularly interesting diagnosis. "It's rather like a rope with two ends, isn't it? We've got hold of one end, and now the Cardassians are reaching for the other. If they get it . . . then, who really owns the rope?" He gazed up at the ceiling. "Or like one of those ancient, land-based transportation systems—what were they called?—a toll highway. We can control who goes into the wormhole, and under what conditions, but if the Cardassians' claim to the sector around the wormhole's other end were upheld, they'd control who'd be able to *exit* from the hole and travel on into the Gamma Quadrant." He stroked his chin. "Very clever . . ."

"Will you just shut up?" Kira glared fiercely at the

doctor. "This isn't a problem in one of your medical textbooks, that you'll get an A for solving. The whole future of my people is jeopardized by this—"

"Exactly, Major. As you see, I have not been wasting your time." Sisko could almost read the thoughts tumbling one after another behind her eyes. "Without effective control over the wormhole, Bajor would become once again a backwater of the universe, a depleted planet with nothing of value to sell. Essentially, it would be another charity case for the Federation. Membership in the Federation for Bajor would become a matter of low priority; the DS Nine station itself would be cut back to minimal functioning or even deactivated. It's simple economics, actually."

"If that's how the Federation would feel about Bajor—if that's how *you* feel, Commander—then we'd find a way of getting by without you." Kira's gaze narrowed. "We survived the Cardassians' rape of our planet; we could survive the Federation's neglect. *And perhaps it would be better that way.*"

"Perhaps." He knew he had evoked the fanatical streak in her beliefs, the sympathy with the Bajoran extremists that lay buried just beneath the surface. It was so tightly interwoven with the anger that constantly simmered inside her, that to produce one was to face the other. "But perhaps it might not be necessary. I suggest that instead of giving way to these emotional displays, we might more profitably turn our attention to finding a way of circumventing the Cardassians' plans."

"What would you suggest?" Her glare didn't soften. "If we had some sort of armed vessel of our own, maybe we could go out through the wormhole and knock them out of commission—"

"That would be an act of war, Major. An unpro-voked act. The fact that we perceive the Cardassians' actions as being contrary to our interests doesn't give us the right to do that. No, I suggest that we beat them at their own game. Even if they knew that we were aware of their intentions, they're still limited as to how quickly they can return to the sector around the wormhole's exit. That provides us with our window of opportunity. If we can get a substation in position there, the Federation can legitimately press a claim for sovereignty over the sector—before the Cardassians can do anything about it. That's why I asked our chief engineer to sit in on this meeting." Sisko swiveled toward O'Brien. "Well? What do you think—is there anything we can put together, and fast, that we can get out through the wormhole to establish a presence with?"

The engineer shrugged. "We've got small craft, runabouts and the like, that we could send—"

"That won't do. The Cardassians would be able to dislodge our claim, based on precedents in interstellar case law. A ship or smaller craft doesn't indicate a serious intention to set up a permanent base." Sisko shook his head. "No, we need something that we can represent, if even just on a temporary basis, as an actual substation. Later, if need be, we can get some-thing larger out there."

"I don't know . . ." O'Brien clenched his hand into a fist. "If we had more time . . . if we had the man-power and the materials . . . we could build you what-ever you wanted. But if you're talking about an enclosed, self-sustaining unit with living quarters, supply replicators, everything a substation would need . . ." The fist squeezed harder. "To put together something like that from scratch . . . there's just no way." His gaze shifted away, as though catching sight of something beyond the commander's office. "Unless . . . unless we used something we already had on hand. . . ."

"What would that be?"

"The quarantine module." Excitement cleared the engineer's previous expression. "It's perfect! It's already designed to operate outside the station. Long-term living quarters, all the facilities—it's certainly big enough to qualify as a permanent base—"

"Wait a minute." A look of alarm moved across Bashir's face. "I've been waiting for that module to come on line for months! It's already *got* a designated function."

"Which will be of little use to anyone, Doctor, if the Cardassians gain control of the other end of the wormhole. If that happens, DS Nine won't be the major transit point we've been anticipating; the Cardassians will be just as happy to shut down all movement through it, if they can't have exclusive access." Sisko held up his palm against any further protest. "I'm sorry, Doctor, but the circumstances force me to overrule you on this matter." He turned back to O'Brien. "How soon can you get the quarantine module ready?"

"It's already close to being finished. Now, we'll have to detach it from the extension gantry, sever the umbilical connections, move the atmospheric and other life-support systems out of the cargo bay and into the module . . . let's see . . ." O'Brien nodded slowly. "We'll have to rig towing mounts on both it and one of the larger utility craft, get some buffers in place . . ." He shrugged. "Five or six shifts, and we'll have it ready to go."

"Make it four. Gul Tahgla isn't going to wait around for us. Major Kira—" He turned back to her. "You're so concerned about protecting Bajor's economic interests in the wormhole—fine. This mission is yours. I can't spare you more than anyone else aboard the station, but the presence of a Bajoran native on our impromptu substation will probably help legitimize our claim to sovereignty over this additional sector. Major—"

She looked up from the computer panel. He could see that she had called up some additional data on it, but she blanked the screen before he could tell what it had been. For a moment, her level gaze burned into his, then she nodded once. "I'll have full operational command?"

"You'll have to—it'll be strictly a one-person operation. We're already critically understaffed here. One of our freight shuttles will be rigged so you can use it as a pusher vehicle. You'll take the retrofitted module out through the wormhole, transfer to it once it's in position, and represent yourself to all approaching vessels—namely, the Cardassians—as having established authority over the sector. It shouldn't be too long before we can rotate a skeleton crew out there to relieve you."

"Very well."

"Let's get to work, people." Sisko pushed back his chair to signal that the meeting was over.

Bashir remained seated after the other officers had left.

"Is there something on your mind, Doctor?"

"You could say that." The chief medical officer spoke slowly, like someone taking a first cautious step into unknown territory. "I think you've overlooked a critical factor in your plans, Commander."

"Oh?"

"You don't have the authority to order that the quarantine module be used for anything other than medical purposes."

Sisko waited a moment before replying. "You seem to forget, Doctor, that I'm the commander of this station."

"I'm well aware of that." Bashir's voice rose in pitch and volume. "But the quarantine module, like all medical equipment aboard DS Nine, is completely under *my* authority. That's by Starfleet regulation, Commander. Those rules were put into effect precisely to keep officers from diverting medical facilities and supplies from their intended use. The only person who can make decisions in that regard is the chief medical officer. I can order O'Brien to not even lay a finger on that module."

"I see." Sisko leaned back, studying the younger man before him. "Doctor Bashir—I would advise you not to press your authority on this. I'm faced with a crisis that threatens the continued operation of this station. If need be, I'll have you thrown in the brig. You won't be discharging much of your responsibilities as chief medical officer there."

Beads of sweat had risen on Bashir's forehead, and his hands trembled. "You could certainly do that, Commander. But then you're going to have to consider how it's going to look to the provisional government on Bajor, when word reaches them that you've stripped their DS Nine station of its first line of defense against epidemic diseases. And not just the station. Since all interstellar traffic to Bajor passes through here, without the quarantine module in place, the likelihood of spreading contagion on the planet's surface is multiplied well beyond tolerable limits. That's a lot to ask of them, just to help repair the damage caused by *your* decision to let the Cardassian vessel go through the wormhole."

"And I suppose you'd be the one to tell the provisional government all this?"

"How could you prevent me?" The look in Bashir's eyes was like that of a gambler at one of Quark's *dabo* tables, who had suddenly realized how far over his head he'd gotten. Only by throwing everything in on one desperate play was there a chance of saving himself. "Throwing me in the brig—that would mean a court-martial before I could be removed from my post on the station. The Bajorans would naturally be interested in something like that—they'd likely send a team of observers to the trial. And when I'm in open court, I'll say whatever I damn well feel like."

"Ah." Sisko pressed his fingertips together and studied Bashir through the cage they formed. "You realize, of course, that to go up against your commanding officer—and by extension, all of Starfleet—is undoubtedly the surest way of scuttling your career in this service? Even if the court-martial were to rule in your favor."

Bashir's neck and jaw muscles were tensed rigid. "And what would *your* career be like after that?" His voice could barely squeeze through as a whisper. "Or is that not really a matter of concern to you anymore?"

So it's gotten out this far, thought Sisko. He knew what the doctor was referring to. That Bashir could speak of it—the resistance he'd put up against taking over the command of DS9, the request he'd made to Picard, and then retracted, for an Earthside transfer —only proved there were few secrets on the station.

"My personal feelings don't enter into this." Sisko's index fingers tapped against each other. "What would make *you* feel better about this mission for which the quarantine module is required? As chief medical officer, that is."

Bashir took a deep breath before replying. "You spoke of it as a one-person operation. I'd like to change that. There's more than enough room—the module's set up for dozens of occupants—for me to go along with Major Kira."

She'll have something to say about that. He kept the comment to himself. "Why would you want to?"

"Commander Sisko, I've been pushing for access to the wormhole since it was discovered. Since you reported the existence of the creatures inside it. These are life-forms whose nature and habitat have no equal in the galaxy—they should be studied. They possess capabilities that we have *no* understanding of—they *created* a stable wormhole! The future of the universe's exploration may rest with them. . . ."

"Of course. And since you're the chief medical officer in this sector, you'd naturally be the one to go into the wormhole and read their temperature and take their pulse."

"Well . . ."

"And *you* would be the one to achieve galactic renown for your groundbreaking studies of the wormhole's inhabitants. I'm sure the number of journal articles you'd get out of it would considerably advance your career."

"Yes, but . . ."

"Perhaps you could even go on the lecture circuit." Sisko smiled. "Doctor Bashir, I think we understand each other very well." He pulled open the bottom desk drawer and took something from it. "Here, catch."

Bashir looked down in bewilderment at the spheroid of stitched leather his hands had reflexively trapped against his chest. "What's this?"

"I thought you might be aware of my love for the ancient Earth sport of baseball—"

"Oh. Yes, of course; you have a library of the old players in the holosuites . . ."

"That," said Sisko, pointing, "is what *hardball* is played with. Perhaps you'd like to keep it as a little souvenir of our discussion today." He leaned back, his smile growing wider. "I can tell when I've been outgunned. It's a two-person mission now. You'll be aboard the retrofitted quarantine module strictly as a scientific observer—you're not to interfere with Major Kira's operations in the slightest degree. I don't think I need to warn you that if you do get in her way, she's likely to make pretty short work of you. Understood?"

Bashir collapsed back in his chair, his entire body suffused with an attitude of relief. "Perfectly, Commander." His upper uniform was soaked with sweat.

What Sisko didn't tell him—and he wasn't about to, either—was that he'd been prepared to grant the doctor's request from the beginning. But now, Bashir had learned to fight for what he believed in; now, he was that much closer to being an officer as well as a doctor.

The commander decided Bashir had had enough for one shift. "I'll run interference for you with Major Kira, and tell her about the change in plans. Maybe you'd better get hold of the chief engineer and let him know."

There was no delay in finding Kira; she was waiting right outside. A drained-looking Bashir slipped past as she strode into the office.

"Commander—" She planted her hands flat on the desk and leaned forward, her eyes pieces of heated steel. "There's something—"

"Let me guess. Something you found in the computer files that didn't sit well with you. What would that be?"

"Just this." She grabbed the edge of the panel and turned it so that they both could see the data she called up. "You removed the restricted access code on Odo's report." Her nail tapped the screen. "And there's the date you logged the original file into your private memory node. And that date is *before* the Cardassian vessel left for the wormhole!" She blanked the screen and stood erect. "Commander, you knew beforehand what Gul Tahgla was up to. You deliberately let the Cardassians go—you even countermanded a hold order that Odo had already placed on their vessel—and thus jeopardized the success of DS Nine's mission here."

He sighed, eyes half-closed in weariness. Facing his first officer's anger was like leaning into a storm wind. "This seems to be my shift for being an educator. Sit down, and I'll give you a small but important lesson."

"I'm only interested in an explanation—"

"Sit down, Major." The thunder in his voice brought an even harder glare from Kira. But she sat. "You may not believe so, but DS Nine's success is my top priority. To ensure that, I've had to do some things that are not in the Starfleet operational manuals. I've been aware of the flaw in our control over the wormhole since practically the first shift we moved the station to this sector—only a fool wouldn't have been. And I've been in constant communication with the Federation authorities, urging them to allocate us the funds and material necessary for placing a substation at the wormhole's other end, before anyone else could do the same. Since you're not as experienced in dealing with the Federation bureaucracy as I am, it may come as a surprise to you that my request is tied up in committee meetings. I know that the only way to get the Federation to act is to manufacture a crisis that it can't ignore. Gul Tahgla's little ploy is exactly what I needed. The threat of the Cardassians gaining any control at all over the wormhole will be enough to force the Federation to provide the means of establishing a permanent substation at the other end." He shrugged. "If I'd known of another way of getting action—other than allowing this situation to go right to the brink—I would have taken it. But there isn't any other way."

"You've thought this all through . . . haven't you?" Kira's anger had been replaced by a look of grudging admiration. "It's something you've been planning for a while."

"I knew we wouldn't have to wait long. The Cardassians' council has the virtue of being more ruthlessly organized than the Federation's decision-making body. They seize opportunities quickly.

That's why it's up to officers on the line, such as ourselves, to anticipate their moves." Sisko leaned across the desk. "And now, I'll tell you something else I've been planning. And that's my putting you in charge of this operation. Even before you allowed that group of Redemptorists aboard a few months ago, I've had my concerns about this division in your loyalties—a division that seems more important to you than to anyone else. You seem to feel there's some kind of conflict between performing your duties as a Starfleet officer and being a Bajoran patriot. I don't see that conflict, Major; as far as I'm concerned, you best serve your people by ensuring the success of this station's mission."

Kira began to say something, then forced herself silent.

"Consider this operation as something of a test." Sisko began sorting through the papers on his desk. "Your attitude toward it is, in some ways, as important to DS Nine's future as actually getting the substation in place. Think about that." He looked up from the papers. "Dismissed."

Her hands squeezed the arms of the chair, words forming at her tongue, before she got up and strode for the door.

He watched her go. When the door had slid shut, he closed his eyes and laid his head back.

CHAPTER
6

ODO KNELT DOWN and turned the corpse onto its back. The body was relatively undamaged, despite having been found inside the massive gears that opened and closed the cargo bay doors. That alone indicated to him a murder that was the work of an amateur, or at least somebody unfamiliar with the operations of DS9. A professional—and he'd admit there were some aboard the station—would have known that sensors activated by the chemical traces of complex organic matter were built into the gear teeth, to prevent crushing accidents to the dock's crew. The machinery could never provide a means of disguising a violent cause of death.

"I suppose we'll need an autopsy." Major Kira leaned over his shoulder. She had been called, as well, to the scene by the cargo bay's foreman. "Maybe

Bashir will have to be pulled off the substation mission to perform it."

He detected a hopeful note in her voice. "I hardly think one is necessary." Kira's sour relations with the chief medical officer were no concern of his; he wasn't about to help her out on that score. "This man's death is obviously due to multiple stab wounds." Odo placed his hand over the bloodied abdomen and let it flow inside; a second later, he extracted the probe. "From the size and shape of the blade, I'd say a personal weapon." Taking a handkerchief from his uniform's pocket, he re-formed his hand and wiped it clean. From the corner of his eye, he noted—with some satisfaction—a wince of distaste from Kira. *That'll teach her to butt in on police work.* "Male Bajoran, early twenties . . ." He spoke into his comm badge, the details being logged into his data base back at the Promenade security office.

"You recognize him?"

"Not by name." He glanced up at Kira. "Or not yet. But I know he was one of that group of Redemptorists, the ones doing microassembly over in the engineering bay." He caught another change of expression, a slight tautening of the corners of her mouth, that told him she had known that much, as well.

He completed the description, then called for a gurney to take the body to the medical unit's morgue. Still kneeling, he made a quick search through the corpse's pockets.

"Find anything?"

Odo stood up. Two small silver squares glittered on his palm. "Just these." He held the recording chips closer to his eye. "The seal's been broken on them. They've been used."

"Oh." Kira squinted at them. "Clues."

"Yes," he said patiently. "That's what they're called."

After the body had been wheeled away, Kira followed him back to the Promenade. He wanted to ask her if she didn't have anything more productive to do, but refrained. She was probably tensed up about the substation mission, he knew, anxious to get through the wormhole and out to the Gamma Quadrant. The last time he had encountered O'Brien in Quark's bar, the chief engineer had complained of her incessant pushing to get the quarantine module ready for travel. O'Brien finally had threatened to have her barred from the engineering bay, so he and his crew could work in peace.

As Odo pushed his way through the nonstop crowds on the Promenade, with Kira in his wake, he pondered the difficulties with humanoid emotions. He hadn't gone to great lengths to cultivate them inside himself, except for the ones useful in his job, such as suspicion and distrust; like the human appearance he bore on the exterior of his form, emotional traits would have been carefully acquired. The advantage to his essentially liquid-based nature, he'd often thought, was that few of the small things that troubled someone such as Kira had the same effect on him. He could let them sink without a trace, like stones dropped into an ocean.

"What's that smell?" Kira scowled as she looked around the security office. "It's like somebody had set fire to their old socks and then—" She used a Bajoran vulgarism that Odo knew meant *to extinguish by urination*.

The memory of Gri Rafod and the cheap tobacco that Quark had unloaded on him did manage to irritate Odo. "Trust me," he told Kira, "there were aspects to our last batch of Cardassian visitors that were worse than you can imagine." The smell had yet to completely fade.

He sat down at his desk and loaded first one chip, then the other, into a player. Neither produced sound. "These were never recorded on." He studied the chip player's small readout screen.

"How can you tell?"

"The type of recording device used with these first lays down an index of tracks. Even if the material is later erased, the index matrix remains. These chips don't have anything like that."

Kira leaned over the desk to look at them. "Not much good as clues, then, are they?"

"That, Major, is why I'm chief of security and you're not." Odo leaned back, holding up a chip between his thumb and forefinger. "Consider. A young Bajoran of known Redemptorist sympathies is found murdered, and in his possession are two recording chips, seals broken but not yet recorded upon." The chip made a small noise when he dropped it onto the desktop. "Perhaps someone wanted him to believe they contained recordings." He nodded slowly. "I'll have to think about this."

Kira made no move toward the office door. After a moment, Odo brought his gaze back round to her. "Is there something further I can do for you, Major?"

She shook her head, as though his voice had woken her. "No . . . nothing . . ."

When she had left, and the door had slid shut

behind her, Odo watched his forefinger push one of the chips around the surface of the desk. It wouldn't have taken any great skill at detection to see that something else had been on Kira's mind.

"What are you going to use for electromagnetic scanning?" Lieutenant Jadzia Dax, the station's chief science officer, looked up at the blueprints on the engineering bay's wall. The thin membrane, some ten meters square, was connected to the DS9 data bases and could call up any magnified schematic within seconds. "I don't see any of the usual data routes—"

"We've taken over the perimeter sensors and reconfigured them." Beside her, Dr. Bashir pointed to a section depicting the exterior of the quarantine module. "They were really needed only for docking maneuvers, but they have a pretty wide spectrum built into them—more than enough for what we need. Computer, give me the control layout." The images blurred and shifted on the membrane, then drew solid. "You see?" He leaned closer than necessary to Dax, reaching around her shoulder to indicate the new set of prints. "There's a lot of carrying capacity for the diagnostic and treatment equipment that we're not going to be using now. We just shunt those aside and use the circuits for whatever we need. Clever, really."

"Very." She ignored his arm—it wasn't actually touching her—and turned her self-possessed Trill smile toward him. "Your idea?"

"Well, no . . ." Bashir followed her toward the QM. "O'Brien's, as a matter of fact. But my approval was needed for it," he hurriedly added. "All these retrofits first have to go by me. . . ."

The chief engineer stood inside the module, sparks raining around him as he prodded a welding torch inside an open ceiling panel. Beyond him, the metal-on-metal sounds of his crew's labors boomed out of the QM's farther recesses. Black power cables snaked around his feet.

"Haven't used one of these since I was an apprentice." Through the noise, O'Brien had heard their approach. He switched off the torch's plasma flow, and the eerie ionic glow that had masked his face vanished. He pushed up his darkened goggles. "So, what's the verdict?"

"Well, I've really only seen the plans," said Dax. "But it seems like a lot to get done. Do you really think you can make your departure date?"

"This pup is going out the door as scheduled, even if I'm still riding on its back with a socket wrench." O'Brien flicked on the torch again. "Now, if you'll excuse me . . ."

"Give me a call at Ops when you have the chance, Doctor." Dax began picking her way out through the QM's clutter. "I've got some ideas on ancillary stat probes you might find interesting."

"How about right now?" Bashir moved to catch up with her, just before O'Brien brought his thickly gloved hand down from the ceiling panel and snagged him by the arm. "I'm not—"

"Not so fast." O'Brien held onto him. "I need you here. We've got some decisions to make." He signaled goodbye to Dax with the welding torch. "I'll send him up to you when he's finished his homework."

Bashir followed the chief engineer to the front exterior of the quarantine module. "So, what exactly is it that's so important?" His words sounded sulky even to himself.

"More important than your hormone level? Practically everything." O'Brien stood beside the intricate mandibles of the towing link that had been grafted onto one end of the QM. A passage large enough for a humanoid to crawl through ran along the center of the four C-shaped locking arms. "Actually, this isn't anything you have to make a decision on—I've already set it up, and I'm not changing it. You and Kira just need to know about it." He pointed to a set of black ovoids around the central channel's rim. "See those? I pulled some of the explosives from the interior walls and formed them into shaped thrust charges. That's because there isn't time to rig up fancy maneuvering jets with enough force to disengage the module from the cargo shuttle we're rigging up as a pusher vessel. Once you and Kira get through the wormhole and into range of your target position, and she transfers over to the substation, one of you will have to calculate your firing angle and let 'er rip." He picked up a cable with bare metal showing at its tip. "The trigger line'll be wired right into the pusher's control panel."

The egg-shaped bomblets seemed less than impressive. Bashir shrugged. "So?"

"I forget—you're a doctor, not a physicist. Well, this'll give you a chance to brush up on your Newton. When these go off, there's going to be a kick. You'd better have yourselves and everything else battened down before you punch the button."

Bashir turned and began to walk away, then halted. He looked over his shoulder. "Wait a minute. You said you took out *some* of the explosives. Where's the rest?"

"Where do you think?" O'Brien went on checking the cable's branching connections to the bomblets. "They're still inside the QM, right where I put them soon as they were delivered from ordnance. If you think I'm going to rip them out, try to seal the walls back up in time to get this thing on its way, and then put the charges *back* in when we want to use this for its original purpose . . ." He glanced over at Bashir, then shook his head. "Life's too short."

"Right—" Bashir looked at him in incredulity. "And I imagine it could get even shorter, what with riding all the way out to the Gamma Quadrant in a craft loaded with high explosives."

"What are you worried about?" O'Brien looped the cable over one of the locking arms and out of the way. "You're the only one who knows the fuse codes. Don't tell them to anyone, and then the charges might as well be cementene bricks for all the damage they could do." He clapped Bashir on the shoulder. "Come on. I need a break. And you look like you need a drink."

As they headed for the engineering bay's exit, they passed the microassembly work benches. A couple of the faces bent over the intricate work lifted and looked at Bashir and O'Brien, then turned back to the circuits beneath the lenses.

"Are those men working on the QM?" Bashir had seen that all the group were Bajorans.

"Of course. We've got everybody in the bay on this one."

"But I heard they're all Redemptorists . . ."

"They can be whatever they want, as long as they get the job done." O'Brien pushed him toward the door. "Let's go."

The voice—mocking, raging, compelling—filled the space. Even if the volume on the chip-player were turned all the way down, so that the words became hardly more than a whisper, they still dominated, hammering at one's ear.

Blood and fire . . . the voice of Hören Rygis spoke of those things, and the death of nonbelievers. *Blood* was the thin, degenerate stuff that flowed in the veins of the faithless; *fire* was the coming day of cleansing, of scouring away the elements that had polluted Bajor's holy soil. A fire that consumed life as its fuel and left the ashes of death behind, corpses facedown on the floors of the temples and council chambers.

"And beyond," cried the voice of the Redemptorists' leader. "The contagion has spread beyond the sky—it hovers above us, rising like the stench from a murderer's hands. Orbiting in empty space, hiding aboard the strangers' machinery of oppression—but even that is far enough to evade our wrath, our justice. She conspires with them, she sups at the table of the wicked, her goblet a martyr's skull, the wine spilling down her chin the blood of innocents. It is a holy act, a sacrament, to rid Bajor of such evil. . . ."

In his office, with the only light that from the stars the voice would pull down from the heavens, Commander Sisko listened. He knew the words that would come next.

"The continued existence of such a person is a sickness." The voice lowered to a mockery of reasoned discourse. "A sickness that infects the spiritual life of all Bajor. To suffer traitors, to endure the beating of their hearts, is to leave a poisoned thorn in our own flesh. It must be plucked out. . . ."

He had listened to the recording twice already. A transcription of the latest broadcast from the Redemptorists' hidden radio transmitters—the security forces of the provisional government had sent it to him on a subspace linkup. He could reach out and switch the chip-player off, plunge the darkened office into a silence that would be as soothing as his wife's touch upon his knotted shoulder muscles once had been—but an almost mesmeric fascination stayed his hand. Whatever else might have been said of Hören Rygis, he could be truthfully described as a *spellbinder*. In historical terms, less of a king and more of a Hitlerian type—the fires of which he spoke burned but did not illuminate.

. . . and the worst are filled with a passionate intensity. Sisko's brooding thoughts pushed the hammering voice away for a moment. The ancient poet had gotten that one right. Things hadn't changed in all the centuries before or since.

A name brought his attention back—a name that the voice spoke, tongue curling as though the syllables were drops of acid upon it.

"Kira Nerys . . ."

The first time he had listened to the chip, a chill had contracted Sisko's spine. That didn't change—it was as if the voice had already killed her and laid the body before him.

"When the blood is tainted, it must be let. That is how disease is cured. . . ."

He roused himself and reached for the player.

"Blood must flow—"

With a tap of his finger, the voice was stilled. For now.

She knew she was dreaming, but that didn't help.

Worse than dreaming. Remembering.

The bed might as well have been on fire, for all the ease that Kira could find there. She writhed in fever, as though the flames she saw had burst from within her veins.

"I'm sorry . . ." she whispered through cracked lips. If there had been anyone else in her quarters, they might have heard.

"Oh, it's much too late for that." The face of the dead, lit a flickering orange, turned toward her. "It was always too late."

Her fists trembled against the sweat-soaked covers. "I didn't mean to . . . I didn't know it would happen like this. . . ."

"You should have thought of that sooner." The burning temple, its walls cracked by explosions, vomited black clouds up to the night sky. The dead's shadow fell across her where she lay, both on the bed in the safety of DS9's encircling steel, and on the barren ground where the impact of the blast had flung her. "But you didn't."

"I'm sorry . . . I'm sorry . . ."

"Too late." The ground was littered with corpses now. Some of them were disfigured by fire, others she could still recognize. All the dead fixed their unforgiving gaze upon her. "Better if you had been with us, inside. You should have been one of us. . . ."

The dream pounded on, its shrinking world battered by new, unseen blows. Kira felt the fabric of the pillow against her cheek, but still couldn't escape. "I know," she said aloud. "But I *am* one of you."

"No—" The dead stepped back, shadows merging with night. "Not yet. But you will be."

Her eyes opened, sudden as the turning of a metal key inside a lock. She saw her quarters around her, bulkheads and shelves and cabinets, the few simple things they held, pieces of her life aboard the DS9 station that were almost as familiar and real as the past—the past that claimed her in dreams and memory.

She drew in her breath, trying to make her heart slow. For a moment, it seemed as if the dream hadn't completely faded away, that the sounds of it still gripped her. Muffled explosions, their impact eroded by falling distance . . .

Someone was knocking with a fist upon the door of her quarters. Nothing more than that; a sense of relief loosened her clenched muscles. The dreaming, and the past, was over, at least for another interval of present time.

"Are you all right, Major?" Commander Sisko stood on the other side of the door. He pointed to the tiny comm panel on the corridor's wall. "I buzzed you, but there wasn't any answer—"

"I'm fine." She moved away, letting him follow her inside. One hand tried to brush her disordered hair into place as she sat down on the edge of the bed. "Nothing wrong—I was just asleep, that's all."

Sisko watched her with concern. "Must have been sleeping pretty heavily. Usually, you're up like a shot."

"Doctor Bashir told me I've been working too hard." Kira shook her head, as though to clear away

the last clinging fragments. She managed a faint smile.
"Seems to be an occupational hazard around here."

"I wonder . . ." He turned the chair around from
the desk and straddled it, arms folded across the top.
"Sometimes people overwork for . . . different reasons. To escape things they don't want to think
about." His gaze shifted inward for a moment. "Or
remember."

The commander's words tensed Kira's spine. "Perhaps so." She couldn't remove a cold edge from her
voice. "But those are personal matters."

"They become significantly less personal, Major,
when they impact upon the performance of an officer's duties." Sisko's attention focused hard upon her,
the touch of his own past shoved aside. "Or say, upon
that officer's life. Or her death, to be more accurate."

"What are you talking about?"

Sisko took a glittering silver square, a recording
chip, from his uniform pocket and held it up. "Perhaps you are aware that there have been threats made
against you."

"Just like the overwork, Commander—it comes
with the territory." She kept a calm exterior, though
her heart ticked faster again. "Not everybody on
Bajor agrees with what we're doing up here. You know
that. Some of the more extreme elements would like
to blow us out of the sky." She shrugged. "But we
don't have to be universally popular to do our job."

"These threats are different. They're directed at you
in particular." The chip sparkled between Sisko's
thumb and forefinger. "I have to take them seriously.
These are people who are capable of following up on
their promises. And their leader speaks of you with a

vehemence that certainly indicates your murder would be a top priority."

Kira sighed. "If you're speaking of the Redemptorists, Commander, then I'm aware of the same things you are." She leaned back and pulled the mattress away from the bulkhead, enough that she could pry open her hiding place. She dropped the handful of chips onto the bed beside her. "You could listen to these, and you'd find that my name comes up at least a couple of times. I've been on the Redemptorist hit list since before I was posted to DS Nine."

With a raised eyebrow, Sisko looked at the chips. "I take it these are all transcriptions of Hören Rygis's broadcasts?"

"Of course. As the Bajoran military attaché aboard this station, I feel it's my duty to stay current with planetside developments."

"So why keep them hidden?"

She shrugged. "Technically, under the emergency regulations that are still in effect, it's illegal for a Bajoran citizen to be in possession of material like this."

"You could be exempted from that prohibition."

"It's just easier to do what I need to, and keep quiet about it. Why should I risk other people not understanding?"

Suspicion lingered in Sisko's eyes. "So you're aware of Hören Rygis's long-standing animosity toward you . . . and you still approved that group of Redemptorists coming aboard."

Her gaze met his head-on. "And I'd do it again, Commander. For the exact same reasons I gave you before. As long as they're Bajorans, they're my brothers."

"Hm." Sisko rubbed his thumb across the chip in his hand. "Perhaps your familial sentiments would be a little less tender if you heard Hören's most recent tirade against you."

"How do you know I haven't?"

"Because this one was never broadcast. The provisional government's security forces finally managed to track down the floating radio transmitter from which all the others picked up their signals. They raided it and confiscated everything, including this." He held the chip higher. "The index date on it shows that it was recorded sometime within the last few shifts. And let's just say that Hören speaks of you at greater length than he's ever done before."

"And was he—"

"Caught?" Sisko shook his head. "No, unfortunately. The Redemptorist underground is, to say the least, secretive. Wherever Hören Rygis is on the surface of Bajor, he continues to elude capture. And, I imagine, as soon as the Redemptorists rebuild their transmitting network, he'll go on spewing his venom into the ears of his followers." His voice lowered. "And continue urging them to kill you."

"I don't think I have much to worry about from a crew of Bajoran microassemblers—"

"Probably not. It's the Redemptorists we don't know about, the ones whose identities Odo doesn't have logged into his data base, who concern me. What I'd like to know is why Hören wants you dead."

"Commander—I wish I could say it was a long story." Kira felt a weariness, from more than the rigors of her dreaming, weigh upon her bones. "But it's not. Before my posting to DS Nine, I had a tour of duty in the provisional government's security forces —it's still a branch of what little military Bajor possesses. I thought I could do the most good there. When the Cardassians abandoned our planet, we were overjoyed, *ecstatic,* to see them go." She pushed her hair back from her brow. "What we didn't anticipate was the chaos that would follow their departure. If nothing else, the Cardassians provided order . . . things like the distribution of food, or the simple knowing from one day to the next what would happen. When that all fell apart, the resistance groups, the ones that had been fighting the Cardassians all along, started scrambling for power. That meant fighting each other." She shook her head. "So much for brotherhood, right?"

Sisko's expression didn't change. "That's why the Federation came here. We've seen it before."

"Well, I hadn't. I didn't know. . . ." Kira took a deep breath. "The Redemptorists got squeezed out of the front organization that eventually formed the provisional government. Hören Rygis was already their leader then. They took over one of the temples by armed force, barricaded themselves inside with nearly a hundred non-Redemptorist hostages. There was a list of demands . . . I don't even remember what most of them were. But Hören and his followers said they would throw one corpse out the temple gate every hour, until the demands were met. And they did— one of them was a twelve-year-old boy. That's how Hören's mind works."

"And you were in charge of doing something about the situation."

She nodded. "And I blew it. Or else I didn't blow it;

I don't know anymore. I directed the whole operation; my security team stormed the gate, we got inside, we pulled out all but a half-dozen of the hostages still alive . . ." She fell silent for a moment. "And the Redemptorists got what they really wanted. They became martyrs. They had enough explosives in there to turn the whole sky red." The words were flat, dead things in her mouth.

"That wasn't any fault of yours. You did what you had to."

She could have closed her eyes and seen the flames, the dreams and memories without end. "Their bodies lay on the ground . . . some of them were still alive, at least for a little while. I recognized some of them. From the camps, when we had been only children, or later, when we had fought side by side . . . when all those things had seemed so much simpler . . ." She closed her eyes, unable now to bear anyone's watching gaze. "I stood there, and I felt my hands and my face withering from the heat . . . I stood there and looked down at them, and they saw me and knew who I was . . . they all must have, before they died . . ." She pressed her fists against her legs to stop their trembling. "They were all my brothers. They died for what they believed in. Maybe I should have, too."

Sisko touched her wrist, and she opened her eyes.

"You can be as hard on yourself as you want, Major. And I wish I could tell you it would help. But I know it doesn't."

Talking about these things had done no good, either; she felt hollowed, as if each word had taken a piece from inside. "Hören survived, of course; he wasn't even in the temple when we broke in. Long gone . . . and already talking about the glorious deaths. . . ." Kira looked down at her whitened knuckles, as if they were small stones, no part of her. "So, of course, the Redemptorist movement became even larger than it was before. That's what always happens, isn't it? Martyrs. The only other thing you need is a target, someone to focus all that righteous hatred against. . . ."

"And is that all it is for Hören? Names on a list?"

"No—" Kira brought her gaze up to Sisko's. "That's not how . . . how his *soul* works. He couldn't be as powerful as he is—his voice couldn't be that powerful—if he didn't really hate. As much as he loved those who died."

Sisko's face was set, grim. "He could find better ways of honoring them."

It's too late for that . . .

"What did you say, Major?"

She realized that she had spoken aloud, the words the dead had spoken to her.

"I . . . I don't know. . . ."

Concern showed in the commander's furrowed brow. "Perhaps the doctor is right. Perhaps you do need a rest."

Kira shook her head. "That'd be the worst thing I could do. Then . . . then, all I'd do would be to remember."

A distance fell between them, as if for a moment he saw something else—or someone—before him. He nodded. "Very well." He pushed himself up from the chair. "The extra security measure I'll be discussing with Odo won't interfere with your preparations for the substation mission." He started toward the door, then turned and scooped up the recording chips she had dropped on the bedcovers. "I don't think you need these anymore."

She could hear the chips scraping against each other, as though he were grinding them to dust inside his fist. "No—" She almost managed to smile gratefully. "No, I don't."

CHAPTER
7

Some things had changed that didn't matter—such
as the location of the hiding place. Other things had
changed for the better—he could tell that by the faces
assembled around him. Hören nodded to himself in
satisfaction. Much had been accomplished with one
simple death. Another—at least, of one of his
followers—wouldn't be necessary.

"Are we all here?" He looked around the circle.
This space was so much larger than the last hole into
which he'd been crammed. That one had been hardly
big enough for him to turn around in, let alone stand
upright; the small of his back and his shoulder muscles still ached from their long confinement. Here, the
bulkheads and ceiling were so far away that the glow
from the portable lantern was quickly swallowed up.
"I asked for everyone to come—"

Beside him, Deyreth Elt leaned forward. "As you

instructed—they're here." Deyreth sat at Hören's right hand, as though at a position of honor he'd newly earned. That, plus the use of the word "they" to indicate the others, indicated his self-appointed status.

Whatever Deyreth thought of himself was inconsequential to Hören. So many things were coming close to fulfillment—these lesser and expendable elements had begun to fade in his sight, like candle flames held against a blazing dawn. He strove to remind himself that they would have their uses for a while longer.

"My heart is gladdened by your presence." Hören let his gaze rest upon each shadowed face in turn. "The communion of the faithful gives us all strength." He sat back upon the cushion of a folded blanket. "How do your labors progress? And theirs?"

None of them spoke. The reforged somberness held them fast.

Deyreth broke the silence. "The quarantine module —or the substation, as *they* have begun calling it—is nearly ready for its voyage. The chief engineer O'Brien and his technicians have finished installing the life-support systems and the various sensors and other equipment for the use of the doctor. Indeed, most of the technical crews have been pulled out in order to complete the preparation of the cargo shuttle that will be used to take the substation through the wormhole."

"And that leaves . . . what? Your work, I take it?"

A conspirator's smile rose on Deyreth's sharp-angled face. "Our true work. There were some, shall we say, *unexpected* problems with the circuitry on which we worked. Microcomponents that did not perform up to specification, or failed under test loads.

Our team has had to go into the substation itself in order to rectify these matters. O'Brien and the others are already stretched too far, for any of them to spend much time supervising us. We've been able to accomplish a great deal—without being observed."

"That's true—" One of the other faces dared to speak. "They don't know at all what we're doing inside the substation. And we've installed bypass circuits on top of everything, so anytime O'Brien runs a diagnostic test, the results all check out the way they should. Nothing can be detected, unless he were to rip out all the interior panels—and there isn't time for that."

Hören let the man go rattling on, though these technical details were of little interest to him. All that mattered were the results, the creation of the next hiding place—the last one—which would bring him within striking distance of the one whose death would be a sweet justice.

He closed his eyes; the follower was speaking of something else, just as unimportant. Hören listened instead to the memory of his own voice, the words he'd recorded to be broadcast across the surface of Bajor to the faithful. *The letting of blood . . . this is how disease is cured.* The mere remembered sounds of the words were sweet. Even more pleasurable were the images they aroused within him, the ancient medical skill of venesection transformed into a holy rite.

There would be more than one doctor on the substation's mission. But his would be the hand that bore the scalpel, the cure for the sickness that had infected his heart as well, that could be purged only with the release of another's blood—her blood . . .

"Does that meet with your approval?"

Of course. . . .

Hören opened his eyes and saw Deyreth, and the others beyond, watching him. He nodded. "Your labors are pleasing to all the eyes of the faithful." He smiled. "I know that you will have everything ready for me."

The slow working of his plans, the coming of that great day . . . that had been the main reason for the change in hiding places. Away from the distant bowels of the station, and closer to, almost inside, the engineering bay. DS9's overefficient security chief was prowling every centimeter of the dark, empty spaces; the principle that had enabled him to evade capture so far, to lodge himself inside the strangers' nest, had been taken to its next logical step. If they knew how close he was to them—to *her* . . . but, of course, they didn't. The shield of his faith protected him from the strangers' eyes.

"Hören . . . I am concerned. . . ."

The few timid words sparked anger inside him. "Oh?" He glared at the one who had spoken. "What troubles you?" He peered more closely at the crouching figure. "Do you find doubts in your heart?"

"No—" The other quickly shook his head. "Of course not. I'm just . . ."

"What?"

"I'm concerned about *you,* Hören." He looked as if he were about to pray to be understood. "You're so important—not just to us, but to all the believers—what would happen to our cause, to our faith, if something happened . . . if something happened to you? What would keep the Redemptorists together? It just seems . . . not foolish, I don't mean that, but . . . risky. That *you* should undertake this task."

"I see." Anger was not called for now. "And what would you suggest? That you do it?"

"I don't know—" The follower seemed mired in his own confusion. "But perhaps . . . if what is desired is Kira Nerys's death . . . we can accomplish that now. So much more easily—and without endangering you. Even if we were to let them go on with their mission— there are hundreds of ways to make sure that she would never come back from it—"

"Ah." Hören nodded. "Your worries for me . . . are very touching." He let his voice soften, become tender as a parent's to a beloved child. "And you are correct: I risk much—I risk everything—by going ahead with what we have planned together, what you have labored to bring about." His gaze moved across the group of men. "But you mustn't forget . . . that my death would mean nothing. To rid the soul of Bajor of this pollution, a small thing is asked of me. And a great thing would be given unto me. The honor of death, to die as our brothers have died . . ." He smiled sadly. "Perhaps I am being selfish, to want that for myself. Would you deny it to me?"

"It's just that . . ." The other's hands tightened into fists. "Is she worth your life?"

"Of course not. Kira Nerys is an insect compared to the least of us, even to that one whose sympathy for the strangers led him into error. But there's more at stake than simply eliminating her pestilential existence. We have it within our power to transform her death—and mine, if need be—into the salvation of Bajor itself." His voice faded to a whisper, which drew the others even closer to him. "The mysteries that our most ancient devotions seek to understand, the gifts that the Bajorans have been chosen to receive, of all the universe . . . the orbs . . ." The whisper turned bitter. "The strangers come here and call the source of our faith a *wormhole*—and we mock our own beliefs when we use that word. That is how the infection spreads. And now, they would make of that sacred mystery a road for their boots to trample on as they carry their wares back and forth to market." The bitterness twisted upon itself. "Shall we not let them make our temples into brothels then? Surely that would bring them money, as well. They might even let us have a few coins of it."

Their heads were bent, even Deyreth's, as though to receive the lash of his words upon their backs.

"Their mere presence here is an abomination." He relented, voice soft again. "But give yourselves this comfort—soon that shall come to an end."

He closed his eyes, knowing that his silence would tell them to leave him. So that he could be alone once more, in the darkness of his meditations.

Soon. Where even his voice, and the words that burned in it, would cease.

Silence at last. He turned off the player and leaned back in his chair, his thoughts deepening inside him.

It had taken some doing to find the right chip, the one that had been confiscated in the raid on the Redemptorist transmitter down on Bajor. Odo realized that not everyone had the same respect for physical clues that, out of necessity, he had developed —but he'd still had to bite his tongue when Commander Sisko had come back to the security office with a fistful of recording chips, the important one mixed in with them. The problem of searching through the chips had been compounded by Hören

Rygis's voice being on all of them, transcriptions of his ranting diatribes—something that Odo found personally offensive. Sentient creatures seemed to already show enough ingenuity at finding crimes to commit—why should they be exhorted to murder in addition?

He scooped up the other chips and sealed them into an evidence bag before extending his arm to drop them in the file cabinet on the other side of the office. Now that he'd found the one he'd been looking for, he wasn't going to risk losing it again. It had been a violation of his own procedural rules to let the commander take away the chip in the first place, but he'd been able to tell that Sisko had had some compelling use for it. His own suspicions about what that might have been were confirmed when Sisko had come back with the handful, and had told him that they had been in Major Kira's possession.

Unfortunately, the commander hadn't seemed to feel any need for sharing what he'd learned from Kira. Inside himself, Odo felt a familiar irritation uncoiling. Like most humanoids, Benjamin Sisko had an obstinate respect for the privacy of others—and at the same time, he wanted his chief of security to snoop out every secret that might threaten the continued functioning of DS9. Odo would have appreciated a little help along that line.

Still, if cooperation wasn't forthcoming from Sisko and the others, there were still inanimate objects to be questioned—they could be much more eloquent. He extracted the chip from the player and held it up to his eye to study it, then laid it back down. He had already taken it over to Dax's lab to glean the information he needed from it. The chief science officer had run it through the subphoton microscope and downloaded the resulting images. Taking out his data padd, he called the file onto the screen.

At the highest magnification, the smooth surface of the recording chip looked as pitted as the surface of an airless moon. Odo scrolled the image to the manufacturer's data inscribed in one corner.

Well, well. Without looking away, Odo punched the long stream of digits into the computer panel. *How interesting.* The chip had spoken, in its own way, with truths far more revealing than the voice of Hören Rygis.

On the larger desktop display was the batch number of the chip that had been found in the raid on the Redemptorist transmitter. He already knew what he'd find as he called up the file on the Bajoran microassembler whose murdered body had been dumped in the engineering bay. And the chip that had been found in the corpse's pocket. . . .

The batch numbers were the same.

Odo leaned back, gazing with satisfaction at the two parallel strings of numbers. He'd previously scanned the corpse's chip, but the one from the transmitter raid had been taken away by Commander Sisko before he'd had a chance to scan it. In the meantime, he'd searched through a massive data base of shipping invoices, and had found another puzzle piece: all the recording chips in that batch had been received and sold by one of the small gadget merchants doing business from an *akhibara* cubicle on the Promenade. Naturally, the merchant—an unusually obtuse Rhaessian—had had no record of his various customers; that would have been too much to ask for.

But even so . . . just those few scraps of information, the silent words from the recording chips, gave him a lot to think about, to piece together, to make sense of.

Inside Odo's head was a world as intricate, and filled with both light and dark corners, as DS9 itself. His pleasure came from working his way through the corridors in both worlds, and finding out the secrets of every thing and person alike.

He set the revealing chip down precisely in the center of the desktop. Soon, he would have enough to make a report to the commander.

"You were warned, I take it?"

Doctor Bashir looked up from the display panel before him. The substation's remote sensors were running through their last circuit checks. "Pardon me?" He glanced over his shoulder to the doorway of the cargo shuttle's pilot area.

"Warned." Kira stood there, arms folded across her breast, her habitual scowl in full force. "Now's not a good time to play around with me, Doctor—we'll be disengaging from the pylon in fifteen minutes. I know Commander Sisko spoke to you. About our . . . working relationship."

He sighed. The length of time it would take to complete the mission—from going through the wormhole and out to the Gamma Quadrant, to bringing the cargo shuttle back to the station by himself—had originally seemed far too short for all he wanted to accomplish. Now, as it had become increasingly clear how much Kira resented his presence on the mission, he had begun to think it might be a long voyage indeed.

"Since you're aware of my conversations with the

commander, why do you bother to ask?" His own temper had started to fray a bit, from the shifts of nonstop work with O'Brien in getting the scientific equipment installed and running before the departure date. As little as an hour ago, Bashir had been inside the cargo shuttle's cramped one-person augmented personnel module, awkwardly adjusting the last few sensors on the substation's exterior. It had been a relief to stow the APM back in its holding bay and step out into the relatively less claustrophobic space of the shuttle's pilot area—at least until Kira had started in on him. "And I don't think that was quite the word Sisko used—*advised* would be more like it."

"Whatever." Kira stood right behind him. "If he didn't warn you, then I will. This mission has great strategic importance, for both the station *and* Bajor. My job is to make sure that everything happens the way it's supposed to. Your job, as far as I'm concerned, is to stay out of my way." She glared at the lights on the display panel, as though they had somehow affronted her as well. "There's still time for you to decide to do that the best way possible."

"And that would be . . . ?" He already knew her answer.

"Don't come along. Your assistance is not required."

"Major Kira." He swiveled the seat around and looked up at her. The time when he had thought there might be a chance of cordial relations between them had passed long ago. She had been ready enough to ask a favor of him when she'd needed it—apparently that had been no indication of her true feelings. "You might as well reconcile yourself to these arrangements. Technically, you may be in charge of this mission, but you should try to remember that, once you transfer to the substation, you'll be on *my* territory. My agreeing to let the quarantine module be used as a substation is the only thing making this trip possible." He had already faced down Commander Sisko about this; he found it comparatively easier to put the major in her place. "I could abort the entire mission right now, and there wouldn't be a thing you could do about it."

She radiated a venomous silence toward him. For a moment, Bashir wondered if her hostility had crossed the line into active derangement. Kira had been missing for a couple of shifts, staying in her quarters —her absence from the engineering bay had enabled him and O'Brien to get a lot more work done—with rumors of a depressive episode floating around the crew on Ops. If that had been the case, she had bounced back from it with a vengeance.

"You'd be surprised, Doctor," she spoke grimly, "at just what I could do about it."

He turned away from her and leaned over the lights flashing on the panel. A *very* long voyage . . .

"Now—"

Hören Rygis stepped to the fore of the group of men. Beside him, Deyreth looked at the readout of the crudely patched together metal box in his hand. It was designed to indicate the status of the final preparations aboard the cargo shuttle.

"They've sealed the pressure locks." Another red dot blinked on the box's surface. "Perimeter checks under way. Let's go."

They were all dressed in the coveralls that were standard issue in the engineering bay. The work on the substation's microcircuitry had continued right up to the last minute—a few well-devised component failures had seen to that. That had ensured that no one would question the microassembly team being on the staging area of the main docking pylon.

Hören felt an unshakable calm settle around his heart. It was at times like this he felt the sure machinery of fate. His followers had done their tasks well; the rest was up to him.

He started walking, shielded by the others. The distance across the pylon's loading ramp had to be traversed, with none of the strangers noticing him. From the corner of his eye, he saw Deyreth surreptitiously press a switch on the box he held by his side.

With a mechanized hiss, the massive docking arms moved a fraction of a meter apart, loosening the connection between the substation and the cargo shuttle that had been modified for its transport.

"What the—" On the other side of the bay, the chief engineer looked in perplexity at the diagnostic cabinet. A bundled set of cables ran from it to a hatch in the machinery mounted on the cargo shuttle's foresection. "We're getting some flaky control feedback here." The rest of the engineering crew looked over his shoulders at the cabinet's gauge panels.

Their voices faded as Hören and the other Redemptorists used the distraction to slip around the substation's distant side.

"Quick—" At Deyreth's order, the largest of the men bent down, cupping his hands to give Hören a boost. Another switch on the box opened one of the substation's curved exterior panels, enough for Hören to pry the gap wide enough for his shoulders to squeeze through. In a few seconds, he had scrambled inside, turning around to grab an improvised handle and pull the panel shut behind himself. The metal grew warm as a low-level fission charge around the panel's edge welded it tight, sealing him in darkness.

He reached up to his ear to activate the tiny comm link there. This close, it was easy to pick up the transmission from Kira Nerys and the doctor in the shuttle connected to the substation.

"Anything wrong?"

That was Kira's voice; he could imagine her up in the pilot area, impatient with the break in the departure procedure.

The chief engineer's reply crackled with static. ". . . looked for a moment like we were having some problem with the mounting arms . . . seems to have cleared up . . ."

Within seconds, a fine vibration moved through the structural beams close around him. There wasn't time to waste—he crawled quickly ahead, shoving aside a panel of lighter weight, then dropping from the ceiling to the substation's interior.

Hören scrambled to his feet and reached up to the ceiling; the dislodged panel was just out of reach of his fingertips. He'd have to take care of it later; he nearly fell as the substation shifted position.

"What are you doing over there . . ." In his ear, he could hear the exit crew's voices. "Come on, clear the area . . ." That must've been addressed to Deyreth and the rest of his group; it didn't sound as if they had aroused any suspicions.

He hurried toward one of the substation's farther sections, with a familiarity born of memorizing the plans Deyreth had provided him. He'd be able to brace himself inside a sickbed unit, secure against the cargo shuttle's acceleration as it left the docking pylon.

Then it would just be a matter of waiting . . .

CHAPTER
8

"We're dead."

He spoke aloud, aware of the figure standing behind him in the doorway of the pilot area. Bashir leaned back from the shuttle's instrument panel and looked over his shoulder. "Completely."

"What are you talking about?" Kira had gone aft to do a visual scan of the connectors for the locking arms; the momentary glitch before they had left DS9 had continued to be a source of worry. If it had been up to Bashir, he would have delayed until it had been thoroughly checked out—but that had been Kira's decision to make. Now, she slipped into the other seat. She quickly looked across the display. "What's going on—"

"As I indicated, we're dead. In the water, so to speak." He pointed. "We've come to a complete halt."

She muttered a few Bajoran swear words, as her

hands moved across the controls. None of the instruments registered any change. She turned and glared at him. "If this is something you've pulled, just so we'd wind up spending more time here in the wormhole, I'll—"

"Major Kira." He tried to control his own temper. "If I'd known beforehand that you were susceptible to paranoid fantasies, I would've prescribed psychiatric treatment for you. I'm getting all the data I need, thank you."

The latter was true; since the cargo shuttle, with the substation mounted before it, had entered the wormhole, the sensors had been operating at full capacity. The various pieces of equipment he and Dax had installed were running perfectly; he had checked the portable data banks and had found the information flow to be running at 110 percent of predicted levels. Commander Sisko himself had instructed Bashir to allow for the additional storage.

"They're smart," Sisko had told him. The commander had been giving him an additional briefing about the wormhole's inhabitants. "They can figure out the purpose of anything that comes into their domain." Sisko had, since his encounter with the creatures, developed a propensity for speaking of them as if they were material, even human. "They can figure out what *you're* doing there. If they decide to, they can pour out information like a naiadene rainstorm."

Perhaps that had already started happening. The wormhole's interior had turned out to be a treasure chest of electromagnetic radiation, dense to either extreme of the sensors' bandwidth, frequencies overlapping and intermingled. A full analysis would have to wait until he got the data banks back to DS9 and could begin going over them with Dax, but his first glance at some of the monitor screens showed indications of order, not just chaotic, random bursts and background noise. If that held up on further investigation, the hypothesis of the wormhole being an artifact produced by its inhabitants, and not just a naturally occurring phenomenon, would be substantiated. And if the underlying structure could be induced from the data . . . then the possibilities were wide open—for accomplishments far beyond the fields of multispecies medicine. Bashir almost had to control his hands from twitching, as though they might otherwise tear right into the secrets filling the banks.

Now, if only the wormhole's inhabitants were to touch his mind, as they had the commander's . . . then he was sure all the doors would open . . .

"I suppose it's just a convenient accident, then?"

In the meantime, he looked at Kira beside him. "Major, perhaps you should lighten up a bit." He'd had enough of her suspicions. "You're well aware of the quality of materials with which O'Brien has had to make do. Probably nothing more than a loose connection somewhere. Here, watch—" He balled up his fist and, as he'd seen the chief engineer do often enough, slammed it into the least fragile-seeming panel in front of him.

Nothing happened, except for a throb of pain that traveled from his knuckles to his elbow. He wasn't about to reveal that to Kira.

"Very impressive," she said dryly. "Now, maybe we'd better try to fix things, and get on our way. If we were able to communicate with DS Nine from this far inside the wormhole, we could've asked O'Brien for some engineering advice. But since we can't—" She stood up. "Come on. Let's check out the engine compartment."

"What do you need me for?" Bashir had already shifted his attention back to the sensor readouts.

"Not much, except to hold the flashlight. Now come on." She strode past him.

As soon as they unsealed the access hatch, the burnt smell struck their nostrils. Not from a fire—the alarm systems would have kicked in if there had been one—but from overloaded circuitry and charred wire.

Bashir leaned over, peering into the opening. "This doesn't look good."

"Thanks for the diagnosis." Kira had already started clambering down the metal rungs into the compartment. "It looks even worse down here."

He breathed through a hand clamped over his mouth and nose as he stood beside her in the narrow space. "What do you think happened?" He watched as she opened a panel on the side of one of the massive cylinders and started the engines' self-test mode.

"Well, it's not the impulse units—they check out fine." More numbers skittered across the readout. "Something to do with the bypass . . . no, it's the buffers." She ran her hand across the surface of the meter-thick shielding that had been placed around the engines, then looked at the sooty ash coating her palm. "They overloaded—something went wrong with the absorb-and-release algorithms."

"What does that mean?"

Kira closed the diagnostic panel. "These buffers are built up from a programmable crystalline matrix. Like an intelligent capacitor—they take in the engines' thrust impulses and modulate them to a sine wave. The propulsive effect is virtually the same, and it doesn't disrupt the wormhole's ionic field. So our little friends out there don't suffer the effects, basically. But something went wrong here; it looks like the buffers were taking in 100 percent of the impulse power but passing on only 90 percent of it. With the additional mass of the substation we're carrying, it's not likely we would've noticed the drop in effective power. At least not until the whole system burned out."

"So, we're stuck here without engines?" Bashir looked across the compartment's silent forms.

"No—" She shook her head. "We can pull out the buffer circuitry easily enough. That would just be putting things back in their original design. The problem is, what happens if we fire these things up—while we're still inside the wormhole—and the buffers aren't working?"

He had to admit it was a good question. Passage through the wormhole was predicated on the understanding that Commander Sisko had reached with the mysterious creatures that were its inhabitants. Creatures for whom the effects of an unbuffered impulse engine were potentially deadly . . .

"Let's get back to the pilot area." Kira started up the rungs to the access hatch above. "We're really going to have to think about this one."

While he waited, he was careful to touch none of the items in the sparsely furnished living quarters. It would have been easy enough for Odo to examine everything the Redemptorist possessed—there wasn't much, clothes and a few sets of microassembly tools

—and to do it undetected. He could have hidden himself as a thin, transparent membrane on the ceiling, and watched whatever the man did when he thought he was alone. But this was a time, Odo had calculated, when a more direct approach was called for.

The door slid open, and the Redemptorist named Deyreth Elt entered. Lost in thought, or just tired—he had let the door close behind him before he saw Odo sitting on the chair pulled over from the desk.

"What's the meaning of this?" Deyreth's reaction was immediately hostile. "What are you doing in here?"

"You needn't be alarmed." Odo kept his own voice level. "I apologize for this intrusion on your privacy. But I thought perhaps you would prefer that any discussions between us were done as discreetly as possible. You know who I am, don't you?"

Deyreth nodded slowly. "The chief of security . . ." He kept his back close to the door, as though he might attempt to flee at any moment.

"It's been my observation," said Odo, "that, for a group whose religious devotions are paramount in their lives, you and your fellow Redemptorists are remarkably well informed about the reality of DS Nine's operations; the personnel in charge, and so forth. Almost as if you'd made it a point of study. At least, that's the impression I've gotten whenever I've talked to the others."

"Why have you been talking to them?" Deyreth's eyes narrowed in suspicion.

Odo observed the change with satisfaction. It always helped to plant a seed that could grow large enough to split conspiracies apart. "It's my job, isn't it? To investigate . . . to talk to people. I would have hoped that you would welcome my attentions, in that it's the murder of one of your own that's being looked into."

Deyreth's expression grew even harder. "Arten was a fool."

"Oh? Do fools deserve to die, then?"

"That . . . that's not a concern of mine." His face showed that he'd spoken too rashly. "But Arten fell among bad companions—nonbelievers—when he came to this place. It was a mistake to bring him with us; he was too young; he didn't have the shield of a confirmed faith to protect him from his errors."

"I see. And those errors were . . .?"

"That is of no concern to you. Investigate his death, if you choose; I have no say about it. But these doctrinal matters are beyond your sphere of authority."

"Very well." Odo leaned forward. "Let's talk of your compatriot's death. I find it . . . *interesting* to hear you tell of these 'bad companions' Arten found here. Especially when my investigations among those who would fit that description—and I know all who are aboard the station—show that none of them had the slightest contact with him. He seemed to lead the same type of reclusive existence here as do you and the rest of the Redemptorists."

A shrug. "I can't answer for all of his comings and goings."

Odo let his gaze wander around the quarters. "Do you like music? Of any kind?" He looked back to Deyreth.

The question seemed to puzzle him. "Such things are frivolities . . ."

"I expected that reaction from you. That's why I'm not surprised to see that there's no chip-player in your quarters. There wasn't one in Arten's, either. Which, of course, made it intriguing that I found a couple of blank chips on his corpse. But then . . . there are other uses for them besides recording music."

Deyreth remained silent, his spine visibly stiffening.

"What use would *you* have for them?"

"I don't know what you're talking about. . . ."

"That statement might have been believable at one time." Odo carefully watched the shift of expressions across the other's face. "But not now—thanks to the services of a certain Ferengi barkeeper. Quark is probably the worst possible 'companion' on the station, but he doesn't mind doing a few little services for me, now and then—it keeps him in my good graces for whatever malfeasances he may commit later on."

A corner of Deyreth's mouth curled in distaste. "What does that sort of creature have to do with me?"

"Quark is in the habit of surreptitiously video recording everything that happens inside his establishment, and most of what happens just outside on the Promenade; the entryway is studded with some cleverly concealed lenses. He is, as one might expect, alert to chances for blackmail."

"I've never patronized such a place."

"No. But quite a few shifts ago, not long after you and the rest of your microassembly team came up here from Bajor, you went into the booth of a Rhaessian gadget merchant just across the Promenade from Quark's place—you show up quite identifiably on the video that he let me have. There you purchased two cartons of recording chips, paying for them with cash scrip issued by the Bajoran provisional government—the Rhaessian cheated you on the exchange rate. At high magnification, the details of the transaction are evident. The manufacturer's batch number of the recording chips you bought is the same as of those that were found on the murdered Arten. Of course, that's not really too significant—you might have given them to him for some obscure purpose that's not really any of my business."

Deyreth had stepped back, right against the door.

"What is significant," continued Odo, "is that the same batch number is on the chips that were found during a raid on an illicit transmitting station on the surface of Bajor—"

In a split second, Deyreth had palmed the door's control and darted out to the corridor beyond.

Odo had been readying himself, altering the muscle mass of his legs into a peak glycogen conversion rate. He was up from the chair like a coiled spring, and pinning Deyreth to the floor within a couple of strides.

"Go about your business," he told the few startled faces in the corridor. With a knee against Deyreth's spine, he jerked the other's wrists back and snapped on a set of hand restraints. "Nothing to see here." He pulled Deyreth upright and pushed him toward the nearest turbolift.

"Any luck?" She knelt down to see how the work was coming along.

Bashir lay on his back, his head and upper torso

wedged into a narrow opening beneath the pilot area's controls. "Wait a minute—" He wriggled out, his tools and light in his hands. "Not bad," he said, leaning his shoulders against the panel. "But it's going to take a while."

He had surprised her by devising a plan for modifying the comm link—Kira had thought that medicine was his only practical field of knowledge. In this case, his leisure activity of restoring ancient audio equipment had proved to be of value: he had done a rough analysis of the electromagnetic spectra surrounding them in the wormhole, and had found a narrow band that seemed to reflect along the limits of the wormhole's curved space. If he shorted out the transmitter's signal on everything but those frequencies, they might be able to hail the Ops deck back on DS9. The drop-off in the signal's strength would occur at a steep exponential rate, but it was still worth a shot.

"Take a break." She almost regretted jumping down his throat the way she had before. "We've got to figure out some strategy here."

Bashir followed her to the pilot seats. While he bandaged the knuckles he had scraped underneath the communicator panel, she ran through her analysis of their situation.

"It's pretty obvious we were sabotaged." Kira squeezed the seat's arm in her fist. "O'Brien put in those impulse buffers himself, and when he checked them out they were functioning perfectly. If they hadn't been, he wouldn't have cleared this shuttle for the mission. So, somebody must've gotten to the buffers afterward." She had her own suspicions about who it might have been, but she didn't want to voice them now. The changes in the buffers' circuitry could have been accomplished only by someone with advanced microassembly skills.

"Maybe that somebody doesn't want us to get out to the Gamma Quadrant." Bashir closed the lid on the first aid kit. "If Odo were here, he'd probably remind us of that old Earth maxim, *Qui bono?* Who benefits? The only ones I can think of would be the Cardassians." He rubbed his thumb across the bandage on his index finger. "But Gul Tahgla and his crew had already left when the buffers were being installed around our engines . . . so, they must have someone else working for them, someone still aboard the station."

His line of thought had diverged light-years away from hers; that was fine, as far as she was concerned. "Right now, it doesn't matter who did it, or why. What we need to figure out is what to do about it. And fast—we've got to get the substation in place before the Cardassians can reach the wormhole's exit sector and claim it for themselves."

"I don't know . . ." Bashir shook his head. "It doesn't do us much good that the engines are still operable. If we fire them up without the buffers, they'll send a shock wave through the ionic field—we can't be sure what the wormhole's inhabitants will do to defend themselves. But when it happened before, with Commander Sisko out here, they collapsed the wormhole's connection with the outside universe. Until they opened it back up, it was as if the wormhole didn't exist anymore. We might not even be able to get out of here using those unbuffered engines."

The same point had been worrying her. She had a

vivid memory of the way the wormhole's swirling entrance, a maelstrom of energies, had blinked out of existence, trapping Sisko inside. The same thing could happen to them now, with even less chance of a resurrection from a tomb sealed with the empty space between stars.

"And beyond that," said Bashir, "there's a certain moral question. Even if we could use the unbuffered engines to get out to the Gamma Quadrant, and if we weren't bound by the understanding Sisko reached with the wormhole's inhabitants—we're still aware of the lethal effect the impulse energy has on them. Do we have the right to hurt them that way?"

"Spoken like a doctor."

"It's still the decision we'd have to make."

She knew he was right. And there were practical concerns beyond the present one: if they did manage to get out and set the substation in the Gamma Quadrant, it wouldn't accomplish much good if the wormhole's inhabitants collapsed it out of existence. Bajor would wind up with sovereignty over nothing but an empty sector of space.

Her fingertips tried to rub away the ache that swelled behind her brow. If there were time to think, if the Cardassians weren't on their way to claim the wormhole's exit sector . . . if she and Bashir were still in touch with DS9, and they could consult with Sisko and the others about a plan of action . . .

There wasn't time. Whatever she decided, even if it were the wrong thing, it would have to be soon.

"All right." She drew in a deep breath, then leaned over and touched Bashir's arm. "Here's what we're going to do."

* * *

"This is all very clever of you." The Redemptorist had managed to regain his composure, enough to snarl at Odo as he was pushed toward the security office. "I imagine your heart is filled with pride over your accomplishment."

"No more than usual." Odo kept a tight grip on his suspect's upper arm. The crowds on the Promenade parted for them, displaying only a mild curiosity; it was a familiar enough sight for them. "I can assure you that it's merely a matter of routine."

Deyreth twisted his neck to look back at him. "Be satisfied with what you can, heathen." The Bajoran's sharp-edged face held a look of maniacal triumph. "What happens to me is less than nothing. A dawn approaches that none of you can forestall—"

"Yes, of course; keep moving." He found religious fanatics to be particularly annoying. There was no complexity to their minds, just a single glaring light that consumed everything else inside their skulls. No challenge to them; this one had already as much as confessed to the other's murder. "Why don't you wait until I can take down a statement from you?"

"Do you need one? Surely, in your cleverness, you have figured out everything you need to know." Spittle flecked Deyreth's lip. "I purchased the chips here, those that the vermin of the provisional government's security forces found in their raid upon our transmitter—what does that mean? Tell me!"

"It means," said Odo, "that your leader, Hören Rygis, is somewhere aboard the station. He's been recording his broadcasts here and having them smuggled back down to Bajor." He hustled Deyreth toward the security office. "That's what you and I are go-

ing to talk about. And then you're going to take me to
him."

Deyreth laughed, eyes wide with delight. "You're
too late! He's gone, you cannot touch him!" The
Bajoran contorted his body even further. *You can't
stop that which is ordained—"*

For a moment, Odo had to turn his gaze away as he
keyed the code upon the door. That inattention was
enough; he heard the metal of the hand restraints
strike the floor, followed by the delicate microassembly tools that Deyreth had stealthily managed
to take from his pocket and use upon the hand restraints. His grip was torn loose from Deyreth's arm
as he was shoved against the wall.

"Stop!" Odo regained his balance, seeing Deyreth
push through the crowd. No one laid a hand upon
him. "Get out of my way—"

In his blind rush, Deyreth collided with the rail
overlooking the deck below. The impact knocked the
breath from him; dazed, he clung to the metal bar, his
torso bent over the empty space.

Odo was still a couple of meters away, battering
against the wall of humanoid and other bodies—there
wasn't time to assume another shape that would have
gotten him past them any more quickly—when he
saw Deyreth turn an agonized glance back toward
him. Deyreth scrambled over the rail just as Odo
reached out to grab him.

Gravity caught him first. Deyreth's grasp of the rail
slipped loose, and he toppled, centimeters away from
Odo's outstretched hand.

The crowd gathered at Odo's back as he looked
down at the body crumpled upon a grid below. Blood

had already begun to seep through the small holes and dot the pipes and wiring underneath.

Odo turned and bulled his way through the gawkers. Someone else would have to gather up the Redemptorist's body. Right now, he had to get to Ops and talk to Commander Sisko.

CHAPTER
9

SHE WALKED THROUGH the dark spaces. In silence; the bulkhead panels curved around her, like the flowing walls of the crypts beneath a Bajoran temple. The passage through what had been the quarantine module, and was now the substation that would secure her people's claim to the stable wormhole, evoked memories in her. Of helping to carry the shrouded body of an uncle, the wounds of the beating he'd received from the Cardassian camp guards still seeping through the thin wrappings, carrying it and laying it down among the sacred bones of their ancestors. She'd hardly been more than ten years old then, and already she'd been pressed into the service of the rituals; there had been so few of her clan left.

Kira stopped for a moment, leaning a hand against a bulkhead to steady herself, and squeezing her eyes in an attempt to get rid of the painful remembrances.

She could recall—she couldn't stop herself—how light her uncle's corpse had seemed; it hadn't been until later that she had realized he had been starving himself, dividing his rations among her and the other children. When the time came, the guards had broken him like a dry stick.

Forget, she told herself. *You've got work to do.* Through sheer force of will, she put the memory, and all the others like it, back inside the chamber she carried inside her head, a chamber as large as Bajor itself, as small as the tear of a girl still weeping as she lay curled on a barracks' dirty straw mat.

The interior of the substation brightened. Aboard the cargo shuttle, Bashir must have managed to switch on the auxiliary power. The central corridor ran ahead of her, branching on either side into the various sections and compartments. In the dim glow of the radiant panels—they wouldn't come to full brightness until the substation's own power source was activated—the substation looked less tomblike, and closer to a regulation Starfleet sickbay. Space was tighter, though, than on either DS9 or an *Enterprise*-class ship; the narrow corridors folded in upon themselves like a maze. When she had inspected the substation during its retrofitting in O'Brien's engineering bay, she had memorized only the routes through it and the areas that she would require on the mission; the other sections she was content to leave sealed off.

"Major Kira—" Bashir's voice crackled from a speaker over her head. "Are you at the control room yet?"

"I'm on my way." The bad memories had snared her, just when there was no time to waste. Perhaps it had been the substation's empty chambers on either side of her, surrounded by the wormhole's darkness, that had triggered deepening thoughts. A wordless feeling had remained, chilling the skin across her arms and shoulders. She pushed it back, and headed for the substation's nerve center.

He wondered why she had stopped. For a moment, as he had crouched silent behind a scrub room door, his hands almost within reach of her throat, he thought that she might have detected his presence. That might have been why she had closed her eyes, head bowed in concentration, her nostrils catching the scent of someone else aboard the substation . . .

She knows, Hören had thought. If that were so, then his careful plans would have to be changed. But the woman's death would still be the final result.

If she had opened her eyes and turned to look toward him, her gaze taking in the miniature lens of the view panel by the door—he had short-circuited the diode that showed it had been activated, but he knew the motions of the phase-sensitive iris inside could still be seen—then that death would have had to be immediate. But she had moved away at last, striding quickly down the central corridor.

Kira stopped again, craning her neck to look at the ceiling above her. He rolled a fingertip across the screen's controls, altering the lens angle. In the corridor's ceiling, he could see now, was the gap he had dropped through when he'd sneaked inside the substation. Still visible at the corner of the opening was the thin metal plate he'd shoved aside.

"What's keeping you?" The microphone inside the

view panel was sensitive enough to pick up the voice of Kira's confederate aboard the cargo shuttle.

"Just admiring the quality of the construction around here." She shook her head, then continued on her way.

Hören let his tensed muscles relax. He was certain that she suspected nothing. Kira Nerys would proceed with her clever plans—he had expected no less of her, finding it within himself to admire her ingenuity as he had listened over the bug that had been placed in the shuttle's pilot area. He could almost regret that her mind, and the determination that pressed it forward, could never serve a righteous cause.

He had his own plans, as well. Soon enough, they would intersect with hers, and she would be shown the errors of her soul. If, in that last moment, her eyes were to widen in sudden understanding . . . then death might encompass some small measure of salvation for her.

It wasn't likely. He knew too well the depth of corruption in the nonbelievers. He switched off the screen and turned away, hurrying to make ready.

He listened to the report. And was not pleased.

"I regret the death of the Redemptorist Deyreth Elt." Odo stood before him in Ops, hands clasped behind his back. "If only for the information that further questioning of him might have provided. As it is, my analysis of his statements awaits confirmation."

Commander Sisko rested his chin upon a fist. He'd almost expected another voice to chime in from the seat beside his own, Major Kira expressing her view of the situation. If she sometimes had spoken too hastily, at least one had never had to wait long to know what she thought. Without her there, the silence seemed to stretch on toward infinity.

Unfortunately, the matter being discussed was Kira's life, along with that of Doctor Bashir. The problem of the cargo shuttle having been detected at a standstill in the wormhole had been compounded by what his chief of security had just told him.

"You're sure of this?" He knew the answer in advance—Odo was not given to low-probability speculations—but he wanted to give himself more time to think. "There's no other interpretation of what he meant?"

"I don't see one, Commander. If we had no corroborating evidence, I might have ascribed his words to just lunatic raving—this Deyreth Elt was seriously disturbed, in my estimation. Whether he was so before, or whether his growing political and religious fanaticism had further impaired his reason . . . it'd be hard to determine now, of course. I haven't had time to thoroughly question the other Redemptorists, but a couple of them have indicated that Hören Rygis was aboard the station. I managed to locate what might have been one of his hiding places; the ventilation was naturally poor there, so the air sample I took might give us some sweat traces that we can DNA-type and match with Hören's records from the Bajoran security forces. . . ."

"We don't have time for all that, Constable."

"Exactly." Odo gave a quick, acknowledging nod. "That is why I feel it's best if we operate on the assumption that Hören Rygis has stowed away somewhere aboard the substation. I'm confident that that is the meaning of what Deyreth Elt said before he died.

We've tightened up security considerably on all vessels docking at or leaving DS Nine, so it's virtually impossible Hören could have gotten off the station by those means. The cargo shuttle is simply too small for him to have concealed himself there for very long. That really leaves only the substation as a possibility."

"I'm afraid you're right." Sisko turned toward Chief Engineer O'Brien. "How much access did this group of Redemptorists have to the substation?"

O'Brien slowly shook his head. "I'm sorry, sir, but they pretty much had total access to it. They were our best team of microassemblers—there was no way we would've been able to get it ready in time without them." His expression darkened, as though brooding over a personal affront. "The big question now is what else they might have done to it while they had the chance."

"The explosives built into the structure naturally concern me—"

"Those would be the least of our worries, Commander. Those are all inert as old bricks; the fuse codes are set into them right at the molecular level. Doctor Bashir's the only person who could set them off." O'Brien scowled as his thoughts moved through their courses. "No, I'm more worried about what other little tricks these jokers might have wired in. And not just on the substation—the monitoring signal we got before we lost contact made it pretty clear that the impulse buffers on the shuttle had been tampered with, as well."

"Very well." Sisko looked behind him to the Ops crew. "Have a runabout prepared for immediate departure." He turned back to the chief security and engineering officers. "If we can't communicate with them from here, we'll just have to go out there to get them. O'Brien, I want you to come along with me; maybe there'll be something you can do to repair those impulse buffers so we can get the substation on its way again. I'm not ready yet to scrub this mission."

"I'll need some time to load up some equipment—"

"Do it." Sisko pushed himself up from the seat. "Constable, I want you to sweat whatever else you can out of those other Redemptorists. The more we know about what we're up against, the better." He strode toward the doorway. "Let's go, gentlemen."

"You ready for this?"

She heard Bashir's voice over the command center's speaker. Kira pulled tighter the fastenings of the seat's harness. "More than ready," she called. Her voice echoed in the silence contained within the substation.

As she pressed her head back against the padding, she could imagine Bashir in the shuttle's pilot area, making the final adjustments on the controls. The two had double-checked their calculations together, crunching the velocity and angle figures on the computer. The numbers had to be perfect: they were going to get only one shot at this.

"All right." Bashir's voice held an edge of tension. "Now, O'Brien warned me that the impact would be pretty sharp—"

"I bet." She made a stab at lightening the mood. "Are you one of those doctors who always warns people about how much something's going to hurt?"

A laugh came over the speaker. "No, I usually try to sneak up on people. Okay, here we go. Locking arms disengaged; separation sequence initiated. Brace yourself—"

She had felt a mechanical shiver run through the substation's frame as the massive C-shaped arms had spread open and the atmospheric seals had snapped into place. That would have been warning enough; a second later, the sudden acceleration from the ring of explosives slammed her back into the seat. The impact knocked the air from her lungs; for a moment, the substation's lights dimmed into spots of darkness swirling before her eyes. She fought to keep them from coalescing, pushing her into unconsciousness.

The pressure eased, and she was able to draw in enough breath to speak. "Bashir—how're we doing?"

After a few more seconds, the doctor answered. "Looks good. The tracking instruments and my own visual check indicate that you're right on target. You're not breaking any speed records, but you don't have that far to go. Shouldn't be much longer before you're out of the wormhole and into the Gamma Quadrant."

Kira relaxed in the seat, feeling a subconsciously held tension drain out of her spine. The plan she had devised seemed to be working. The cargo shuttle's maneuvering and docking jets didn't require any energy from the impulse engines, so they could be safely used even with the buffers out of commission. Once the correct attitude had been determined, it was only a matter of "aiming" the shuttle like an old-fashioned gunpowder weapon, with the substation as its cannonball. The force of the bomblets built into the coupling's disengage mechanism was enough to send the cargo shuttle and the substation in opposite directions, the shuttle farther back into the wormhole, the substation forward to its exit point. The wormhole was its own linear pocket universe, so the relative motions couldn't go too far astray; the trick had been to make sure that the substation continued down the center of the wormhole without getting mired in the gravitational field around the edges and losing its precious momentum.

She unstrapped the harness, and let it retract into the sides of the seat. Another stricture seemed to have been loosened from her. For the first time in a great while, she felt that things were working out as they should. As she wanted them to. Even with these delays, the substation would reach the wormhole's exit sector well before Gul Tahgla's retrofitted vessel could return to it; the Federation's claim would be established, and Bajor's future protected. The other details, the source of the sabotage . . . that could all be cleaned up when she eventually made her way back to DS9.

"Julian—" It was the first time she had addressed him by his first name. "Will you be all right?"

"You needn't worry about me . . ." His voice faded for a moment, then came back as the transmitter compensated for the increasing distance. "All the sensors are up and running, and I've got gigaquads of data to start rummaging through." She could imagine him smiling. "You were quite right when you suspected that I wanted to spend more time in here. Though I don't know how much longer it'll be—the station probably sent out a runabout as soon as our communications broke down."

"Enjoy yourself while you can, then."

"Maybe when we're all back at the station, we can have a celebratory drink together at Quark's—"

"Don't push it." She reached out and switched off the comm link.

It had been worth a shot. He told himself that, as he told himself after any rejection. Or *striking out,* as one of Commander Sisko's ancient ballplayers might have termed it. The fact that the substation, with Kira aboard, was on its way to its destination reaffirmed that persistence had its eventual rewards. He'd have to try to remember that.

Bashir stood up and stretched, working out the kink that had settled between his shoulder blades. The sensors and their rapidly accumulating data would have to wait; after this much work, he felt more like a nap, after a perusal of whatever had been coded into the shuttle's food replicator.

There wasn't time for that. No sooner had Bashir checked the tracking monitor—it showed the substation just approaching the wormhole's exit—than he was thrown from his feet by a sudden surge of power. He landed on his hands and knees, feeling the vibration coming up through the pilot area's floor.

Below him, in the bowels of the cargo shuttle, the impulse engines had come to life.

"What the—" He grabbed a corner of the control panel to lift himself up; he barely managed to hold onto it as the cargo shuttle was shaken by an even stronger force, caught by a shock wave that dwarfed the bomblets' explosion. The instrument readouts of the exterior sensors peaked, then were overloaded by the fury of electromagnetic radiation pouring into them. A blinding red light sliced through the visual ports.

It's them—Bashir's thoughts slammed against the

confines of his skull. *Out there . . . they felt the engines—*

Impossible to stand; he crawled, fingers clawing at the seams of metal, as the keening of the shuttle's alarms mounted. He reached desperately for the access panel that would take him down to the lower compartments, as the blow of an invisible hammer twisted a darkening cage around him.

"Julian!"

She had cried out his name, as she had seen the fabric of stars tear open. At the mouth of the wormhole, the open space of the Gamma Quadrant just beyond, as though her goal could be gathered by reaching out her arm . . .

The shock wave hit, a shuddering convulsion, the wormhole itself turned into a living thing. The substation had tumbled crazily, sending Kira shoulder-first into the corner of a bulkhead and the ceiling, then sliding across the command center's operations panel. She clung to it with one hand, bringing her other fist down upon the comm buttons.

"Julian . . . what happened . . ." No reply came over the speaker. As the tremors died, she scanned through the transmitter's frequencies; all of them were dead.

One by one, the lights came back up on the panel, as the computer ran its autodiagnostics and reestablished its core functions. Kira felt blood trickling down from her temple, but ignored it as she called up a visual scan.

Behind the substation, the vast, churning image of the wormhole blotted out uncountable worlds. She had seen it before, from its terminus close to DS9: a thing of radiance and terrible beauty, a pouring forth of wonders, a thunder that was not sound but the trembling fibers of one's being, atoms become suns. . . .

Now, the wormhole screamed.

She sensed rather than heard it, as though the spine inside her shivered at the same mute pitch. A living thing—its pain struck her once more.

No light—the wormhole drew darkness into itself, a writhing contraction of space itself.

Kira leaned over the viewscreen; a drop of blood spattered between her hand and the glass.

He's in there. The thoughts inside her head had contracted to one alone. *Inside . . . somewhere . . .*

They both saw it. And then saw nothing.

That was what dismayed Commander Sisko and Chief Engineer O'Brien. For a moment, as they had come within the final approach to the wormhole, they had been enveloped in light. Different than ever before: a light that blinded in its fury, a rage that shouted the length of their optic nerves, that, even as they raised their arms to shield themselves, sank into the night of dead worlds.

"It's gone." O'Brien looked down at the instruments' readouts. "The wormhole—it's collapsed." He turned toward the commander. *"It's gone—"*

Sisko gazed at the silent, mocking stars. A hollow space had opened beneath his breastbone.

"God help them." He shook his head slowly. "We can't."

He tore at the circuits, the deep throb of the engines rubbing his bones against each other, as though they might grind to pieces and fly apart. Wires thin as human hair tangled between his fingers, the sharp edges of the microcomponents bit into his palms; the compartment bucked around him again and he fell, squeezing his hands into fists, the guts of the controls stretching taut, then snapping. The ends stung across his face like quick hornets.

With a groan, the impulse engines halted. Bashir lay panting against the bulkhead. He opened his eyes when he realized that his own ragged breath was the only sound he heard.

Outside the cargo shuttle, the wormhole had stilled itself.

Silence.

And then she heard something.

In the empty spaces of the substation, the branching corridors, the sealed rooms; where nothing moved.

Nothing but her pulse, stepping from one beat to the next. Kira turned away from the control panel, and listened.

A voice . . .

She had heard it before, long ago. In another world, her life before this moment, this place light-years away from anyone else.

It spoke her name.

"Kira . . ."

Then she knew.

She wasn't alone.

PART
TWO

CHAPTER
10

It DIDN'T MATTER if she were dreaming or not. All that mattered was the firepower in her hands.

More than Kira had ever known before—if she closed her eyes, the weapon's weight drew her to the center of Bajor, as though her world's heart had been given to her to bear. The metal sweated in her palms, a living thing with its own desires. *Her* desires—the killing machine she held had read the fire in her soul, the part of her that had consumed the rest, that wanted revenge and the bestowing of pain equal to her own. Now, the fire was locked inside the weapon, ready to be released with the slightest motion of her finger.

"Sure you can handle that thing?" The assault team's oldest member, a grizzled veteran of anti-Cardassian campaigns, watched her. He sat with his back to the wall of the drainage ditch, his face and gear smeared so that he looked as though he were made of the same mud and wet stone. Kira knew that the man had been going on raids against occupation facilities while she had been a hollow-ribbed child in the refugee camps—but it hadn't been that long ago. "We could maybe equip you with something a little more . . . suited to you." He turned his head, drawing in the scent of the predawn air and whatever it could tell him.

"I can handle it." She knew she was being tested. There was no room in the assault team for weaklings. She had already packed the shoulder cannon and a brace of its shells enough kilometers to leave her legs trembling from exhaustion. A patch of skin on the small of her back had been worn raw by the weapon's metal stock. It was antique military tech, heavy and loud, and coated in the same dirty grease as everything else the Bajoran resistance carried; worse, it was completely outclassed by the Cardassian guards' armaments. Well-aimed, though, it could do an impressive—and soul-satisfying—amount of damage. The one time she'd fired it—the resistance didn't have enough shells to waste any on target practice— the power transfer link for one of the largest stripmining complexes on the planet had been reduced to glowing scrap. "I've done it this far." Kira shifted the cannon's bulk, making sure that its delicate electronic sights were shielded from the drizzling mist.

"Here they come." The team's scout ducked his head back below the wall's top ridge. "Six of 'em."

Kira saw the older man, the team's *de facto* leader, stiffen. "We were told five," he said.

"You go up and count them, then." The scout handed over his binoculars. The sniper fire from the

Cardassians' perimeter pickets had taken out the team's fourth member, and had made them all jumpy.

She watched as the leader, standing with his head hunched low, adjusted the binocs' tracking range. A faint green light shaded the rims of his eye sockets. After a few seconds, he dropped back down and crouched between Kira and the scout.

"All right—the five I recognize. I've been on operations with all of them before. The sixth one I don't know, but he appears to be unarmed."

"Bajoran?" Kira looked up to the ridge. "A prisoner, maybe?" The Cardassians had a wide range of techniques for pressuring the weak-willed into becoming collaborators. Some didn't need to be convinced.

The leader shook his head. "I don't think so. We'll just have to wait and see."

When the larger group came within a few meters distance, the scout signaled to them with a flashlight shuttered to a single radiant point. A minute later, they had all scrambled into the ditch.

"Who's this?" Kira's leader nodded toward the sixth man.

"Political officer." The point man for the larger group propped his rifle against the stones. "Sent out from headquarters."

"That's all we need." He looked in disgust at the black-clad figure.

"Perhaps it is." The political officer spoke in a low voice, a surface calm darkened by a brooding judgment. His unsmiling gaze measured his critic. "There have been reports . . . of dissension among those who seek to overthrow the oppressor. A failure of unity in our purpose. Such things are wounds, brother, by which Bajor itself is bled. That dawn is coming when the oppressor's vanities will be trampled in the dust; we must purge our own hearts and make of them vessels of light, to be worthy of that which shall be granted to us."

Talk and fine words . . . Kira crouched with the shoulder cannon, listening and mocking inside herself the overly dramatic words. They seemed so pointless to her. Hearing them made her feel like a child again, listening in on the elders' endless debates and theological discussions in the camps' barracks, tired old men splitting infinitely finer hairs and formulating political agendas that would never come to pass. That, as much as her hatred of the Cardassians, had finally pushed her into picking up the gun and joining the resistance. It had been a good thing for her that she'd been starved skinny and breastless; she had barely been able to crawl beneath the last camp's barbed wire, the metal thorns tearing the thin fabric of her shirt and leaving a set of bleeding stripes down her back, stripes that she'd worn as a badge of honor until they healed and faded.

Words . . . and at the same time, this man's voice. The part of her that mocked fell into silence inside herself. And listened. The way that his companions listened, a leaning forward, as though every sense must gather in what he said.

Her team's leader was the only one who didn't partake of this communion. His gaze flicked across the other men and then, eyes narrowing, came back to the political officer. "You can save your little inquisition for later. Right now, the rest of us have work to do. If you're not toting weight, the best you can do is stay out of our way."

"As you wish." The political officer, broader across

the chest and a head taller than the team's leader, nodded once. "Let the righteousness of your faith be the shield that protects you in your endeavors."

The team's leader grumbled something under his breath as he turned away. "All right, let's move out."

Kira lifted the shoulder cannon. . . .

And then, for a moment that stretched to the night's horizon, her hands were empty. She squeezed her eyes shut in confusion, wondering if she were dreaming now or at the edge of waking. She didn't seem to be standing in a muddy ditch with the familiar stars of Bajor overhead; she crouched in a narrow metal chamber, its low ceiling pressing against her back. And she herself was different: not a skinny teenager, hair beginning to grow out after being shaved for lice in the camp from which she'd fled; and not in the dirt-colored field gear of the resistance, but in a uniform with an emblem that she could almost recognize. . . .

The dreaming or the waking, whichever it was, faded away. She clambered out of the ditch, the shoulder cannon's harness tugging her back into the ground, and hurried to catch up with the others.

Then, things didn't go well.

I remember that, she murmured to herself. She pressed her hands against the metal walls binding her, as though they were the weight of memories pressing the breath from her lungs. *I remember . . . but you're dead. . . .*

The metallurgical installation went up in a fireball that resembled a new sun, straining against the hot leash rooted in the blackened towers. It had serviced the largest of the Cardassian construction yards based on Bajor—the alloys and massive framing girders going from its forges into the starships and heavy cargo freighters hauling away the rest of the planet's wealth. The plant's tailings and chemical wastes seeped into the groundwater, and into the lungs of the Bajorans unlucky enough to work there, a forced assignment that was little more than a five-year-long death sentence. To see a cancer like that erased from Bajoran soil . . . Kira had felt the flames leap up in her heart as well, as she had taken her eye away from the cannon's sight. Two of the shells she had gotten off, as she had knelt beneath her comrades' covering fire, had torn open the plant's central power source, the overload surge igniting the rest of the facility.

That part had gone all right—the dead had the comfort of knowing they had succeeded in their task.

It had been a suicide mission all along; Kira had known that and accepted it without a second thought. What surprised her was how quickly it changed, from the near-sexual glow of triumph inside herself, to the sudden adrenaline rush of fear that blocked out all except the animal desire to survive.

"They're behind us—"

She didn't know which one of the assault team had spoken; she turned her head and saw the dark shapes ranged along the crest of the hill, and knew that they were a unit of the Cardassian defense forces that had managed to circle them undetected. The hot barrel of the cannon burned her hands as she scrambled to swing it around. She didn't make it.

The first impact lifted her off her feet and into a tumbling flight surrounded by shattered rock. If it had been a direct hit, she would have been torn to bleeding pieces as quickly as her comrades at one side.

More luck: she landed in a bank of soil that crumbled beneath her, her half-conscious form sliding into a ravine a few meters deep, the water at its base tangled with exposed tree roots. The wet dirt covered her face and torso, shutting off her breath. Her hands pawed feebly at her mouth and nose, but were too weak to clear them.

Just before she passed out from lack of oxygen, she felt another's hand grasp her by the arm. The figure— she saw only a silhouette outlined by stars—pulled, drawing her up onto her feet, legs trembling beneath her.

"Kira—" The political officer kept her from collapsing with an arm clasped around her shoulders. She didn't wonder then how he knew her name; later, she realized it had been part of his duties. "Can you walk?"

She nodded, coughing to clear the mud from her throat. His voice, even though no more than a whisper, seemed to impart its strength, evoking her own. The sound of heavy military machinery drew her gaze. Adrenaline sped her pulse as she spotted the Cardassian defense forces prowling the ridge above.

The political officer drew her back into the shadows. "They're sweeping the area." He turned his face toward hers. "We'll have a better chance if we split up. At least one of us should make it, then." He pointed along the ravine's course. "Head north. There's a resistance encampment in the Tohrmah hills."

Crouching low to avoid being seen, Kira moved off. Behind her, she heard only a few softly spoken words, telling her to remember that her faith was a shield. When she was several meters away, she glanced back and saw the man's silhouette as he watched for his chance; then he broke out of the ditch's shelter. In a second, he had vanished into the darkness. She turned and continued on her own silent way, expecting fire to roll over her back at any moment.

She never saw him again. But she knew of him, and realized who the political officer had been—the name linked to the powerful voice—when, only a few years later, she first heard the broadcasts of the man who had become the leader of the Redemptorist wing of the resistance.

That voice had spoken her name once, in a crevice soaked with rain and blood. And then later, when both she and the man had become different from what they once had been. And yet the same. The voice spoke her name differently then, in a thunder of wrath and vengeance.

And then a whisper again, close to her as her own heartbeat.

Kira . . .

A whisper that promised death.

Her eyes snapped open, and she knew where she was.

Not dreaming, or lost in memory. Her hands pressed against the tight confines of the space where she had managed to hide herself, deep inside the substation's maze of corridors and rooms. Beyond, she knew, were the empty reaches of the Gamma Quadrant, its ranks of stars cold needles of light.

And inside the substation, with her . . . *he* was there. The voice that had spoken her name. She turned her head, listening through the enclosing silence for a footstep, or a breath that wasn't her own.

Nothing—but she could still feel his presence.

She had run from the substation's command center,

losing herself in the branching network of doorways
and compartments. All she had known was that she
had to find somewhere safe, if only for a little while,
just long enough to think. To plan, to find a way of
surviving.

Exhaustion had felled her, more quickly than whatever weapon was in the hand of Hören Rygis. Curled
inside a remote storage locker, its hatch pulled tight,
she had panted for air, feeling herself falling, as if the
metal at her back had parted beneath the weight of the
memories she bore.

They had claimed her. As though she had never
been able to escape them.

Forget, she commanded herself, as she had done so
many times before. She knew it was impossible. But
still . . .

Kira drew in a deep breath, feeling her muscles
tense in readiness. *For now*—she willed the dark,
unforgiving thoughts back into the chamber from
which they had escaped. *Just until you've done what
you must.* To survive.

She reached out her hand and pushed open the
locker's hatch, then leaned forward and peered into
the waiting shadows.

CHAPTER
11

HE LEANED across the desk toward the station's chief officers. They had gathered in Ops and then, for security reasons, relocated their meeting to the private office. "All right," said Commander Sisko. "Status report on the substation mission."

"There have been some developments." Jadzia Dax, DS9's chief science officer, had taken on some of the duties that would ordinarily have been performed by Major Kira. "We've picked up a monitoring signal that indicates the substation actually managed to exit the wormhole. It's relatively close to the position in the Gamma Quadrant that had been its original destination."

"Any communications?"

Dax shook her head. "Negative. Our own diagnostic signals show evidence that the transmitting and receiving equipment aboard the substation was either damaged during the convulsive event inside the wormhole, or had been tampered with before leaving the station—possibly with some sort of delay trigger, to keep the sabotage from being detected until it was too late for us to do anything about it."

"What about the cargo shuttle? Any sign of it?"

"That will be a much more difficult question to answer, Commander. As far as I've been able to determine, the stable wormhole has transmuted from a bipolar to a unipolar state, anchored in the Gamma Quadrant. This is an entirely different cosmological anomaly. In a very real way, for us, *the wormhole no longer exists.* At least, not as we had begun to understand it. If the cargo shuttle is still inside what might be termed a cul-de-sac or pocket universe, we presently have no way of determining its status. I'm sorry."

Sisko swiveled toward his chief engineer. "What do you think? Is there anybody still aboard the cargo shuttle?"

"There would have to be, Commander." O'Brien's expression was grim. "The only way they could've gotten the substation out of the wormhole was to fire off the disengagement bomblets—use that force like the propulsive element in a cannon shell. I was wondering if they'd figure that out. Evidently they did; but, for it to work, one of them would have to stay aboard the shuttle, to initiate the trigger sequence. My guess would be that it was Doctor Bashir."

"Undoubtedly." Sisko nodded. "It's Kira's mission —she'd want to see it all the way through. And there would've been no way for her to know what was about to happen with the wormhole."

Dax spoke more softly. "It's still possible that

Bashir is alive. Before our end of the wormhole collapsed, sensors seemed to indicate that the shuttle's impulse engines had been activated—*without* the buffers being on line. It's a reasonable assumption that that was the cause of the convulsion; essentially, a defensive reaction on the part of the wormhole's inhabitants to a potentially lethal shock. If Bashir was able to shut down the engines, soon after we lost contact, then the shuttle might not have been destroyed. At this point, we just don't know."

"Yes . . ." For a moment, Sisko's gaze drifted from the faces arrayed before him. Inside himself, he saw images shift and merge together, a kaleidoscope of memory. He knew more about the wormhole's inhabitants than any other sentient creature, and they remained enigmatic to him. They had spoken to him through the masks of his own history; the dead had spoken to him. Even his wife, the emptiness he carried beneath his breastbone, an emptiness with a name that he murmured aloud in sleepless dark hours. What had the wormhole's inhabitants learned of the human mind and soul by studying him? That there was violence and grieving in the outside universe. *Better if a saint had found his way in there*—the words he'd told himself before mocked him again. Perhaps a saint would have been wise enough not to make promises that would wind up being broken. And now, Bashir might be the one who would have to pay for that.

"It *is* possible that he shut down the impulse engines in time—" Dax's voice tugged at his awareness, bringing him back to those around him. "There are indications that the wormhole, in its altered state, still exists in the Gamma Quadrant; our monitor beacons in that sector are still picking up several band segments of the wormhole's signature energy emissions. The cargo shuttle could be simply drifting inside the wormhole, with Bashir aboard."

"*If* he's still alive." Sisko saw no value in analyzing the situation in anything except the harshest possible light. He turned to the security officer. "What have you been able to get out of the other Redemptorists?"

"Not much." Odo shook his head. "We have enough evidence to hold them indefinitely, on suspicion of complicity in the sabotage of the substation mission and the murder of their fellow group member. *And* the smuggling aboard of a known terrorist leader wanted by the Bajoran security forces. If you were to order it as my top priority, I could almost certainly assemble airtight cases against them. But as far as getting information out of them, at least in time to do us any good . . ." He shrugged. "They're a closemouthed bunch. Fanatics. Their ideology is more religious than political in nature, and they're certainly willing to die for as well as kill for it." A certain self-satisfaction could almost be seen in the security chief's face. "As I've indicated before, it was an error to ever have allowed such types aboard the station in the first place."

"We'll deal with those regrets later. Have you managed to confirm that Hören Rygis is aboard the substation?"

Odo gave a curt nod. "That is something on which the Redemptorists are not keeping silent. They're rather boastful about it, actually."

"You'll have to keep the pressure on them. Any useful information we can get—"

"May I remind you, Commander, that my interrogation of these men is not unhindered by other considerations? Word has gone through the whole station that I've taken them into custody; the news is bound to reach Bajor soon, if it hasn't already. You're aware of how volatile the provisional government is right now; when the legitimate political wing of the Redemptorists hears about these men being held, it's going to demand either a complete explanation or their immediate release—"

"Those are not concerns of yours, Constable." Sisko's voice grew stern. "I'll deal with the political situation on Bajor. Your job is security, and right now the security of this station and its personnel depends upon the outcome of the substation mission. That's why we need you to get those Redemptorists to open up."

Odo betrayed no sign of emotion. "As you wish, Commander."

One of Sisko's hands rubbed at the ache that pulsed behind his forehead. "All right, then. Keep pushing for establishing communication with Major Kira. By this point, I don't think we need to warn her about Hören—she's almost certain to be aware of his presence. But we still might be able to assist her somehow." He pushed his chair back and stood up. "I'll be in contact with all of you, so I can be given updates on any developments."

Dax regarded him with a raised eyebrow. "Where are you going, Commander?"

"To Bajor." Sisko stepped behind her and the other officers as they headed for the door. "There's someone else I need to talk to."

* * *

"Now," he said, "we are going to have a little conversation." His words bounced off the barren metal walls. The other cells along the corridor outside were empty. "You have much to tell me, and I'm sure that I'll find all of it of interest."

On the other side of the table, the four Bajoran microassemblers—once there had been six of them aboard the station—shifted uneasily. Odo had entered the cell without using a key, flowing between the close-set bars and then reassembling his humanoid form on the other side. He assumed that the Redemptorists had been aware of the shapeshifting abilities of DS9's security chief, but he had found in the past that a demonstration often worked to unnerve suspects and make them more receptive to his pressure techniques. Once someone began to doubt the true nature of the physical objects around him, and began wondering whether the chair on which he sat might not be listening to every word he said, then disorientation and helplessness could seep in.

Sometimes, in moments of quiet reflection, savoring an accomplished investigation—his greatest pleasure—he found himself admiring his self-sufficiency. In other places, other times, the police had had to conduct interrogations in pairs, "good cop" and "bad cop." If he worked it right, he could be both.

"We have nothing to say to you." One of the Redemptorists kept his arms folded across his chest. "Leave us in peace."

So this is their new spokesman, thought Odo. He had observed the others' glances from the corners of their eyes, waiting for the one in the middle to answer. A definite intellectual cut below the late Deyreth Elt, who at least had had a measure of intensity, a second-

or third-generation copy of the Redemptorist movement's leader. The survivors of the group that had come aboard the station all had a sullen obstinacy about them, as though most of their brainpower had been devoted to their intricate craft, with the iron dictates of their faith filling in their inadequate personalities. Such types, he knew from experience, were often more difficult to crack than a superior mind — they could always lapse into a defensive silence, whereas a genius wouldn't be able to resist proving how much cleverer he was than a mere security chief. As long as they kept talking, Odo would eventually find out what he needed to know.

"I thought we might talk about Hören Rygis." For one of his physiology, all sitting positions were equally comfortable; now, he assumed one that clearly signaled a relaxed, even casual attitude. "Surely that's a subject that you don't tire of."

A smug expression rose on the spokesman's face. "Didn't you hear enough of him before? We told you where he is."

"Yes, of course. I was just wondering what he might be doing out there, so far away from his devoted little flock."

"He . . ." The smugness changed to caution. "He performs the obligations laid upon him by our faith."

A canned phrase; Odo nodded slowly. "I see. You mean murder."

All the Redemptorists glared at him sullenly. "Such acts," said the spokesman, "are not murder. They're justice."

"Ah. Like what happened to your compatriot Arten."

Silence.

"The problem," said Odo, "is that you're going to be tried as accessories to that 'justice.' Others might not take such a . . . complex view of these things. They might simply regard murder as murder."

"So?" The spokesman shrugged. "A glorious martyrdom is welcomed by the faithful."

"Yes, it usually is. Which is a good thing for you, since Hören certainly set you up for it." He let the remark sink in for a moment before continuing. "That is, of course, if it actually was Hören . . ."

The spokesman stiffened in his chair, as the others glanced nervously toward him. "What do you mean?"

Odo knew that the simplest deception would never have worked on the Redemptorists. These were men who had spent years in close contact with each other, and with Hören Rygis; small conspiratorial units, the smells of their own blood and sweat locked into their subconscious memories. There were a thousand little clues that even he, with his shapeshifting abilities, could never have gotten right. If he had disguised himself, taken on Hören's face and body structure, and come walking into the cell, ordering his followers to confess all to their captors—they would have seen right through him. Their contempt would have been justified.

But to do it in front of them, the way he had come through the bars . . . to plant the tiniest of seeds in their minds . . . that would burrow deeper and deeper, and do its slow damage to the sureness of their beliefs. . . .

The body was easy enough; Odo had studied the photographs and the few available tapes of the

Redemptorists' leader, and had memorized Hören's distinctive broad-shouldered form. He could even manage a reasonable approximation of Hören's face, one that could pass muster for a few seconds, as long as the light silhouetted him from behind, shining into the Redemptorists' eyes.

The voice had taken more effort: he'd had to experiment in private, sculpting inside himself the thickness of the larynx's cords, the dimensions of the thoracic cavity, and the smaller, more intricate chambers of the sinuses, all that gave the voice on the recording chips its resonance. Even when he'd judged his mimicry a success, he knew that there was still some irreducible element, a power not in the material form, that he wouldn't be able to reproduce.

But he was still close enough.

Across the table from the team of Bajoran microassemblers, the form and image of Hören Rygis leaned toward their startled gazes. The face of Hören Rygis smiled thinly, then his voice spoke.

"Your faith should be a shield. To guard you during the great task of cutting this pollution away from the soul of your world."

They were all shocked into a dismayed silence. They stared at him as he resumed his usual appearance. He remembered the old entertainers' maxim that it was best to hit one's audience and then get offstage before they could pick the act apart.

Odo now tried to make himself sound as kind as possible. "The problem is, gentlemen, that you don't know how much *I* know . . . how much of what you may have said before wasn't spoken to your grand and glorious leader . . . but to me."

He pushed the chair back and stood up. It didn't matter how messy the logic of what he'd told them might be; in some ways, it was better like that. It gave their brains more to be puzzled about, to endlessly twist and turn in their thoughts. Just as long as the elements of doubt and suspicion were there.

"I'll leave you now." He stood with his back against the bars; a moment later, he was on the other side of them. The Redemptorists flinched. "I'm sure you have a lot to discuss with each other." He turned and walked down the corridor between the cells, feeling satisfied with his work.

It would have been comforting to have someone to talk to. Humans were by nature social creatures, and he perhaps more than most. Julian Bashir wouldn't have become a doctor, otherwise.

He let such musings roll around the back part of his head as he continued working on the circuitry of the cargo shuttle's engines. His forebrain was preoccupied with repairing the damage he'd caused in his desperate haste to shut down the unbuffered impulse energy pouring out, before the wormhole's convulsions had thrashed the shuttle to pieces.

"Damn . . ." Another sharp corner of metal had bit his fingertips. Clearances were tight inside the panels, and he lacked most of the appropriate tools. Open-heart surgery on an exoskeletoned Thallasinite with a butter knife would have been easier. He sucked the blood from under his nail and leaned forward to peer into the electronic innards. Besides conversation, it would have been handy to have Kira here—so *she* could hold the flashlight.

Fortunately, the cargo shuttle's engines had been equipped with a modular repair kit, updated by DS9's Chief Engineer O'Brien, with most of the circuitry duplicated on plug-in cards. The control schematics could be scrolled through on a small readout screen; with that and a miniaturized logic probe, Bashir had been able to trace and reconnect most of the thin-filament wires he'd pulled loose before.

In doing so, he had also located parts that didn't belong there at all. He had tugged them free and examined them on the palm of his hand. Some he could recognize, enough to be sure that they were what had caused the unexpected firing of the engines. A few override modules, a short-range remote trigger, some kind of delay device—nothing that O'Brien would have had any reason to install. They would have to have been wired in place back on DS9 by someone else—probably that group of Redemptorist microassemblers—at the same time the impulse buffers had been tampered with. But set off from close by; given the shuttle's close quarters, the only possibility was that it had been done from aboard the substation while it had still been attached. The setting on the in-line delay circuit had given just enough time for the disengagement sequence to have been completed and for the substation to have reached the wormhole's exit before activating the engines. The saboteur—Hören Rygis, of course; who else could it have been?—would not have anticipated that a way would have been found to get the substation out of the wormhole; Bashir figured that the Redemptorists had planned only to collapse the entrance to the wormhole, to prevent any outside assistance from reaching him and Kira. Once the triggering device had been set off, the delay circuit would have been needed for Hören to scramble back to whatever hiding place he had had in the far reaches of the substation. It was just a turn of bad luck that things had worked out even better for Hören, with Kira in the substation with him, while Bashir remained stuck in the wormhole.

That thought—that there was someone else on the substation besides Kira, now drifting somewhere out in the Gamma Quadrant, someone with apparently a wealth of bad intentions—kept him working long after his eyes burned with the fatigue of squinting into the dimly lit space. Before he'd found the trigger and delay, he'd only wanted to ensure that the engines wouldn't come on again unexpectedly; otherwise, he would have gone on fine-tuning the shuttle's transmission and reception equipment, trying to establish a communication link with Kira. To warn her, if nothing else. From this close to the wormhole's exit, there was a chance of a signal reaching the substation.

He straightened his knotted back and rubbed the sweat away from his eyes. As far as he could tell, he'd gotten the controls for one of the engines back in working order—he wasn't sure if there were enough cards in the repair kit to get the others back on line. The shuttle would be able to proceed on one engine, although at a reduced velocity. He'd have to run the autodiagnostics first, then go back in and patch up anything he hadn't gotten close enough to spec. It was a simple matter of closing the hatch and pushing a few buttons. . . .

"Well done, Doctor," he said aloud. His voice boomed hollow in the space. An old med school joke surfaced unbidden in his mind: *The operation was a success. Too bad the patient died.* He realized he didn't have the least idea of what he should do next.

If he had managed to get the engine operational—a big *if*—then what? There had been some vague notion floating around inside his head, that he could come charging to her rescue. But if he fired up the engine, got as much thrust as he could from it, what would the chances be of getting the cargo shuttle all the way out of the wormhole in one piece? Or if he did, would the wormhole then collapse completely out of existence behind him? Without the wormhole's shortcut, the Gamma Quadrant was sixty years' travel from the edge of the Federation's inhabited worlds, even at maximum warp speeds. He and Kira would have a long uninterrupted time to get to know each other.

Another *if*. If she were still alive.

Bashir closed the panel and punched in the code to initiate the autodiagnostic tests. Despite the darkness of his thoughts, he was pleasantly surprised when the small readout indicated that the impulse engine was functional within 70 percent of its rated load capacity.

Eyes shut, he leaned his forehead against the panel. The temptation to get the shuttle moving was strengthened by the dread of staying frozen in this spot, inert, cut off from all the rest of the universe . . .

"I should just do it," he said aloud. "Just go—"

Is that what you wish to do?

He heard her voice behind him, and almost answered. Before he realized . . .

Slowly, he looked over his shoulder. He saw Kira watching him from the shadows at the far end of the engine chamber.

But not Kira. He saw that her eyes were empty, holding nothing but black space and scattered stars.

CHAPTER
12

WHEN SURROUNDED BY METAL, bound by the energy fields that keep an artificial world intact, a constant vibration settles into the fibers of one's being, so small as to signal only the rubbing of one molecule against another. He had forgotten about that—it became buried in the subconscious for all aboard a Starfleet vessel or a station such as DS9, and was remembered only when one stepped onto the surface of a planet.

The reverberations of DS9, from the metal-on-metal clashes that shook the drydock bay, to the motion of subatomic particles inside the computers' circuitry, was the sound of a machine, essentially a dead thing. The silence of Bajor was of something living.

Sisko stood in the central garden of the Kai's temple. The high, enfolded walls shut out the distant street noises of the Bajoran capital. Here, the only sound was the ripple of water, the touch of a sheltered breeze on the courtyard's small, shallow pool.

"Your thoughts are much disturbed, Benjamin."

He turned and saw her. Kai Opaka's attendants withdrew discreetly back into the temple's cloistered halls, leaving them alone. The Kai's calm, meditative appearance, Sisko knew, was like the surface of the pool they stood beside; hidden beneath, as had been revealed to him more than once, were quiet depths, chambers of secrets and truths.

One of his eyebrows raised. "Are they really so obvious to you?"

Kai Opaka smiled. "They would be obvious to anyone. Particularly"—the smile widened a bit—"if one stayed informed about developments here on Bajor, and on your station."

"I see." He wished, not for the first time, that there were time. Not the stuff of hours and minutes racing by, the continuing round of crises writhing like a basketful of snakes, missions and lives hanging in the balance of his decisions—but the endless dimension contained within the temple's walls. If he had that sort of time, he could spend it in the presence of the Kai, if only to absorb the slightest measure of her wisdom. . . .

But he didn't. "I regret," he said, "that I can be here for but a brief moment. To consult with you."

She sat down, her robes settling over the tiled edge of the pool. Her plump hands folded across each other. "I understand, Benjamin. More than you think. You mistake the nature of my contemplations here if you believe I have no awareness of the outside world's urgencies."

Sisko sat beside her. "Perhaps it's not what I believe. But what I'd like to believe." At the back of his thoughts, the digits of a clock's readout sped faster and faster.

"You must beware the temptations of mysticism. Though you are not as other men—the things that you have seen, that no one else has, changed and are still changing you—yet you are inextricably linked to the physical universe. There are others besides your son who depend upon you." She touched his hand. "I depend upon you, Benjamin. I am not such a foolish old woman as not to be grateful for the protection you represent for our order."

Changed . . . he knew what she referred to. A body of secret knowledge shared between them. Some things that he knew, and others that were the Kai's alone. The infinitely slow revelation of the wormhole's mysteries . . .

The clock's numbers raced into a blur.

He shook his head. "We'll have to talk of these matters on another occasion. Right now, I've got the lives of two of my officers to worry about."

"Of course, Benjamin. Your esteemed doctor and our Major Kira. My thoughts dwell upon them also."

Someday, he would have to find out whether Kai Opaka received her surprising amount of information about the station's affairs from leaks among the DS9 staff, or through some arcane ability of her own. "What do you know of them?"

Kai Opaka didn't waste time telling him things he already knew. "The doctor . . . his fate is unknown to me. Or perhaps *unknowable* would be the better word. I cannot see. The inhabitants of what you call the wormhole have suffered a grievous injury; how they will connect that trauma to another outsider—another human being—in their midst, is a question only they can answer. Much will depend upon the doctor's wisdom; what he chooses to do or not do, to extricate himself from his plight. And much will depend upon *your* wisdom, Benjamin."

"How do you mean?"

"Their understanding of the universe beyond their little one, and their understanding of any entity other than their own, is derived from what they know of you. You are the one whose mind and soul they examined so minutely; you are the one who was judged by them. Or to put it more accurately, all of us were judged through you. Thus, you became an inter-cessor, pleading the universe's case; that great responsibility was thrust upon one who was unprepared for it."

He nodded slowly. "I know . . ."

"What they found in your heart, Benjamin, they have placed in their store of knowledge."

The Kai's words weighed heavy upon him. If he could have switched places with Bashir, he would have. *Let the fire fall upon me.* He had gone into the wormhole with rage and loss darkening his soul. They still did; to think of them poisoning a formless world, whose inhabitants had never known pain because they had never known time itself . . . it was almost more than he could bear.

He might as well have spoken aloud; the Kai's hand rested gently upon his. "You must remember," she said, "that you bore light in there, as well. As much as any that ever emerged from them. You just haven't seen it yet."

171

"Perhaps I will, someday." Sisko drew in his breath as he straightened his spine. "Very well. What about Kira?"

Kai Opaka looked away from him. "I do see her." The Kai spoke in hushed tones. "More than I wish. Kira is surrounded by darkness. There is one who has sealed her fate inside his fist, as though he could crush her like an insect—though an insect's life would mean more to him."

"You speak of Hören Rygis . . ."

"Yes. The enmity he bears her, among others, is well known."

"Tell me about him. Anything might be of use to me."

Her expression grew sadder. "Benjamin. You are looking for answers where there are none. There is nothing to tell of him. *Hören no longer exists.* There is a thing that wears his form and speaks with his voice, and carries within the flames of hatred that he ignited. But the rest is ashes. It has been consumed, burned away by his anger. Just as your anger, your loss, your pain would have consumed you if you had let them."

He knew she spoke truth, as always. "Then tell me what I can do. To help Kira."

"You can do nothing." An iron thread tightened in Kai Opaka's throat. "You understand that already, and you do not understand it. You could do nothing before, when you lost someone—someone closer to you than Kira could ever be—and you can do nothing now. That is why some part of you is still at war with both the universe and your own heart, as though they were one and the same, and equally guilty."

He said nothing, letting her words fall through him like stones into the pool's still water.

"That remains the hardest thing for you to do, Benjamin. To do nothing."

"Of course." He looked up at her, even managing a thin smile. "As you said, I'm linked to the world outside my skin. I can't yet allow myself to be as wise as you."

"Ah. But you didn't come here for wisdom. You came here hoping that I had some kind of magic, a wave of my hand that would bring your doctor and Kira back from their fates." Kai Opaka shook her head. "But I don't. Not the way you think."

"I suppose you're right." Sisko stood up. "I should go back to the station and . . . do nothing."

"But you won't." Her smile chided him. "That is something we both know."

Without any signal from the Kai, her attendants had appeared to escort Sisko from the temple. "Until another time." The clock inside his skull had resumed its relentless progress.

"The same time, Benjamin. It's always the same."

He nodded, then turned and left her presence.

As close to her as her breath, her heartbeat; as if he walked behind like her shadow, turning when she did, stopping when she paused to listen to the silence held by the dark spaces. He watched her, feeling inside himself a glow of satisfaction, even of pleasure, that came from the power of observing without being observed in turn.

Hōren crouched beside a doorway, studying the display screen he held. A pair of wires mounted with fusion-weld tips ran into the corner of the security panel that he had pried open. His prey showed on the screen as a simple red dot, alternately moving or stopping in a scrolling chart of the substation's maze. His followers had done well in adapting the corridors' web of sensors and communication lines for this new purpose. The expanded visual aspect was something he generated inside himself: on his mind's screen he could picture Kira's face as she gazed anxiously around herself, her body coiled with apprehension as she took a step into a sector where anything could be waiting for her.

He closed his eyes, savoring that vision. This moment had been so long in coming, from the first dark seed that had been planted in his soul, a seed of fire as he had watched the temple torn open by explosion and had known that his Redemptorist brethren, his children, were things of charred flesh and shattered bone, their corpses lying before the boots of traitors. The dead he had been able to forget—they had all known that sacrifices would be necessary to achieve the sanctification of Bajor—but not the face and name of their murderer. One whom he had saved before from fire and the crushing grip of the Cardassians—that memory was gall on his tongue.

If he had been as wise then as he had become . . . if he could have foreseen the evil that would grow in Kira Nerys's heart, as the desire for justice had grown inside his . . . he would have let her die, breath choked by the soil of the world she would betray. Better if he had. But instead, that seed, the image of her laughing and triumphant, had been nurtured inside him, carefully tended, flourishing where he had uprooted every soft and tender part of himself. Thus,

he had transformed her crime into his righteousness; the burning of that fire, a red flower that would
never extinguish itself in his memory, had made steel
of his will, sharper than before. Every Redemptorist
had been touched by that new metal, the movement
made stronger, the weak cut away, blood purged to
holiness.

And now, the time had come for the final blossom-
ing of that seed, the unfolding of intermingled fire
and steel. If the price of taking her life was his own,
he was more than prepared. All his labor, and the
work of his followers, had gone to bring about this
moment. When there would be no one but himself
and Kira, no one to stand in the way of his uplifted blade, no one to shield her from the justice that
now descended upon her. That had been the function
of the various devices that the faithful, the small
group of microassemblers aboard the strangers' station, had so cleverly wired into the circuitry of the
cargo shuttle. First, to cripple the vessel and leave it
stranded in the midst of the wormhole, and then to
separate Kira from her partner on the mission. All
that had been done, to greater effect than he could
have wished for.

Hören opened his eyes, gathering his strength inside
himself. So much more was about to be accomplished:
not just Kira's death, but the banishment of the
strangers, the lying Federation and all its servants,
from the skies of Bajor. The only reason that the
DS9 station's commander and the others stayed
was to exploit the wealth they thought could be
obtained from defiling the wormhole, the source
of Bajor's most precious mysteries. And there
were certainly enough traitorous factions in the

provisional government, who maintained their ruling coalition by debasing themselves for the scraps of wealth dealt out by their off-world masters. All that would change now, or already had been changed; he had felt the shock wave that had hit the substation, as the unbuffered engines aboard the cargo shuttle had inflicted their wound upon the wormhole's inhabitants. The triggering device, with its corresponding delay circuit, that Deyreth Elt had built for him had done its job. A regretful necessity—but how else could the Federation's hold on Bajor be broken? Perhaps someday, when the faithful prevailed in righteousness, and Bajor had returned to the purity of isolation, then the wormhole might open onto its chosen world again, bestowing the crystalline gift that indicated its sanctity. . . .

He didn't know if he would live to see that day. It was enough that he could help usher in its dawn.

The red dot on the display screen moved. Hören watched it, quickly calculating that she was heading for the substation's control center, from which she had fled before. He smiled to himself.

It would be a pleasure to speak to Kira Nerys once more. Nearly as pleasant as what would come afterward.

She stood before him. "Kira—" He reached out his hand, hesitating, as though he wanted to, yet was afraid to touch her.

The image regarded him with its gaze filled with the bright points of stars. "Who are you?" Its voice was flat and hollow, with not even a pretense of human emotion. "You are not the same. You are not the one who is here . . ." The voice drifted silent, as though the creature behind the image were searching for a word, a concept.

"Before," said Doctor Bashir. He knew he was addressing one—or more—of the wormhole's inhabitants. This was how Sisko had reported their manifestation to him, the incorporeal entities taking on faces and bodies from the perceivers' memory, like empty clothing dangling in a forgotten closet. "That was another human being. Another man."

"'Was' . . ." The stars showed in the Kira image's mouth when it spoke. Without substance, the image hung suspended in front of Bashir, unable to cast a shadow among the others in the shuttle's engine chamber. "That is the language of *time*. In that you are the same."

"Yes." He nodded slowly. More of his self-possession, and the scientist's intent that had brought him here, had returned. He felt like a biological field researcher, carefully approaching a member of an undiscovered species, a *rara avis* perched on a tree limb, that might flutter away and be lost if startled by any sudden move. "The same . . . but different."

"How can that be?" The image's voice altered slightly, into an almost hostile, demanding tone. "You change in *time*. You are not the same in one *time* as another. And yet you are also different at the same *time*. Explain."

It would be impossible, he knew. The wormhole's inhabitants were of a different order of existence from himself; the pocket universe in which they dwelt was bound inside the larger one's spatial dimensions, but transcended it in all considerations of past, present, and future. A metaphysician would be required then, to determine if in *time*, the universe that held all the galaxies was itself contained within the wormhole.

There might have been an occasion when Bashir would have been interested in puzzling these matters out; the doctor in him could already see the implications of a temporal continuum where the onset, progress, diagnosis, and cure of a disease were simultaneous; where death itself was equivalent to birth, both of them gems on the same necklace.

But not now. Not when Kira's and his own life might still be at stake.

"The one to whom you showed yourself before—the one named Benjamin Sisko—he and I are both *men*, but we're not the same *man*." Bashir struggled to find means of communicating with the entities that shuffled in and out of the image before him. "We're both the same kind of creature, but not the same individual."

The Kira image frowned. "Your kind speaks in riddles, just as . . . *before*. You change from point to point in this *time;* yet you claim to be the same creature. How can you know that?"

"Well . . ." He started feeling desperate. "That's the function of memory. Part of us is a record of the changes we go through in time." That sounded right to him; he decided to go with it. "It could be maintained that all we are—all that creatures such as myself are—is the sum of those changes."

"Then you might *change*, in *time*, into the one called Sisko."

"I don't think that's very likely."

A pensive expression formed on the image's face. "We do not *change*. We are . . . eternal. That is your word."

He saw an opening. "But the universe outside us—the small one, that my kind calls the wormhole —that's part of your kind, isn't it?"

"Yes . . ." Kira's image nodded. "Our kind and the wormhole—we are the same . . ." Its eyelids closed for a moment, hiding the empty space of stars behind. "The same *flesh*. That is what you would say."

"Maybe 'substance' would be better. But it doesn't matter." Bashir resisted the urge to step closer, to touch the image's hand, to feel whatever energy it was composed of. "The wormhole changed, though, didn't it? Because of what happened—"

The stars changed to blazing suns, bright in the engine compartment's dim space; he winced at their sudden fury.

"Yes!" The image's other voice thundered from it. "The hurt—the wounding! As *before,* when one of your kind came among us. That one, the one named Sisko—he made a promise to us. He made *time* a thing to be bound, to be held in his hands; he said *never*. Never would the wounding happen, never would your kind come amongst us and *hurt* us—"

The image of Kira seemed to swell with rage, as though absorbing the physical dimensions of the compartment. Bashir found himself looking up into its black gaze. His hands, in a reflexive panic, clawed for the rungs at his back.

"Never is a thing of time—so he told us!" The image's voice mounted. "So *you* told us! Your kind!

But it is not so—it is a lie. There is no such thing as *never*—you come here and *hurt* us again. And *always*—"

His courage wavered for a moment, long enough for him to turn without thinking and scramble up the ladder. He pulled himself out of the access hatch and collapsed onto the deck above.

She was already there, waiting. For a moment, he thought it actually was Kira, kneeling down beside him. Until he rolled, exhausted, onto his shoulder and could see the blackness and the starry points inside the image's eye sockets.

Its first voice spoke, gentler if only because it betrayed no emotion. "There is no need to speak in your defense. We know the nature of your kind; we have listened to, and gone deep inside, one who is both different and the same as you. What decision we make depends not on your words."

The momentary panic had drained away from Bashir; he could faintly see his line of attack again, the way he had been trying to shape this strange discussion's course. "'Decision' . . ." He hoisted himself into a sitting posture against the bulkhead. "Don't you see? That word alone implies an operation in time. Your kind will *decide,* and that will make things different now from what they were."

The Kira image nodded, almost sadly. "Yes . . . our kind has already been changed by this *time* you have brought us. *We are not as we were.* To exist as your kind does . . . we do not know yet if this is a good thing. We look inside you and see that you are something called a *doctor,* as the other one is a *commander.* Know then, Doctor Bashir, that *time* and *change* and all the other aspects of your peculiar existence may be only a disease. And one for which you possess no cure."

"That may be." Another thought came to his mind, unbidden.

The image peered more closely at him, as though seeing through the bone shell of his brow. "That is true, Doctor. As you speak inside yourself: *The cure for time is death.* We know that."

"It's not a cure that my kind accepts."

"Pity." The Kira image regarded him with no change in expression. "See how much more suffering and pain you cause by not doing so."

Anger, born of the entity's incomprehension and his own failure, flared inside Bashir. "There is another one of my kind, whose semblance you have taken on—"

"Yes. That one's exterior appearance was uppermost in your thoughts."

"She's in danger. I need to speak with her."

Lines appeared on the image's brow, as though the entity beyond it were puzzled. "That one is in no danger from us. That one no longer exists here."

"Nevertheless . . ." He made an effort to contain his frayed temper. "She exists elsewhere."

The image shrugged. "Speak with her, then."

"I can't. The electromagnetic radiation . . . certain aspects of your nature make it impossible for me."

Eyes closed, the image was silent, as though in deliberation or conference. Then its gaze settled upon him again. "That has been *changed,* as your kind would say." It pointed down the passageway to the shuttle's pilot area. "Go to that material object that enables you to speak with nonexistent ones. You will find it functions as you wish."

As Bashir got to his feet, he saw the kneeling image begin to fade, bands of darkness rising through the visible form. Kira's face, with its eyes of stars, looked up at him.

"We will speak again, Doctor. It is—also as you would say—simply a matter of *time.*"

He thought he saw its face evolve to a trace of a smile, before it was gone. When he was alone once more, he turned and hurried to the pilot area.

CHAPTER
13

SHE HEARD HIS VOICE, even as she inched forward in the corridor's shadows.

"Kira . . . come on, answer . . ."

Static crackled through the words, the background noise of a barely maintained comm connection. The source of the transmission was in some sense not far away at all, and in another, a universe away. It didn't matter; the touch of that voice at her ear was as welcome as a rope tossed to one who was drowning.

"Kira . . ." An anxious edge filtered into Bashir's voice, detectable even through the haze of electronics. "Are you there . . ."

The initial impulse that Kira felt was to push herself away from the bulkhead and sprint the last twenty or so meters to the substation's command center. She fought that urge back; she had made her way as stealthily as possible through the substation; she was now completing the circuit that she had begun when another—and closer—voice had spoken her name. The voice of Hören Rygis had come from the substation's internal comm system, one of the concealed overhead speakers being activated by a remote circuit whose other end could have been anywhere aboard. It had been an unreasoning animal response to have fled the command center, as though the voice had been an armed Hören suddenly revealed standing behind her. In actuality, she might have been running straight toward him; the hiding place she had found in one of the storage lockers could have been separated from the blade of his weapon by no more than a few centimeters of reinforced metal.

Stupid, she had told herself. She hadn't survived a childhood in the refugee camps, and then her years in the Bajoran resistance, by giving in to panic like that. Her own instincts, and the military training she'd been given on top of them, were sharper; the only explanation she could give herself was that here in the Gamma Quadrant was the farthest she'd ever been from the soil on which she'd been born. Bajor was no longer even a pinprick of light in the field of stars ranged in DS9's observation ports. A thread had been broken for her, through which she had received some unknowable strength . . .

"Come on, Major—" Bashir's voice broke into her wordless thoughts. "I know you're there . . . you *have* to be there. . . ."

She had to reach the command center and respond to Bashir's transmission before he gave up and broke the link. At the same time, she knew that the stowaway Hören had detected her presence in this area before, and would logically assume that she would return to it at some point. Being at the farthest extension of one of the substation's sectors, the command center formed a perfect cul-de-sac, a trap with no exit. To step into it, no matter how urgent the reason, might be the same as stepping into the center of Hören's lethal plans.

Carefully, she crouched and peered around the next corner of the passageway. For what must have been the thousandth time since she had first heard her name spoken aloud, she reached down to the belt at her uniform's waist, for the personal armament that would be holstered there . . . and found nothing. The weapon had been left behind at her DS9 quarters, part of a decision she had fully concurred with at the time. The substation was supposed to represent a permanent settlement, not a military expedition; it would be easier to maintain that position in a court of interstellar law if the substation was effectively unarmed, down to the lowest possible level. The only hostilities that might have been expected would have come from the Cardassian vessel under Gul Tahgla's command, and he would be smart enough to realize that any warlike action would automatically invalidate any claim he might make on the sector surrounding the wormhole's exit.

There were times when, paradoxically, defenselessness was the best strategy; unfortunately, the present situation—or what it had become for Kira—wasn't one of them. She would have given a great deal to have a fully charged phaser filling her hand right now.

The command center's doorway was open. She couldn't remember if her fist had hit the retract lock switch on the inside control panel, or if she had heard the door slide back into position after she had bolted through it. Light spilled down the corridor from the center's overhead panels. Keeping her back close to the bulkhead, she could see most of the interior, the control stations curving around the sides, the two empty operations seats . . .

And no sign of another living being.

Minutes had passed since she had last heard Bashir's voice over the command center's speaker. She prayed that he was still on the comm link, waiting for a reply or fine-tuning the cargo shuttle's transmitter.

You've come this far, she told herself. *You might as well go for it.* She shoved herself away from the metal beside her and ran for the doorway.

Within seconds, she had dived inside, twisted, and rolled onto her feet, coming up with hands readied in an elementary defense posture. A quick visual scan showed that the center was empty; she slapped the doorway's control panel and let her tensed spine relax only a fraction as the metal slid into place. She felt no safer than before, but a small measure of power had been reestablished.

"Bashir—" She leaned over the command center's transmitter, one fingertip jabbing the respond switch. "This is Kira—"

"Great . . . I was just about to give up on this," Bashir's voice answered her. "Are you all right?"

"For the moment." Kira looked over her shoulder, keeping an eye on the doorway.

"I was afraid you might've gotten banged up, when everything went crazy."

"Negative on that; I came through fine." She assumed, since Bashir had gotten the transmitter working, that *he* was in working condition, as well. "Now, listen; I need—"

"There's something important I have to tell you, Kira." His words broke through hers. "You're not alone out there. Someone else is aboard the substation with you—"

"I'm well aware of that. He's already revealed his presence to me. It's Hören Rygis."

"The Redemptorist," Bashir said, nodding. "I guessed as much."

"He's been making broadcasts for months about how I should be killed. I don't imagine he came along now just to talk politics with me."

Bashir nodded again. Kira was simply confirming what he'd already surmised. "Then he had some way of firing off the cargo shuttle's engines. It was his bunch that installed the devices I found. . . ."

"Good guess." She found that it was easier to turn her back to the comm panel, her hand behind her on its switches, and keep watch on the closed doorway. "What's your current situation? Are you in communication with DS Nine?"

"No—and there's no way I can be, either. At least, not for the time being. When the shuttle engines activated without their buffers, the wormhole went through some major changes. The convulsion you felt was the least of it. The wormhole's inhabitants collapsed the other end by the station. It was a purely defensive reaction, to keep out anything else that might harm them. Unfortunately, it means that as far as DS Nine's concerned, the wormhole doesn't even really exist. Whether I'm stuck inside it or not."

"You've had contact with the wormhole's inhabitants?"

"With mixed results." Bashir sounded annoyed with himself. "They allowed me to get in touch with you. That's about it for now."

Kira nodded as she processed the new data. "You'll have to keep working with them. Somehow, you've got to persuade them to open up the wormhole again. The comm equipment has either been damaged or tampered with, so I can't get in touch with DS Nine. And even if I could, without the wormhole, there's no way for Sisko to send any assistance out here to me—"

"There is another way. To get assistance to you, I mean." Bashir's voice grew excited. "I did manage to get one of the cargo shuttle's engines operational; the diagnostics all check out on it. I could activate it and rendezvous with your position pretty quickly. We wouldn't even have to do anything about Hören; you could be waiting by one of the hatches, we could get you transferred onto the shuttle in no time, and he could rot aboard the substation for all we care."

"Are you out of your mind?" Kira took her gaze away from the door and stared at the comm panel. "The engines firing without their buffers is how things got screwed up in the first place. That was all part of Hören's plan. If you activate them again, there's no telling what the wormhole's inhabitants will do."

"Maybe that's a chance we'll have to take. If I gave it all the thrust it's capable of bearing, I might be able to get the shuttle to the wormhole's exit and get it outside before the inhabitants could do anything. Or they might expel the shuttle, like an immune system rejecting a foreign object—"

"Right, or they could crush it like an egg and spit out the pieces. Or dissolve it—and you—into subatomic particles. There's no way of knowing what they're capable of." She shook her head in exasperation, leaning her weight on the panel. "And what if you did manage to get out? They've already shut down one end of the wormhole; why wouldn't they shut down this one as well? Then we'd be stuck out here in the Gamma Quadrant—without the wormhole, that's a *sixty-year* voyage at maximum warp velocity—with nobody else in this sector except for a shipful of pissed-off Cardassians. Hören Rygis wouldn't *have* to kill me; he could just watch us die of old age."

She didn't speak of what else the disappearance of the wormhole would mean: the complete triumph of the Redemptorists' plans for Bajor—to render the planet valueless to the Federation and isolate it from all the other developed worlds. If her death was necessary to keep that from happening, she was ready.

Bashir wouldn't be deterred, though. "Then what would you have me do instead? Your life's in danger from that maniac. Do you expect me to sit here and do nothing?"

"That's exactly what I expect you to do. More than that—I'm ordering you to do nothing. I'm still the commanding officer for this mission; its success matters more than either of us. As far as I'm concerned, my arrival at this sector at least gives the Federation a chance of making a claim of sovereignty over it—"

"That claim's going to be pretty shaky if you're dead."

"A court of law would have to determine that. Look, I know you're right, Doctor; if the Cardassians reach this sector and find nothing but a murdered Starfleet officer and a homicidal lunatic running around the substation, then they're going to be in a strong position. The Cardassians could blow away the substation, assert their own claim, and justify it all with a legal defense of necessity. Maybe it would stand up, maybe it wouldn't. *But it's not going to happen that way.*" Kira leaned closer to the comm panel. "I can handle Hören; he's a known quantity to me. I understand how his mind works. He's already lost the element of surprise; if he was planning on sneaking up on me, there's no way he can do that now. This isn't your area of expertise—but I spent years fighting on different kinds of terrain. This substation is just one more. And I've got the advantage; the defense always does. Especially if I just have to hold out until we do come up with a way of getting some assistance to me."

It was all a lot of big talk, she knew, designed to convince Bashir; she wouldn't have bought it herself. She didn't know what other surprises—booby traps —Hören and his followers might have wired into the substation. Or what weapons he might be carrying— if she were going to arm herself, she would have to cobble together something from the medical equipment aboard. If she had the time, and the means of getting to it before Hören intercepted her. It wasn't a matter of defensive strategy at all; it was more like walking naked through a forest of knives.

"I don't know . . ." Bashir sounded unconvinced. "It still strikes me as risky."

The real risk, Kira knew, was in Bashir's emotional, impulsive nature. She played her final card. "There's something else to consider, Doctor; something that I heard *you* talk about, before we ever left the station. *We can't do anything that would harm the wormhole's inhabitants*—not any more than we've already done. We don't have the right to do that."

His lack of response over the comm link indicated that her words had hit their target.

"All right." Bashir's voice finally came through the speaker. "If that's what you think is best. But I still don't like it."

She wanted to tell him that she didn't like it, either, but stopped herself. Already she had spent far more time than she had intended, convincing him of the need for inaction on his part. Hören and an army of Redemptorists could have marched on her by now.

"I'll stay in touch with you," she said. "As much as I can. But don't worry—I've got everything under control."

She broke the link before he could make any reply. With that connection gone, and with it the human touch of his voice, the substation's silence folded around her.

He leaned back in his seat, looking at the shuttle's comm panel. A blinking light told him that the link between him and Major Kira had been terminated—for the time being—on her command.

"Great," said Bashir disgustedly. He laced his fingers behind the back of his head and stretched out his cramped shoulder muscles. He still felt the effects of spending several hours in a tight space, hunched over as he had worked to get one of the shuttle's engines back on line. A fat lot of good he had accomplished by doing so; the shuttle now had the motive power to possibly get out of the wormhole and come to Kira's rescue—a not inconsiderable goal in his mind, for several reasons—but he didn't have the authority to fire the engine up and *do* it. His hands clenched tighter together in frustration.

And the worst of it, the logical and emotionless part of his brain had to admit, was that Kira was almost certainly right. He had to admire anew her *sangfroid* in going through her list of reasons justifying his inaction; all the while some demented religious maniac might have been creeping up on her. The angry-at-the-universe attitude that she had always carried around herself like a shield, back at the station, had concealed a mind fitted with precision-cut steel gears. Yet, one that could also factor human elements into the equations; the business about not harming the wormhole's inhabitants had been almost perfectly calculated to evoke the maximum desired reaction from him.

She's the one who should've been a doctor, thought Bashir. The control of patients—really a form of benign psychological manipulation—had been a topic at medical schools for centuries. Plus, Kira wouldn't be one to shrink from using a scalpel, if necessary.

Bashir slumped forward, hands in lap, then glanced over his shoulder at another section of the pilot area's control panels. The readouts showed that the external sensors that had been installed in the cargo shuttle were still operating at peak capacity, soaking up every fluctuation in the wormhole's complicated soup of electromagnetic radiation. There would be some interesting data, once he got it all back to DS9, where he and Chief Science Officer Dax could start breaking it down. The data would have been significant enough, if this had turned out to be a routine voyage through the wormhole. Now—with the convulsion triggered by the firing of the unbuffered shuttle engines, the manifestation of the wormhole's inhabitants inside the shuttle, and the changes in the bands of radiation to allow the comm link to function—the accumulated information could be the basis for not just a ground-breaking but a definitive study of the wormhole's fundamental nature. A ticket to the Federation's highest scientific awards might just as well have been tucked inside the data collectors.

There was a certain temptation, he had to admit, to blank out the rest of the universe and its problems, Kira's included, and just concentrate on the input from the sensors, monitoring the data stream to make sure that it was coming in as pure and unhindered as possible. He had already been ordered to do as much by the mission's commanding officer. No one could blame him for following those instructions to the letter. . . .

No one but himself.

"Even worse than that—" He nodded slowly. "I've started talking to myself." The isolation of being stranded in the middle of this pocket universe was no doubt affecting his sanity. That was his clinical self-diagnosis. Now would be a good time for the floating committee of the wormhole's inhabitants to make a reappearance. He could use someone to talk to. Whether it, or they, wore Kira's face or not no longer mattered to him.

"Hello?" He raised his voice as he swiveled the chair around toward the center of the pilot area. "Anybody home?"

Silence. They were probably listening to him, and laughing. If they *could* laugh; that hadn't been estab-lished yet. Bashir had to ruefully congratulate himself for providing the focus point for yet another investi-gation into the physiology of nonmaterial entities.

He glanced once more at the panel showing the activities of the shuttle's external sensors. That, he knew, was what he should be doing, giving over his entire attention to that scientific process.

Instead, he remained seated, the point of his chin pressed against his doubled fists. His thoughts had already exited the wormhole, and now moved through their persistent calculations out beyond, in the Gamma Quadrant.

She didn't know what he was thinking. That was the problem.

The layout of the substation was becoming more familiar to Kira, from her having already traversed it more than once. It was too late to kick herself for not having memorized the chart of the branching corridors and rooms before leaving DS9; there had been no reason to expect that she would ever need to be familiar with more than a few different sectors around the substation's command center. Now, however, a functional map was slowly being ingrained at a subconscious level, a system of passageways and enclosed areas that she could almost recognize from the trace of her own sweat that had touched the bulkheads.

Kira crouched down in a dark intersection of the shuttle's main corridor. The problem with the map inside her head was that it didn't show the most important element: where Hören was. For all of her confident talk to Bashir, the Redemptorist leader's thought processes remained cloudy to her. She could reason out some things, based on her own past experiences with him and what she had learned from others' encounters, but that still left out a crucial emotional component. It would be as much an oversimplification to characterize Hören Rygis as completely insane—no matter how demented-sounding his broadcast diatribes against her had become—as it would be to view him as coldly rational in his calculations. That he was obsessed with her—and with her death—there was no question; what form that obsession might take was still a mystery.

In the corridor's silence, Kira let her thoughts roll on as she gathered her breath. The big question was how Hören viewed his own death. Always, in his broadcasts to his fellow Redemptorists, there had been talk of the need for all of them to make the ultimate sacrifice that would bring about Bajor's purification. The cross between political and religious fanaticism always produced that kind of obligation on its followers, with the assumption that it held equally true for the movement's leaders. Historically, it didn't always work out that way: the pasts of any number of planets were littered with accounts of holy men sending the faithful off to die in battle, while they stayed safe inside their temples. She was convinced that wasn't the case with Hören; he'd already put himself on the line by smuggling himself aboard the substation.

But if Hören was prepared for his own death, how glorious did he want it to be? After that one contact, the speaking aloud of her name over the internal comm system, he had as much as disappeared. He could be taking his time stalking her . . . or he could be preparing another surprise, on a far grander scale. It still worried her—*putting it mildly,* she thought— that the substation was constructed with high explosives throughout its framework. Both Bashir and Chief Engineer O'Brien had assured her that the explosives were as inert as clay without the fuse codes being read into them—but the Redemptorists had already proved themselves clever at rewiring the substation's functions. Could they also have figured out some kind of a bypass, a way of igniting the explosives without the codes? If so, that would give Hören the ability to destroy himself as well as her, in a fiery cataclysm whose impact would be felt, symbolically at least, all the way back on Bajor.

That thought nagged at her, as well as the simple suspicion that all Hören wanted to do was move soundlessly upon her from behind, unexpected, snare her, and draw a sharpened blade across her throat. All that talk of *blood*. . . . Deep inside herself, she felt that the words, the thundering way he had spoken them, had to be more than empty verbiage. There was a physical longing expressed in them, the desire for a consummation that couldn't be satisfied through cleansing fire, but only by the yielding of one body to another. A yielding where her blood would flow over his wrists, gathering in a shining pool at their feet, until he let her go, and whatever was left of her fell, broken.

Stop. Negative on that—her own voice inside her head short-circuited those images. That was a violation of all training and the survival instinct beneath; indulging one's fears, letting them fester and grow along one's spine, was a sure way of programming them to come true. Hören Rygis was as human as she, despite the voice of a wrathful god that he had summoned out of himself. He could be defeated, neutralized . . . killed, if necessary.

Kira saw nothing moving down the length of the central corridor. She stepped out of the shadows and along the bulkhead to the next sector. Her quick strides left the silence unbroken.

She had already decided that, whatever Hören's plans might be, hers had to go on the offensive. He was obviously giving himself the luxury of time, the savoring of his prey's trapped and cornered condition. That could come to an end all too quickly if Bashir, back aboard the cargo shuttle, found a way to persuade the wormhole's inhabitants to reestablish its entrance zone. If that happened, Sisko would have an armed runabout from the DS9 station through the wormhole and out to the Gamma Quadrant in virtually no time . . . and that would be all it would take to push Hören over the edge. Whatever plans he had would go immediately to their climax; if he had a way of blowing up the substation, that would be when he'd push the button. If, on the other hand, Kira figured, all he wanted was to plunge a knife into her heart, he'd cut short this sadistic foreplay and move in on her before he could be stopped from the outside.

Either way, she needed to locate Hören and render him inoperative—that had been the usual Resistance phrase for all violent actions, up to and including murder—before he could carry out his plans.

A shape suddenly loomed in front of her. She quickly snapped back against the bulkhead, spine flattened against the metal. Holding her breath, she listened for the slightest noise, the least motion in the substation's still air. A closed door was within reach behind her; she raised her hand toward its small control panel, ready to punch it, and dart through the opening, if necessary.

She heard nothing. Carefully, she leaned forward, enough to see a few meters farther on. The silhouette of her head and one corner of her shoulder slid along the flooring's grid. The faint luminescence from an overhead panel had cast her shadow ahead of her; that was the only enemy within striking distance. She relaxed—only a fraction, still maintaining her scanning alertness—and moved on.

There was another reason behind her actions, that she could acknowledge only to herself. Inaction was something she could order Bashir into, but she would never be able to endure it for herself. Even if that had been the best strategy, to find a sector of the substation that she could barricade and defend, holding out until help came—she would have gone crazy, passively waiting for Hören's attack. Anything would be better . . . to find him and fly straight at him, whatever weapon she'd been able to improvise raised in her hand . . . no matter what the outcome of that final, long delayed encounter might be.

That was the emotion burning in her gut. The force of it was just barely controlled by her brain. She would have to act in a precise, logical method, not just wander aimlessly around the substation. Already, as she had made her way from the command center, she had been planning how she would use the rough map forming in her head to make a systematic sweep of the substation's corridors and sectors, how she could move through every space one by one, driving the hunter turned prey before her.

She had a dim memory, from when she had regained consciousness, of seeing something she might be able to use, in the dark hiding place she'd found herself in. A fusion welding rig, just barely compact enough to sling onto her shoulders and carry with her—it must have been equipment left behind by one of O'Brien's work crews, or part of the substation's own emergency gear. With that, she could seal off sectors as she cleared them, and bit by bit render a growing area of the substation out of bounds to Hören. Even if she could cut off just some of the routes through the substation that he must have mapped out for himself, that would still be a lessening of the advantage with which he'd started.

Now, her brain was working the way it was supposed to. She could already visualize everything happening the way she wanted, the methodical process by which Hören would be caught in his own trap. The best result would be if she could take him alive, corner him and seal him into a section where he would be rendered harmless, unable to get back at her. Then she would be happy to sit down and wait for assistance to arrive. It would be a crushing blow to the Redemptorist movement on Bajor to have its leader brought back in such humiliation, captured by the very woman he had launched such a holy war to destroy. She could see it all . . . and there was enough malice in her heart to relish the prospect.

That was still in the future, though. It was a satisfying enough vision to hang in front of her like a gauzy curtain, almost obscuring the length of the final branching corridor that led to the storage locker where she had hidden before. Kira put her head down and hurried toward the hatchway and the welding gear beyond it.

The future obscured the present. Enough for her to forget, to let her senses grow dull for a second—

And that was enough.

She felt a change in air pressure before she heard anything. Then above, something was dropping toward her. She turned, raising her arm to defend herself, but it was already too late. She was knocked sprawling onto the corridor's flooring.

The human form's knees pressed against her abdomen, pinning her flat. A hand grabbed the collar of her uniform, pulling her head forward. Dazed, she felt something thin and cold at her throat.

"Kira . . ."

The voice spoke her name again. A whisper, almost loving in its softness. But this time she saw him. Hören Rygis lifted the knife blade under her throat, and smiled.

CHAPTER
14

HE NEEDED TO KNOW everything that had happened. That was why he called his remaining officers into his private office.

The image of Kai Opaka was still uppermost in Commander Sisko's mind. Not just from this last visit to her temple, but from the cumulative effect her contact had upon him. In some ways, he didn't know what had changed him more, his brain-dazzling experiences when he had first entered the wormhole, or the slow, stilled—and on the surface, much less dramatic—working of the Kai's influence upon him. One had been a thunderbolt, cracking open a stone to reveal its hidden interior; the other, carefully measured and patient drops of water, one by one, accomplishing the same revelations.

"Let's have an update," he ordered as he swiveled his chair around to face the DS9 crew members. He almost shook his head, as though that would clear away anything obstructing his concentration on the job at hand. But he knew it was pointless; the touch of Kai Opaka was locked into a level deeper than his conscious brain. His soul, perhaps. He focused his gaze on the station's security chief. "Any luck with our little band of Redemptorists?"

"Some." Odo gave a noncommittal shrug. "I used on them a certain psychological ploy that I've found valuable in the past. It yielded a few . . . *interesting* results."

"Anything we can use now?"

"That's always the question, Commander. I've certainly been able to dig out a great deal of background information on Hören Rygis. If we're successful in bringing him back here to DS Nine, it'll be a toss-up as to what sort of legal procedure we should initiate against him—a criminal trial or a clinical determination of his sanity." Odo gazed up at the ceiling for a moment. "Of course, you're probably aware of my own preference in such matters. I am of the school of thought that defenses based upon the perpetrator's alleged mental condition are inevitably fraudulent. I would rather simply, as the old police phrase goes, 'nail the bastard.' "

"In this case, so would I, Constable. But we're not at that point yet. If there's something you've found out that we can use to get a handle on Hören Rygis, open him up—"

"Given enough time, Commander, we could do all that; we could psychoanalyze him *in absentia* until we were familiar with every facet of his mind. We already know, from what was in the records of the Bajoran security forces and from what Major Kira herself told you, most of the root causes of Hören's murderous obsession. The Redemptorists that I've been interrogating have filled me in on some of the past details of which we had been unaware—apparently there was some contact between Hören and Kira some years preceding the raid she led on the hostage situation. And there will undoubtedly be other things the Redemptorists will tell us, and perhaps soon; once the first cracks appear in their psychological defenses, the total disintegration of that armor follows shortly thereafter. At least, that's been my experience." Odo's gaze sharpened as he addressed the figure on the other side of the desk. "What must be answered, Commander, is what good the information I can extract from these men will be, if we can neither act upon it ourselves, nor relay it to Kira so she can use it."

Sisko knew that his security chief was right. He turned toward Chief Engineer O'Brien. "What about it, then? Any progress on establishing communications with Bashir or Kira?"

"Negative, sir." O'Brien shook his head. He nodded toward the chief science officer standing next to him. "Dax and I both have been working flat out on that one. There's just no way—"

Dax spoke up. "We're running into some hard physical realities, Commander. The intermittent bending effect we've detected before in the subspatial matrix actually seems to have been heightened by the wormhole's change to a unipolar condition; as long as that persists, communications with the Gamma Quadrant are considerably accelerated. The problem is that the mission's only subspace equipment is on the cargo shuttle with Bashir. The wormhole is still nonexistent for us here; until its entrance reappears, there's no one to whom we can even send a subspace transmission."

"There is one possibility—" O'Brien's words were accompanied by a doubting grimace. "We thought of it but . . . I don't know . . . it might not be something you'd want to consider."

"By now, I'm willing to consider anything." Sisko leaned forward across the desk. "What is it?"

"Well, technically speaking, the substation is not completely alone out there. There is someone else approaching that sector of the Gamma Quadrant. And that's Gul Tahgla." O'Brien shrugged. "And the Cardassian vessel does have subspace transmission and reception gear aboard."

Sisko gazed at his chief engineer in astonishment. His initial reaction had been to tell O'Brien that he was out of his mind.

"You see," said Dax, "it would be possible for us to make a request of Gul Tahgla, that he relay an encoded message to the substation. There are precedents for such actions, between parties that are not officially in a state of war with each other. Maintaining reciprocal confidentiality has been an element of diplomatic relations for centuries."

"I'm not sure Gul Tahgla would see this matter in such an enlightened way." Sisko rubbed the corner of his brow. "In fact, I'm sure of it. If he's aware of our substation being in that sector, he's bound to have figured out that we sent it there to frustrate the Cardassian empire's claim of sovereignty over the wormhole's exit. Why should he cooperate in the process of defeating himself? Especially, when he would know that he didn't have to—by asking him to relay a message, we'd be as much as telling him that the mission had gone wrong somehow, that the substation might as well be disabled."

"That was exactly our analysis, Commander." The calm tone of Dax's voice remained steady. "However, we cannot be sure of how Gul Tahgla would analyze the situation. He might assume that our claim of sovereignty had already been established and, after the subterfuge he committed to get his vessel through the wormhole, that it would be prudent for him to reestablish a cordial relationship with us. Also, he could be reminded that he and his crew now have no way of returning from the Gamma Quadrant, unless we here at DS Nine find a means of opening up the wormhole again."

"If Cardassians were reasonable creatures, Gul Tahgla might assume those things." Sisko tapped a finger against the desktop. "The reasonableness of Cardassians, however, has rarely been demonstrated."

"True. I would not estimate our chances of success along these lines as very high. But—given our lack of other options and what's at stake—it might be worth a try."

Beside Dax, O'Brien's scowl deepened. "I just have an aversion to asking Cardassians to do anything except kiss my posterior."

"As do we all. However . . ." Sisko drew in a deep breath. "Let's give it a shot. Have the communications officer initiate contact with Gul Tahgla's vessel." He turned to his security chief. "Prepare a synopsis of everything you've gotten out of the Redemptorists— anything that Kira might be able to use."

Outside the private office, he took his seat in Ops. "Screen." His officers stood behind.

The Cardassian's image wavered before him. At this distance, with the signal shuttled through a string of relay beacons, visual static crawled erratically across Gul Tahgla's face. A delay factor of several seconds had to be dealt with; a moment passed before the image nodded with a self-satisfied smile.

"Ah, Commander Sisko. Always a pleasure. I wouldn't have thought we would be communicating again . . . so soon."

Sisko pressed his palms against the seat's arms. "I wouldn't have troubled you if it weren't a matter of some urgency." The overly polite diplomatic language stuck in his throat like a sharp-edged stone. "I know that your own mission demands your full attention. But I have a request to make of you. Your assistance will be greatly appreciated by all of Starfleet, and by me in particular."

"Indeed." A higher level of interest appeared in Gul Tahgla's eyes. "Then proceed, Commander Sisko. Consider me to be . . . at your service."

"We're having difficulties communicating with a unit of ours that is currently in the Gamma Quadrant, just outside the wormhole's exit. It should be within normal comm range for your vessel, however. We'd like you to relay an encoded message to the unit."

"Encoded?" The Cardassian feigned surprise. "What is the necessity for that?"

"Come, Gul Tahgla." He held his palms spread out before him. "It indicates no degree of distrust between us. It's simply a matter of . . . standard operating procedure. Surely it would be the same for communications between vessels of your fleet."

"I see." Gul Tahgla leaned forward, his image growing larger on the screen. His smile vanished, as though it had been part of a mask now discarded. "Let me say, Commander, that you display a remarkable degree of presumption. To ask this of me . . ." The Cardassian's gaze grew harder. "Perhaps you would like me to thrust a dagger into my own heart as well?"

"I'm afraid I don't know what you're talking about." But he did know.

The smile returned, but as a much crueler thing than before. "What is that old Earth word that I've heard our mutual friend Quark use on occasion? *Chutzpah*—that's it. For sheer nerve, you carry away the baked goods, as I believe the Ferengi would also say."

Sisko stiffened in the chair. "You seem to display some unusual linguistic interests."

"I'm making a study of exotic languages, Commander. I expect they will come in handy very soon . . . when I'm overseeing the passage of all the developed worlds' ships out of the wormhole and into the Gamma Quadrant. I have time for these studies, as well; my crew and I are having quite a leisurely voyage back to the sector surrounding the wormhole's exit. Where nothing—not all your little schemes, Commander—will prevent us from establishing sovereignty over that sector for the Cardassian empire."

"Gul Tahgla . . . this isn't what you—"

"Don't indulge in these pretenses with me, Sisko." The smile twisted into a sneer. "I'm well aware of your reasons for positioning that unit right where it is. My only regret is that you were able to figure out my intentions in time to make this abortive attempt at frustrating them. But your own haste has foiled you. And now, you expect me to help you repair whatever has gone wrong? Really, Commander."

"You have my assurances—"

"Ah. Assurances from a Federation officer." Gul Tahgla's image wavered through another burst of static, then formed again. "I leave it to you to imagine what those *assurances* mean to us. Especially after having trusted your previous guarantees that the privacy of my vessel would be observed while in the DS Nine drydock. Obviously, those assurances meant nothing, or you would never have discerned what mission I had been sent upon."

Sisko felt a twinge of revulsion in his gut, both at the *gul*'s self-indicting logic and at the awareness that in his own dealings with the Cardassians, his words and actions had begun to mirror theirs.

He made one more attempt. "There are lives at risk aboard that unit."

"I hardly think so, Commander. You see, we have already been trying to communicate with it—*and we have received no response to our signals*. Please accept my sincerest condolences regarding whatever members of your crew were lost in your foolhardy attempt to circumvent the legitimate aims of the Cardassian empire. These are the hazards of command, are they not?" Gul Tahgla's expression mocked sympathy. "When we reach the sector, we will make some attempt to retrieve whatever bodies may be aboard the unit, so they can be sent back to you for whatever religious observances you may consider to be appropriate—of course, only if we can do so safely. You have made many public comments about the shoddy materials and construction of the station you took over from the Cardassians; I doubt if anyone will blame us if we find ourselves compelled to . . . *eliminate* in as forthright a manner as possible this piece of DS Nine you sent out here. It is, after all, adrift right in the middle of what will be the traffic conduit into and out of the Gamma Quadrant. We would be performing a service to the developed worlds by disposing of this menace to navigation."

Sisko perceived an opening. "Then, since you acknowledge that the unit presents no threat to you or your plans, you would naturally have no objection to relaying—or at least attempting to—our encoded message to it?"

"That would need to be determined, Commander. Feel free to send us the encoded message, and once my cryptographic analysis officers have broken it, read it, and made sure that its contents cannot compromise Cardassian interests—we might send it on."

"Gul Tahgla—you're aware of the degrees of Starfleet message security. It would take your computers years to decode the message."

"Well, then." The Cardassian shrugged. "Simplify matters for all of us—send the message unencoded."

"That's absolutely not possible."

"I expected as much. For the sake of your crew members—if any of them are still alive—I hope the message you wished to get to them was nothing *too* urgent. Request denied. End of transmission."

Sisko gazed up at the blanked screen. "Well," he said. "That could have gone better."

She looked at the face before her. The knife blade had been drawn back a few centimeters, the edge still cold against her throat, but allowing her to breathe. Kira worked at keeping her pulse steady, her muscles tensed for the smallest opportunity that might be presented to her.

"How many years, Kira?" Over the gleam of light on the weapon, Hören regarded her. "Since we were in each other's presence . . . not that many, really. Not when you think about it. It's just that . . . so much has happened since we were together."

Her hands braced flat against the deck. "What do you want?"

"Why do you waste the little time you have left? Asking stupid questions—" His fist remained locked tight around the knife's handle. "Surely I've made my desires—the desires of many people—clear to you by now. But then . . . you feel you have the luxury of time, don't you?" Hören tilted his head, peering into the eyes of his captured prey. "And you do—much more than the ones you murdered had. Those brethren's deaths were in fire and pain, though mercifully brief. They also died in the righteousness of their faith. That is a comfort I'm afraid will be denied to you."

She felt the blade scrape across her throat as she arched her neck. "You know—I'm not really used to discussing theological issues when I'm flat on my back, with a knife drawn on me. Maybe we could go on talking under some slightly different conditions?"

"We could go on talking forever, Kira. But we won't. Time is not infinite for us, though the consequences of our actions outlive our days. Your betrayal of your fellow Bajorans—not just the ones who died at the temple, but all of your race—that was but the blink of an eye, a moment come and gone. No doubt you little expected how long others' memories would be, how that moment would eventually come full circle." Hören leaned forward, closer above her. The knife blade pressed down, almost breaking the skin. "This is where the circle closes, Kira." His gaze narrowed, as though the eyes were glittering steel within slits of thin flesh. "And time ends—for you."

There had been no chance of him letting her up, dragging her up against the bulkhead with the knife still readied underneath her jaw—she had known that. Whatever depths Hören's insanity had reached, he remained smart enough not to let the situation go on too much longer. An egotist who wanted to savor his triumph and the sound of his own words, but not a fool. Or at least not a total one.

She closed her eyes and gasped, as though fear had gripped her breath. "I . . . I can't hear you . . ." The whisper barely emerged on her lips.

His face came closer to hers, his words almost a kiss touching her ear. "You don't need to—"

That was what she needed, a trick to take him off balance. Literally; his weight had shifted forward, poised awkwardly for a second. But that was enough —the sudden thrust of her bent legs against the deck, and her doubled fists striking beneath his ribs, toppled him over her. Just as quickly, she twisted her head to one side, feeling the knife graze a centimeter away from the corner of her brow.

She heard Hören's weight hit the bulkhead, as she followed through on her own shoulder-first roll. Scrambling to her feet, she dived forward, hands outstretched. Her vaulting arc was broken when she felt her ankle snared from behind. She managed to contort enough to land braced against her forearm, protecting her ribs from the jarring impact.

Hören's grasp tightened. He grunted with the effort

of tugging her back toward him, his torso rearing up from where he knelt. The knife sparked in his raised hand.

Kira didn't resist, but pushed instead against the deck, doubling the force of Hören's pull. The heel of one boot struck him in the chest; his eyes widened from the unexpected blow. A split second later, as her fingertips clawed into the deck and twisted her onto her other shoulder, a scissors kick caught him on the angle of his jaw. His head snapped back, and the knife flew from his hand, disappearing into the darkness behind him.

He recovered faster than she expected. Panting for breath, Kira saw him grabbing for the knife, his hand falling instinctively upon its handle. His gaze broke from her, long enough for her to pull herself upright.

She turned and ran, shoulder colliding with an angle of the bulkhead as she pushed through a hatchway into one of the branching corridors.

She didn't hear running footsteps at her back. But laughter.

"Is that what you wish to do?"

He heard the voice behind him. Turning his head, he looked over his shoulder and saw the image standing there. He had already opened the access hatch leading down to the engine compartment; he sat at its rim, legs reaching down to the rungs.

"I don't know," said Bashir. "But I knew you were watching me—all of you. I couldn't think of any other way to make you show yourselves."

A different voice, the angry one, came from the Kira image. "You see?" The image tilted its head back, the star-filled gaze directed toward an invisible audience. "So lightly this one threatens us! Our existence means nothing to such a creature!"

"That's not true. I would never have come here among you if . . . if I didn't think you mattered a great deal. Like all living creatures." He craned his neck, trying to peer into the blackness of the image's eyes, as if he might see all the wormhole's inhabitants mingled in that small universe. "I wanted to understand you; that's all. Curiosity is in the nature of my kind."

"That comes from being in *time*." The softer voice spoke once again. "You are blind things, attempting to *see*. If you were outside *time,* you would *know*."

Bashir shook his head, sensing the gulf opening up between him and these bodiless entities. He could wander in that space for ages, trying to make himself understood by them in turn. "That may be. But we don't have a choice about it."

"That is not truth. There is one of your kind who exists both in *time* and not in *time*."

The statement puzzled him. "Do you mean Sisko?"

"Not that one. He is still of the same nature as you. But there is another—do you not know?"

The riddles had started to make his head spin. "I don't know . . . and I guess right now I don't care, either. You can talk metaphysics all you want, but you'll have to do it without me. I've still got to figure out what to do about Kira."

Looking down at itself, the image studied the human form it had taken. "This one—" It laid a hand upon its breast. "That exists in your mind—that part you call *memory*—but not here."

"Yes. She exists somewhere else, though. Outside the wormhole." He gestured toward the bulkhead and the space beyond the cargo shuttle. "Outside where you exist."

"The fate of this one concerns you. You are troubled that this one might cease to exist in *time*. Would this one still not exist in *memory?*"

He took a deep breath. "Yes . . . she would. But it's not the same thing. Memory isn't alive . . . not the way I am, and she is. Memory is like your kind. It doesn't change."

"Perhaps then it is a better way to exist. Changeless and eternal."

His shoulders slumped. "I'm not going to argue with you about that. Maybe our kind is wrong, and you're right. But it's just in our nature. To prefer the living, and the changing, to what we think of as being dead." The irony of the situation weighed upon him: before he had left DS9, this would have been the making real of dreams beyond his most grandiose ambitions. To have not only established contact with the wormhole's inhabitants, but to go even further than Sisko had in understanding their nature. . . .

But there was no time for that. Not now. The wormhole's inhabitants were right; his kind did exist in another way, one where the illusions of eternity slowly faded, to reveal the cruel steel gears of the universe.

The image regarded him with a frown. "Your nature makes you suffer. You exist in pain."

"That is what's sometimes called the human condition." Bashir almost felt like laughing, a humorless noise collecting inside his throat. His immediate diagnosis would have indicated the cumulative effects of fatigue. "That's why I keep thinking about activating the engine—even without the impulse buffers, and with the effects it would have on your kind—and heading out there. To see if I could do anything to help her."

A shake of the image's head. "That cannot be allowed. You have already brought pain and wounding to our kind. There are those among us who would cause your existence to cease, in order to defend us."

"Still . . . you can't expect me to just forget about a friend. And what's going to happen to her."

"You see that one in *memory*—but it is not enough. Perhaps if you could see that one in that other place—that place that is not here. Then your suffering would cease."

He raised his head. "What're you talking about? Can you do that?"

The expression on the image's face remained placid. "It is close enough. What we can perceive can be shown to you."

Bashir swung his legs out of the hatchway and scrambled to his feet. "Then show me. Now—"

The Kira image stepped toward him, bringing its face close to his. If there had been any substance behind the surface phenomenon, it could have brought its lips to his for a kiss. Instead, he found himself gazing into the blackness of its eyes and the stars swimming there.

"Look. If that is what you wish."

He saw a brighter spot of light, and knew it was the substation drifting just outside the mouth of the wormhole. It grew larger, the stars disappearing behind it. Then it vanished, as he felt himself falling toward it.

Another dark space, its walls curving around him.

He could almost sense them pressing against his shoulders, and at the same time he knew he was still aboard the cargo shuttle, gazing into the empty eyes before him.

He saw her then—Kira, the real one. Running before him, into the corridor's distance. His hand reached out involuntarily, as though he could stop her. She looked over her shoulder, but her gaze went through him, toward another point. He called her name, but she didn't hear; she ran without stopping.

Then he saw the other, the silhouette of a man, looming up before him, blocking out everything else. The man took a few steps forward, and Bashir saw the broad shoulders, the heavy arms dangling at his sides. In one of the man's fists, a star glittered, a bright flare of light. But not a star. The man continued on his relentless path, and in the corridor's shadows, the object in his hand resolved into a sharp-bladed knife.

"What is wrong?"

Bashir had stepped backward, away from the image before him. His own hand came up, shielding his eyes from the vision it had presented him.

"Did you not see this one?" A puzzled tone came into the image's voice. "Does this one not exist out there, in *time?*"

He couldn't answer. His fists trembled as he turned away, his gaze falling to the open hatchway and the engines in the dark space below.

CHAPTER
15

HE BROUGHT OUT the good stuff. From a locked cabinet by the welding equipment lockers; the deactivated jacksledge, hunkered down on its pile-driver feet, seemed to stand guard as he pulled out the bottle of Powers.

"All the way from Earth itself." O'Brien broke the seal with his thumbnail and poured two fingers of Irish whisky into each of the glasses he'd set out on the workbench. "I've been saving it for special occasions." He shrugged, shaking his head wearily. "Though we certainly don't have much to celebrate. Your health."

Sisko matched the toast and knocked back a mouthful. It tasted like a rain-drenched peat bog on his tongue and felt like fire sliding down his throat. "Thanks." He could understand why the chief engineer was fond of the stuff, though he also knew it wasn't going to do any good for either of them; they would get just about as inebriated by upending the bottle and pouring its contents out on the engineering bay's deck.

It was the sentiment that mattered, however. Far better to have been invited here, amid the smells of raw metal and spent fuel—the bay always reminded him of one of the programmed modules in the holo-suites, a re-creation of a nineteenth-century black-smith's shop, complete with eye-stinging black smoke and iron heated to a glowing red—than to be sitting in a booth in Quark's lounge, an untouched synthale in front of him. If nonaction was the prescription he'd have to take whether he liked it or not—Kai Opaka's words still weighed heavy in Sisko's memory—it was best practiced in congenial, if cruder, surroundings.

"You can't beat yourself up over these things, Commander." O'Brien had drained his glass; he re-filled it and topped up Sisko's. "There's a limit to what you can do."

He managed a smile. "It seems to be my curse to be surrounded by people wiser than I am."

"I don't know about that. To be frank, I'm still puzzled about what happened up there in Ops." O'Brien leaned over his arms folded on the bench. "When you had Gul Tahgla on the screen—why didn't you give him an unencoded message to relay to Kira on the substation? Hell, he already knew we were in trouble with it."

"Perhaps he did." Sisko rolled a drop of the whisky around on his tongue. "And perhaps Gul Tahgla didn't. The problem is, *we can't be sure*. Tahgla might've just been fishing for confirmation of his suspicions—a confirmation that we would have handed over to him on a plate if we had given him an unencoded message. And, as long as there's any doubt in his mind, he's going to proceed that much more cautiously. When the Cardassians' vessel gets within range of the substation, he's going to stop and sniff around it, looking for any sign of a trap, anything that we could possibly spring on him." He took another swallow. "That's Gul Tahgla's problem—and it's one he shares with most Cardassian officers. They're so constitutionally devious that they can't imagine anyone else not being the same way. They can all waste shift upon shift, first creating suspicions inside their own heads, then chasing them down. Endlessly; even when they get proof that nothing underhanded is going on, they still won't believe it." The alcohol hadn't cheered him up any, but had loosened his tongue; that was more of a lecture than he had intended to give.

"Hm." The chief engineer had made significant progress on the bottle's contents. The potential loss of Major Kira and Doctor Bashir had set him off. "Is that a good enough reason not to do it, though?" His tone was almost belligerent as he hunched over his glass. "Because *you* were the one who decided to contact Gul Tahgla in the first place. You said that helping our officers was more important than any reservations we might have about dealing with the Darcass . . . Cardassians."

"True. Up to a point." Sisko tapped a finger against his own glass. "And that point is reached when we do anything that might negatively affect Kira's successful completion of her mission. *She still might have a chance*—and I owe her that much. When I gave her the mission, I indicated my trust that she'd be able to carry it out. I can't second-guess her now. Because of circumstances that we were unable to predict, Kira is operating on her own, cut off from any communication with us." He raised his hands, palms outward. "Fine—that's what we'll have to accept. But until we have hard evidence that she is in fact dead, we also have to assume that she's continuing on the mission. If we could have gotten potentially useful information to her, we would have; but to do so at the cost of jeopardizing the mission itself would be cutting the ground out from beneath her feet." Sisko shook his head. "I can't treat a subordinate officer that way."

"Not even if she might wind up dying? Because you didn't?"

It took a few seconds before he could reply, seconds in which a hollow space seemed to open inside him. "Kira assumed a certain responsibility when she accepted the mission. And I assumed it when I gave it to her." The words, though true, echoed bleakly through the emptiness. "That's the nature of our job here. This is not a settled territory, where someone might reasonably expect a degree of safety. Things can go wrong very quickly. And then we have to deal with them, as best we can. That's all."

O'Brien contemplated the dregs in his glass. "I guess that's why I'm glad you're the commander here, and I'm not."

"I wish I were glad about it." He pushed his chair back. "Take it easy on that stuff, will you? You're still on duty until this crisis is over."

Deliberately, the chief engineer picked up the bottle —it was still more than half-full—held it out at arm's length, and let it drop. It shattered on the deck, the brown liquid spattering across his boots.

"I wasn't thirsty, anyway." O'Brien kicked away a wet shard of glass. "At least, not right now."

She leaned her back against the metal. As soon as she had gotten through the doorway, she had hit its control panel with her fist. The door had slid shut, cutting off the passageway. Panting for breath, Kira pressed her palms behind her, as though she could keep the door locked that way.

Her eyes slowly adjusted to the dim light. The farther from the central corridor, the more the substation was set in darkness. By the faint bluish glow from an instrument panel, she saw the outlines of a row of pedestaled biobeds, most with surgical support frames hanging above. The frames were larger than the ones in the sickbays set aside for oxygen-breathing organisms, the clamshell forms capable of extending sealed atmospheric chambers around the beds. When the substation was still being designed for use as a quarantine module, the area would have been employed for the benefit of some of DS9's more exotic visitors.

Its original function didn't matter now. Kira pushed herself away from the door and ran to the rows of medical equipment drawers. She yanked them open, each gleaming metal tray clattering to the end of its track. All of them were empty.

"Damn—" She flung the last one closed in frustration. She had hoped to find something that could be used as a weapon. Even a simple manual scalpel would be better than her bare hands. Obviously, Bashir's progress in fitting out the QM had been interrupted by it being commandeered for its new mission. There were probably crates full of implements that she could have used—surgical instruments were fundamentally variations on cutting edges, no matter how advanced the technology for making the incisions might be—and all of them were sitting in a storage locker back on DS9.

In her flight through the substation's maze, she had come across a few cartons of simple bandages and other soft materials. *Wonderful,* she had thought grimly. *Maybe I could wad them up and shove them down Hören's throat—if I could just get him to say "Ah."*

She clambered onto one of the biobeds and looked up at the overhead surgical frame. The curved lens of its focused-beam spotlight glinted a transparent green. She stood on her toes and struck the lens with her fist. A shard of glass—a big one with an end wrapped in a bandage for a handle—could draw blood as well as sharpened steel. She ground her teeth together as the thick lens shivered with each blow, but didn't break.

"Kira—"

The voice didn't startle her; she had been expecting it at any moment. She quickly crouched down on the bed's padded surface, scanning across the area's darkness, ready to spring from it and run again.

Silence.

Carefully, she stepped down from the bed's pedestal. Nothing moved in the darkened space. The voice had come from an overhead speaker—Hören could be at any point in the substation.

She called out. "Where are you?"

"I'm everywhere, Kira." The whisper was overamplified, but still recognizable as Hören's.

"That's why you can't escape me. You never could. Because I'm in your heart, as well."

"That's a lovely thought." Looking over her shoulder, she calculated the distance to the doorway. The impulse to dash for it, into the corridor beyond, was almost overpowering. "Sometime, you'll have to show me the rest of your poetry."

"Yes . . ." Hören's voice betrayed no anger. "We should talk, Kira. I admit I made an error in judgment. I underestimated how well you could resist your own guilty conscience. If we sat down and talked . . . perhaps that part of you that still acknowledges righteousness would accept that which comes with it. That is, justice."

She heard something beyond the voice coming from the speaker above her. From another direction, and closer.

"You mean my death." Kira kept her head motionless, looking out the corner of her eye.

"Such a harsh word. Don't torment yourself with it."

"Right, I forgot; that's your job." How had he traced her to this area of the substation? She had thought she had lost him all the way back at the storage lockers. And he couldn't be talking through the entire comm system—there was another overhead speaker in the passageway beyond, and she would have heard the voice filtering through the door, if that had been the case.

It was a question that would have to wait for her to figure out the answer. She heard the other sound again, the slight disturbance in the still air. Behind her, somewhere down the row of beds.

"A regrettable necessity, Kira." The voice oozed smooth from the speaker. "A movement such as the Redemptorists is fueled by the passions of its followers. Anger against a traitor is an effective spark for those emotions. I serve my followers by evoking it in them."

"How noble of you." She realized what the sound was. Someone's breath, one bed closer to her now. "I wonder . . . if there's something else that fuels *your* anger."

"Oh? And what would that be?"

Slowly, Kira reached behind her, bracing her hands against the edge of the bed. "Guilt." She listened to the area's silence. "Not mine, but yours."

The other sound, the careful inhalation and release, halted for a moment. "What do you mean by that?" The voice from the speaker above tightened a fraction.

"You survived, Hören. And they didn't." She flexed her knees slightly, rising a centimeter onto her toes. "The ones back at the temple, all those years ago. They died . . . your faithful brethren. I remember standing there, looking down at some of them . . . with the flames at my back. . . ." She raised her voice, so it echoed from the corners of the space. "It wasn't pretty. Some of them lived just long enough to maybe wonder . . . where you were, Hören. And why you didn't die with them."

The breathing sound grew louder; she could picture the nostrils flaring, the cords tightening in the neck. She knew it came from only a few beds down the row.

"Really quite a common reaction, Hören." Kira felt her palms sweating in anticipation. "Survivor's guilt.

Because in *your* heart, you don't believe that I'm the traitor. You're the one who betrayed them—"

A cry rang from both above and behind her. She sprang to one side, pushing the corner of the bed so that it rotated on the axis of the pedestal. The other end caught Hōren across his abdomen, toppling him forward. Kira ducked beneath the arc of his knife; for a moment she saw plainly the contact microphone taped to his throat, which had picked up and magnified his almost inaudible whispering. A wire ran from the black dot of the microphone to a short-range transmitter clipped to his belt. She rammed the butt of her palm into the side of his head, but his momentum carried him on top of her.

The knife swung again, closer, and she felt a streak of fire along one arm. She thrust herself upright, her hands against Hōren's waist and shoulders, and heard him land heavy against the angle of the bulkhead and the floor.

Blood streamed down to her elbow; she was unable to draw her left hand into a fist. She glanced over her shoulder and saw Hōren on his knees, pushing himself upright with one hand, his other arm dangling as though broken. Rage contorted his face.

She made it to the doorway before he could launch himself toward her. A quick stab at the control panel and she had stumbled out to the passageway, the door sliding shut behind. The narrow space tilted dizzily around her. Hōren's footsteps pounded closer, only slightly muffled by the door.

Reaching up with her good hand, she grabbed the edge of the metal surrounding the luminescent panel above her. It came free as she drew her legs up, her weight breaking the seal. A thin strip peeled loose, a few meters long, flexing in her grip. She jabbed the broken end into the doorway's sliding track, just as Hören struck the control on the other side. The door ground to a halt as the metal strip, its other end still fastened to the ceiling, bowed to the snapping point. Through a gap of a few centimeters, she could hear Hören cursing incoherently.

Kira turned and staggered into a run. She clutched her wounded arm tight against her breast, the blood soaking into her uniform.

He heard her even before she spoke. Before she responded to the signal transmitted from within the wormhole—her ragged breathing spoke of exhaustion close to collapse.

"Kira—are you all right?" Bashir pressed his hand flat upon the comm panel's switches. He had been trying to hail the substation for over an hour. "What's wrong?"

"Under . . . under control." Her voice broke into a crude simulation of a laugh. "I can't believe it. I thought this was supposed to be some kind of a hospital unit, and I can't even find a damn first aid kit . . ."

The comment worried him even more. "What happened?"

"Let's just say . . . I made contact with Hören. It wasn't fun."

"How badly are you hurt?"

"Like I said . . . under control." The sound of her breathing steadied. "Surface wound from a knife; lots of blood, no major tissue damage. I was able to pull an insulation sheet loose from one of the control panel modules and bind it up with that. I seem to be getting function back in my hand—anyway, that's the least of my worries right now."

"What about Hören?"

"That is what I'm worried about." Kira's voice grew tense. "He's still out there, roaming around the substation. That's the worst of it—I don't know where he is, but somehow he's able to track me. Somehow . . . somehow, he's able to pinpoint my location, no matter where I go. He was waiting for me; that's how I got nicked by him." Her voice paused for a moment. "You weren't still going to try to get out here, were you? With that engine unbuffered—"

"I couldn't, even if I made the attempt." Bashir's fingertip whitened from pressing against the switch. "Our friends here in the wormhole made it clear to me that they wouldn't allow it. Remember what you said about them crushing the shuttle like an egg? It'd be something like that—I'd never reach the exit zone."

"That's one decision you don't have to worry about making, then. If I could just figure out how he's tracking me . . . then maybe I could lay a trap for him. . . ."

The answer struck him. "The thermal sensors. That must be how he's doing it."

"What're you talking about?"

"In the control panels for the doorways—" The explanation came rushing out. "The whole substation's wired with them; it was supposed to be a way of monitoring patient movement through the quarantine module. There's a microscanner right beside the door release switch on all the panels—Hören must have some way of tapping into the data grid they feed into. He just sets the readout sensitivity for your body temperature, and he can tell when you move from one sector to the next. It's the only possible way he could do it."

"Great—is there any way of shutting down the system?"

Bashir shook his head, though he knew she couldn't see him. "Not from the command center. The data line's bonded to the structural members; you'd have to practically disassemble the whole substation to get rid of it." His thoughts raced ahead; they were the only way of reaching out to help her. "But you can fool the system. Now, listen carefully—he knows where you are right now, so you don't have much time. You're going to need some things; there's a group of supply cabinets a couple of sectors over . . ."

At first, he had thought he would have to do something about his arm. He had heard the crack of bone when he had landed, his full weight impacting against his own flesh. Now, the arm dangled uselessly at his side, the wrist curled outward. A net of loose wiring that he had torn from the control of one of the biobeds would have served as a makeshift sling, but he had at last balled it up and thrown it away from him. The pain served a better purpose, the grating of the splintered ends against each other with each step he took; it honed his anger to a brighter, sharper edge. It had been sharp enough to kill before; now Hören felt as if he could slash the metal of the substation apart if need be, to reach through and grip her throat in his good hand.

He leaned his shoulder against a bulkhead, close to a doorway, fumbling with the buttons of the small tracking device. It had taken some effort to wedge open the control panel and get the device's wires into place. Effort, and time—Kira had already gotten away from him, more than once, and he blamed his own slow delight in her trapped situation. A weakness, for which he now bitterly lashed himself. Vengeance, the justice of the Redemptorist faith, was to have been a sword, quick and irrevocable, and he had almost dropped it. No more.

The grid showing the substation's layout came up on the device's small display. Hören thumbed the button below it, scrolling through sector after sector, until a red dot blinked on. Somewhere close to the command center; that made sense. He knew that Kira had been using the comm equipment there, to link up with the other Federation officer, who had been left behind in the wormhole. Not that it would do her any good.

He was about to pull the wires free and stow the device in his pocket, where the knife lay waiting, when another red dot appeared. The grip of his good hand tightened convulsively on the tracking device as he stared at it. At a point that would be a few meters away from the first, the thermal sensors had picked up another source of body heat.

It can't be— He jabbed at the buttons, but the red dots remained, blinking steadily. There couldn't be another person on the substation; he would have felt through the frame the shudder of the docking hooks grappling onto any vessel that had approached. Unless the person had been able to beam aboard the substation—but the cargo shuttle, even if it had been able to exit the wormhole, lacked personnel transporter equipment. And there were no other vessels in the area. . . .

A third dot appeared on the display. Then a fourth, and a few seconds later, a fifth.

An army, a dozen or more, showed by the time a wordless cry of anger escaped from Hören's lips. He smashed the lying device against the bulkhead, the display going blank as the microcomponents fell out of the broken case and onto the deck.

Hören struck the control panel and rushed through the door before it had slid halfway open. With his head lowered, he drew out the knife and headed down the corridor.

She pulled the silvery blanket closer around her, careful to keep her head covered by it. Bashir had told her that shielding her arms and legs wasn't so important—the main sources of body heat radiation, that the doorway sensors were set to pick up, were her torso and head. A chill leaked from the thermonic blanket, raising gooseflesh across her shoulders. Its medical purpose was for the treatment of fever patients, its activated thermal-exchange circuits the equivalent of an old-fashioned ice bath, but more controllable. Now, for Kira, it served as an even more effective form of camouflage.

The blanket's hem trailed behind her as she hurried toward the next doorway. From within the hooded folds, she took one of the blanket's counterparts, a catalytic heating patch. Squeezing the patch's edge, she initiated the chemical reaction inside—she could feel it begin to warm in her palm—and set the processor-controlled temperature to match her own. She peeled away the tape guards and slapped the patch onto the doorway panel beside her. Down the length of the corridor, and into several of its branches, similar patches had already been stuck across all the sensors.

She heard him approaching. The sound of footsteps ringing through the enclosed spaces—that was a good sign. It showed that she had managed to push him even farther over the edge. Hören's mounting anger was washing away before it all his stealth and hunter's cunning. The substation had been a psychological extension of his own body, both a substance and an environment that he had controlled. The fight in the other sector, when he had used the diversion of the throat-mounted microphone to sneak up on her, had been the first blow to that armored self-image. Whatever physical harm he had suffered wasn't as important as the eroding of his self-command. And now, to effectively blind him, rendering useless the sensors by which he had as much as seen into every corner of the substation . . . *This ought to be good,* thought Kira, as she rushed to get one more thermal patch up.

She ducked into the shadows of the nearest corridor branch, pulling the bottom of the silver blanket in behind her. The branch's angle gave her a clear line of vision down the main corridor.

Hören appeared, knife in hand, his other arm hanging at his side. His shoulders hunched bull-like, chest laboring from exertion. He stepped forward, his glaring eyes scanning across the bulkheads.

Holding her breath, Kira watched as he stopped beside one of the doorways. He reached up, using the knife to poke at what he had spotted on the control panel. The blade slipped under the patch and lifted it away. Hören knelt down and rubbed the back of his fist across the patch lying on the deck, the heat still seeping from it. His face tautened as realization set in; the knife suddenly rose, then slashed the patch open, the chemicals spurting out.

That was what she had wanted. Hören strode down the corridor, teeth clenched in anger at the sight of the thermal patches fastened onto each doorway panel. He ripped one loose and flung it down, then the next.

As he came closer, Kira silently pulled the blanket from around her shoulders and held it ready before her. When her target crossed in front of the branch's opening, she leapt forward, the blanket lifted like a net. Her momentum toppled Hören from his feet; she fell with him, the blanket's folds billowing between them.

Even with just one arm, his strength surprised her. The knife point tore through the blanket, nearly grazing her ribs. She was thrown clear as Hören reared up. He tossed the blanket aside with another sweeping motion of his arm. Kira scrambled to her feet, crouching with hands forward in combat position.

Instead of coming at her, Hören scooped up the blanket and tossed it at her face. In the few seconds it took her to duck and push it away, Hören had turned and vanished into the opposite reaches of the corridor. She heard his footsteps dwindling away in the darkness.

She breathed deep. gathering her strength around her racing pulse. She had hoped for better, but still . . .

From this point on, it would be closer to a fair fight. She could deal with that.

CHAPTER
16

HE ACCEPTED ANOTHER DRINK, though he had already altered his metabolism so that it, and the ones preceding, would have no effect on him. The fresh synthale was set down in front of him, and the empty mug taken away.

Quark slid into the seat across the table from him. "Your health, Constable." The Ferengi had picked up the term from hearing Commander Sisko use it. "You know your patronage is always most welcome in my humble establishment."

"Is it, indeed?" The other's sharp-toothed smile grated on Odo's sensibilities to a greater degree than usual. His brooding about the situation on Ops, with everyone tensely waiting for any communication from the wormhole or the Gamma Quadrant, was not lightened by Quark's impersonation of a charming host. "Don't get ideas about what it means. I only come here because it makes a convenient vantage point for the comings and goings on the Promenade."

"You're too kind." Nothing fazed Quark. "I seek to provide every amenity for my customers." He leaned forward, the smile replaced by an expression of heartfelt solicitude. "Really too bad, isn't it, about Major Kira and Doctor Bashir? I'd like to be counted among the many friends who are concerned about them."

"What do you know about that?"

"My dear Odo. One hears things. As you yourself just indicated—this is a wonderful location for keeping an eye on things." Quark gestured toward the other booths and tables, and the multi-species clientele lined up at the bar. "Really . . . it's like the *heart* of DS Nine, don't you agree?"

He made no reply. Once again, he was reluctantly impressed by the Ferengi's network of informants, gossips, and other data conduits—a network that rivaled his own. A total security clampdown had been put in effect on the mission to the Gamma Quadrant, even before things had gone wrong. And here was Quark, making it a point to show that he was aware of the details. *I should deputize him*—the thought had occurred to Odo before. *If I could trust him.* At least, Quark wouldn't be privy to any more sensitive material than he already was.

Odo took a drink and set the mug back down. "I hope I can rely on your discretion."

"Oh, but of course." Quark made a little bow where he sat. "And more than that, Constable. I want to *help.*"

"You'll help by keeping your mouth shut." He

looked around to see if anyone else in the bar could overhear their conversation.

A sigh came from Quark. "I always encounter such hostility from you . . . and I don't know why. Oh, well—" He started to slide from the booth. "Perhaps you're just not interested. . . ."

Odo grabbed the Ferengi's wrist and drew him back. "Do you think you have something to tell me that I don't already know?"

"Your problem is that you think you know everything." Quark adjusted his cuff. "Just because you can pass yourself off as a fly on the wall, if you want to. But you can't be everywhere at once, can you? You certainly weren't here on the Promenade when that Redemptorist Deyreth Elt was purchasing certain *interesting* items."

"Those recording chips?" Odo shook his head in disgust; Quark was obviously beginning to slip. "You already gave me that tape."

"Not the chips—anyone can buy those legally. I'm referring to a transaction that occurred right here in my bar, between Deyreth Elt and a pair of tech smugglers."

"I see." Odo's interest had been aroused. "And were these smugglers friends of yours?"

"Well, they weren't Ferengi, but they were certainly smart enough to make a little extra money by telling me what the Redemptorist had bought from them." A smug expression settled on Quark's face. "Most intriguing; lots of possibilities."

"And these items were . . . ?"

"Constable. We're both men of the universe." Quark looked across the bar, then turned back to Odo. "If I satisfy your curiosity—what's in it for me?"

"I thought you were so concerned about Kira and Bashir."

"Oh, I *am*. Nearly as much as I am about myself."

"Very well, then." Odo shrugged. "You could expect a measure of forbearance on my part when it comes time to relicense your establishment. I'd be willing to overlook certain problems that have come to my attention, concerning the adulteration of beverages and irregularities in the operation of your *dabo* tables."

"Thank you. I *like* a security chief I can do business with." Quark drew a set of folded papers from inside his jacket. "Here's the complete technical data on the items Deyreth Elt purchased. I don't mean to insult you, but the information is somewhat specialized; it may be a little bit outside your realm of expertise. I suggest you consult with Chief Engineer O'Brien on this matter."

He glanced through the sheets before refolding them. The Ferengi was right. "That's exactly what I'll do." He drained the last of the synthale and stood up, then leaned over Quark. "If nothing else, he'll be able to tell me whether or not you just pushed some worthless trash on me."

"Constable!" Quark feigned shock. "I would *never*—"

"I know. Not unless there was a profit to be made from it." Odo turned and headed for the exit.

"Have you changed your minds?"

The image regarded him with its eyes of blackness and stars. "That is not the correct word of your language. Our kind does not have *minds* as you would know them. It is something different."

"Whatever." Bashir resisted the temptation of getting into another protracted metaphysical discussion with the entity. It would have been so easy to do that, to forget all about matters of life and death in the universe outside. . . . He shook his head, as though struggling for a moment to stay focused, and laid his hands flat upon the arms of the pilot area's seat. "Perhaps I should have asked if you had come to another decision."

"We have not. The concern you feel for this other one of your kind, the one who exists here no more— we are *intrigued* by that. Your kind seeks to mold *time*, to make it different from what it is or will be; that is strange to us. But as you say, it is in your nature." The image of Kira closed its eyes for a moment, silent, as it communed with the unseen others behind it. "Nevertheless, we cannot permit you to go to that other one. That which moves you from point to point, in *space* rather than *time*—this engine, as you call it—it wounds us terribly. We had not even known what pain and not-pain were, until such a thing came upon us. Now, we even know what death is; that is how severe the engine's effects are upon our kind. All these things of *time* were brought to us by the one called Benjamin Sisko—but he also promised us that it would not be that way again. We accept that it was not your intent to harm us. But we cannot allow it to happen again."

Bashir clenched his jaw in frustration. There was no telling what was going on with Kira, out in the Gamma Quadrant—he had reached the limit of how much good he could do her at this distance. He had received no communication from her in the last few hours; she could already be dead, for all he knew.

Hören could have caught her as she was fetching the thermal patches and blanket from the storage cabinets. Caught her with an arm around her neck, and the knife rising up in his other hand—

He pushed the image out of his head. "If only . . ." He shook his head. There was no way to explain to them.

There was no need to. The Kira image's gaze penetrated his thoughts. "You do not believe us. In your *mind* and in your *soul,* you think we tell you something that is not truth."

After a moment, Bashir nodded. "You're right. That is what I think. There must be some way that I can activate the engine, and not have it hurt you. Or . . . or maybe it wouldn't be as bad as you think; maybe you're just afraid of it, because of the pain. It would be for only a little while, and then I would be out of the wormhole—"

"You see?" The harsh, angry voice came from the image again, its expression changing to a scowl. Bashir knew it wasn't addressing him, but the rest of the wormhole's inhabitants instead. "This also is in the nature of these creatures! The pain and death of others is not real to them—thus they find it easy to kill all not of their kind!"

"No . . . it's not like that. . . ."

"These words are such clumsy things." The gentler voice returned to Kira's image. "Even for your own kind. It was the same with the one called Sisko—there were things he would not believe until he could see them himself. Perhaps it is the same for you. We should show you that of which we speak."

"What do you mean?"

"This is not the only *time* that exists." The image

raised a hand toward the shuttle's bulkheads. "All of what you see—both in this universe and the one outside it—that is but one *time* of many. There are others, different from this."

He leaned forward in the seat. "You mean parallel realities? Something like that?"

"Words—your kind is so fond of them. You name things and believe you know them." A smile played on the image's face. "Yes, if it pleases you to call them such."

"All right. What is it you would show me, then?" He felt like a character in an old Earth story, talking to the ghosts who had visited him. "I'm ready."

More than ghostlike; a phantom of suffering. Suddenly, the image of Kira threw its head back, the cords of its neck tautening, mouth grimacing in pain. The image grew translucent; for a moment, the stars filled its outline, twined with bones of glass. Then it was gone.

He was alone in the cargo shuttle. More so than ever before; he realized that even when the image had chosen not to show itself to him, the wormhole's inhabitants had always been there with him, watching. Their presence had filled the shuttle like oxygen. He could breathe, but the stuff inside his lungs was something colder and thinner; a bitter metallic taste formed on his tongue.

"Where are you?" Bashir called aloud, then slid down from the seat. He stood in the middle of the pilot area, looking slowly around the empty space.

Something else had stopped that had almost become as much a part of him as his pulse. He looked toward the panel that held the instruments for the external sensors. All the readouts had pegged down to zero, the same blank red numeral showing on all the gauges. He stepped toward the panel and laid his hand on it. The equipment was still working; a faint electronic hum seeped through the skin of his palm. The data storage units continued to operate, absorbing the flat output of the wormhole's dead universe.

Appalled, Bashir stepped back from the readouts. He spun to face the pilot area's center. "Where are you?" A cry now, as much of anger as fright.

We are not here. Not now. A soundless voice spoke at his ear. *This is the place where we are not. Because of what you would do to us. We can look into this other time, and touch you in it, but we cannot be here.*

He went to the front of the area, and leaned over the control panel, to gaze out the observation ports. The swirling play, the visible bands of the wormhole's electromagnetic radiation, had vanished. Darkness without stars surrounded the shuttle.

"This . . ." He touched the cold inner surface of the port. "This is what the engines would do?"

Without that which you call the buffers . . . yes. The wounding it causes, the hurt to us . . . the death. You would kill us with the engines. And when we die, the wormhole becomes a dead thing, as well. Its flesh is our flesh; we are the same as it. It would not happen at once, but slowly in your time. Whenever the engines come upon us, a little more death. Until there is no more.

There was something else they weren't telling him; he sensed it, out beyond the fragile skin of the shuttle, beyond the limits of the wormhole itself.

"What about the rest? Out there?" He pointed to

where the stars had once been, cold light swarming at the point where this small universe opened onto the larger one. "What happens there?"

We know not. The voice seemed to come from a place almost as distant. *That is not our concern.*

An idea had already formed inside him; all he needed to do was speak it aloud. Even though he was afraid to.

"Leave me here, then." Bashir looked over his shoulder, half hoping to see the Kira image standing behind him. "In this time, in this place."

This is the time of the dead.

"I know. But I can do you no more harm here. Your kind exists in another time, apart from this. I can activate the engine without causing any more suffering, any more death, to you. We're all beyond that, here, in this time. There would be no more wounding, yet I could go to the aid of the other one of my kind. That's all that matters to me now."

The voice was silent for a long moment. Then it came again. *You do this at peril to yourself. We cannot tell you what lies beyond this place, this time, our flesh. We are not out there, where you wish to go. You will cease to exist for us, as the other one did. You will have no way of speaking to us again.*

He nodded slowly. "But there's no other way."

You will be lost.

"I'll have to take that chance. But like everything else out there—it won't be your concern anymore." He shrugged. "Maybe you won't even remember me."

Too late. Now, you exist in memory, as well.

"All right." Bashir pushed himself away from the panel and stood in the center of the pilot area. "Let's do it."

It is done already. The voice was barely perceptible. *Goodbye . . .*

He was truly alone. The instrument gauges stared at him like empty eye sockets. He walked past them, heading for the hatchway that led down to the engine compartment.

A few minutes later—if time could have been measured in this universe—he came back up and settled himself in the pilot area's chair. He reached out and pressed the main thrust control. Below him, he felt the surge of power emitted by the unbuffered engine.

Gathering speed, the cargo shuttle moved toward the wormhole's exit.

"I've brought someone with me this time." He pulled another chair toward the table in the center of the cell. "I think you know our Chief Engineer O'Brien."

Odo watched as the Redemptorists, sitting in a row on the other side of the table, nodded toward their former boss. They all looked puzzled as to why he had come.

"The chief engineer and I have been having an interesting conversation." Odo unfolded the papers that Quark had given him and spread them out on the table. "Much the same as you and I have had. Only concerning things that I wasn't quite aware of before."

The Redemptorists shifted in their chairs, appearing nervous and uncomfortable. He had observed this condition in interrogation subjects before, especially after they had had time to reflect upon various psychological ploys he might have used upon them. This bunch now radiated an uneasy fear when confronted by him, undoubtedly worrying—if only subconsciously—about what he might turn to next.

"It seems certain devices were purchased by your late comrade Deyreth Elt." Odo looked down at the sheets of paper. "Devices that the chief engineer informs me are called *parasitic echo relays.*" He looked up at his audience. "Ring any bells with you?"

The Redemptorists glanced from the corners of their eyes at one another, but remained silent.

"These devices have some striking properties. It was an education, hearing about them. It seems that these echo relays can be placed in parallel with circuits that might have a coded signal sent along them—the input circuits, let us say, for a chain of high explosives that requires a fuse code in order to be triggered." Odo looked at O'Brien sitting next to him. He sensed the hot-tempered human's impatience with what must have seemed like a roundabout mode of questioning. The engineer would have been much more likely to have reached across the table and banged a couple of heads together to get them talking. Even if he hadn't gotten any answers that way, he would have felt better. "These echo relays don't require the code signal; they can pick it up from the circuits they've been placed on, and hold it for a variable length of time before allowing it to pass on to the next stage of the circuit. Now, does that sound familiar?"

They were trembling, right at the verge of cracking; Odo saw one of the Redemptorists open his mouth, as though he were about to speak. Sweat dotted all their brows. The softening up he had done before was about to pay off. To confront them now, with a spiel of information that they had thought was known only to themselves, was the final step in the process.

244

"Come on," growled O'Brien. "There's people's lives at stake—"

The Redemptorists didn't even seem to hear the chief engineer. They were still staring at Odo, like small animals hypnotized by a venomous reptile.

"You know you want to tell me." He pitched his voice low, almost soothing. "Think how good it will make you feel. Why not now?"

"It's so they won't all go off at once—" The one in the center of the row broke his silence, his words blurting out, propelled by the pressure inside him. "And that way—"

"That's right," another one quickly added. "So the force isn't cumulative, it's dispersed—"

They all began talking at once, their voices tumbling over each other.

Odo turned toward O'Brien. "Are you getting all this?"

She swiveled her chair toward him. "There have been some highly unusual developments in that sector, Commander."

Sisko stood behind Dax on the Ops deck, looking at the panel display she had called him to see. "Exactly what's going on?"

Dax ran a fingertip across the glowing numerals. "I've been keeping a monitoring scan on the sector where the entrance to the wormhole was before it collapsed out of existence. Look at this." The numbers she pointed to were rows of zeros. "There's been a near-total drop in the background electromagnetic activity. Virtually nothing is happening in that sector. I've never seen anything like that before."

He felt his brow creasing in puzzlement. "What do you think it means?"

"Hard to tell, Commander." She studied the readouts. "It's as if that sector has shifted in time somehow—to a point approaching the theoretical end of the universe itself. This flattening out of the EM distribution is a kind of death on a cosmological scale. It's what we would anticipate seeing—if there were anyone still around to see it—when the universe begins collapsing in upon itself. It's just that here it's confined to this one relatively small area."

"Something must be going on in there. Inside the wormhole."

Dax nodded. "That sector of space and the wormhole must somehow still be connected—just as if the wormhole left a gap in the outside universe's fabric when it disappeared. And now we're seeing some kind of resonance effect between them."

"It's Bashir." One of Sisko's fists struck the panel. "He must have done something. He must have figured out some way of dealing with the wormhole's inhabitants."

"Perhaps. But then, the wormhole's entrance hasn't reappeared."

"Commander—" A voice called from the Ops doorway. He looked up and saw Odo and O'Brien striding toward him.

"What is it, gentlemen?"

"My interrogation of the Redemptorists has yielded some results at last." Odo appeared pleased with himself. "We've come up with some information that may be of considerable value."

"It's just as we thought," said O'Brien. "They've wired some additional surprises into the substation."

Sisko led them back to his office. He leaned forward across his desk, chin braced against his fists, and listened to the chief engineer's explanation.

"—and that's what they've cooked up." O'Brien had finished the technical details. "These parasitic echo relays turn the autodestruct function of the original quarantine module into something almost completely different. The original destruct sequence was set for all the explosives to go off simultaneously, as soon as the fuse codes were transmitted to them. That way, the QM would have been completely destroyed; there wouldn't have been any pieces bigger than your hand floating around afterward. Now, with these echo delays wired into the circuits aboard the substation, they will go off one after another, with several seconds between charges. The cumulative effect won't be present; all the substation's atmospheric seals will be blown out, but the structural framework and most of the exterior shielding will still be intact."

"Apparently, the plan was something devised by Deyreth Elt and Hören Rygis." Odo turned his gaze toward the commander. "They anticipated that once we discovered Hören was aboard the substation—particularly if we also found out that he had been successful in murdering Major Kira—we would initiate the autodestruct sequence as the quickest means of eradicating him, so that he couldn't be brought to trial on Bajor. He couldn't eliminate the explosives and their circuitry on the substation, but with the echo relays they could be sufficiently altered so that he would stand a reasonable chance of survival. With one of the portable emergency life-support systems aboard, he could hold out for some time. Long enough for the Bajoran provisional government to become aware of the situation and press for him to be brought back to the planet's surface. Any trial would become a show for gathering even more support for the Redemptorist cause. Hören would come out of it an even bigger hero than before."

"Indeed." Sisko leaned back. "Now that we have this information, gentlemen, what do we do with it?"

"If we could get this information to Major Kira, she could use it against Hören." Odo's voice remained dispassionately logical. "We know that the other end of the wormhole is still in existence; it's also reasonable to assume that the cargo shuttle is still close to the wormhole's exit. Though the internal curvature of the wormhole normally renders impossible any transmissions to or from vessels that have traveled significant distances inside, the cargo shuttle might be within effective comm range. If so, there's a chance that Kira is in contact with Doctor Bashir. He could transmit to her the fuse codes for the explosives. As soon as she had acquired a portable life-support system for herself, she could initiate the autodestruct sequence and blow Hören into space. An entirely appropriate conclusion to him, I would maintain."

"The problem is in getting the information to her." Sisko rubbed his chin. "I think we need to have another little discussion with Gul Tahgla. . . ."

He used the augmented personnel module to transfer from the cargo shuttle to the substation. The APM, stowed in its own bay just off the shuttle's freight hold, was almost a complete small spacecraft in its own right, nearly two meters across at its widest point and close to four meters from the base of its propulsion unit to the signal lights and sensors mounted above the multiwindowed head. The six utility arms positioned around the APM's elongated trapezoidal form were equipped with a variety of tools, from heavy-duty grappling pincers to fusion weld cutters. Bashir didn't know what it would take to get inside the substation, but he wanted to be prepared for any eventuality.

The safety of the cargo shuttle dwindled behind as he steered the APM toward the substation's docking port, where it had once been connected to the vessel taking it through the wormhole. In all directions lay the field of stars, the coldness of their scattered light prickling Bashir's skin. The memory of the Kira image's eyes haunted him; that, and the dead pocket universe, the wormhole wounded by the unbuffered engines, from which he had finally piloted the shuttle.

Around the docking port were the black scorch marks from the bomblets that had originally cannoned the substation out here to the Gamma Quadrant. Inside the APM, Bashir rotated a control on the small panel before him, playing an exterior work light across the massive C-shaped arms splayed out from the port. Reaching behind him in the APM's cramped space, he found the glovelike hand-piece that operated the smaller grappling arm. The APM turned on its axis as the arm extended and seized hold of the port's emergency release bolts.

He breathed a sigh of relief when the bolts gave way, the grappling arm slowly twisting them to their unlocked position. The explosive force of the bomblets hadn't damaged the entry system. He had been worried about the possible need to cut his way in with the fusion torch, and compromise the substation's atmospheric seals.

Backing the APM off a few meters, he watched the hexagonal door of the port swing open. Within minutes, he had guided the APM inside; using one of the grappling arms, he struck the red manual-activate switch protruding from the side of the airlock. Through the APM's sensors, he could hear the hissing sound grow louder as oxygen flooded the chamber. As soon as the pressure-match light came on on the panel, he unsealed the APM—a vertical slit appeared between two of the segmented windows, widening as the metal edges retracted from each other, down to the APM's base. Bashir quickly stepped out and hurried to the doorway leading to the interior of the substation.

In the central corridor, with the door sliding shut behind him, caution suddenly held him back. There was no telling where Hören might be—the Redemptorist would undoubtedly have been able to tell that someone new had come aboard. Bashir resisted the impulse to call out Kira's name, and instead, tried to make as little noise as possible as he headed for the command center.

He found he needn't have worried.

When the command center's door slid back, he spotted the two corpses lying on the deck. Or what had been corpses; slow centuries had reduced them to skeletons, the soft tissues reduced to a thin, wrinkled leather.

The larger one he assumed had been Hören; the other, he was able to recognize as Kira from the few faded scraps of her uniform, the white fingers of her ribs visible through the gaps. The skull's eye sockets held nothing as they gazed up at the ceiling.

He knelt down and touched what had been her

head. The small bones crumbled to dust with the slightest pressure.

Cold, deeper than that between the stars, seemed to radiate from inside him. He quickly stepped to the control panels; the instrument lights came up, slowly and dimly, beneath his fingertips. "DS Nine—this is the substation mission calling Deep Space Nine. Do you read me?" He could hear his own voice tautening, as dread seized hold of his throat and breath. "Is there anyone there? *Anyone* . . ."

Silence answered him. Silence that he knew now was the wordless speech of the dead, an emptiness large enough to swallow galaxies, small enough to be held inside jaws of whitening bone. He stepped back from the panel and turned toward the dead, who still had remnants of faces.

"They have been here a long time. Just like this. Waiting for you."

Somehow, the unexpected voice failed to startle him. He looked over his shoulder and saw a woman standing behind him. She was dressed in the enfolding robes of a Bajoran priestess.

"There is no blame to be ascribed to you." The woman's expression was one of gentle forgiveness. "As I told your commander, Benjamin Sisko, there are limits to human effort. One must learn to accept what one can and cannot do."

He recognized her then. He had never met the Kai Opaka in the flesh—though she seemed real enough now, standing with placid calm in the substation's command center—but had seen photos and tapes of her, millennia ago back on DS9. Her soft voice confirmed her identity.

Slowly, Bashir stood up and turned toward her.

After so much that had happened, his capacity for being surprised had been erased. But not the questions inside his head. "What is this place?"

"This?" Kai Opaka lifted her small hand and gestured toward the substation's bulkheads, then toward the observation ports to indicate the stars beyond. "This is everything, Doctor Bashir. This is the universe, the one to which the inhabitants of the wormhole brought you—at your request, remember. The universe you remember—the universe of living things—exists, and doesn't exist, somewhere else. You have left all that behind."

"Are we . . ."

She read his thought. "We are the only living things here. And everywhere. This is the universe of the dead." She pointed to the observation ports. "Go and see for yourself, Doctor."

He stepped toward the ports and looked out. At the stars and the worlds hidden in the darkness between them. His skin felt cold, as though the hollow in his gut was a piece of the same vacuum.

"Do you not sense it?" The Kai's voice came from behind him. "Or rather, you do not sense it. That which was as familiar to you as your breath, so much a part of you that it could be forgotten. The sense of being surrounded by a living organism, the universe itself. That is what you miss now."

"Yes. . . ." He nodded slowly. "That . . . that's all gone. Everything. . . ." He turned away from the empty vision. "It was the wounding, wasn't it? That did this. They told me . . . about the suffering, and the death. . . ."

"Of course. Are you not a doctor? Did you not

know that one part of a living thing is connected to all other parts? Even the wormhole, as separate as it is, still is of that greater substance. By wounding it, by its death, the death of all was brought about. It could not be otherwise."

He had known the answer even before she had spoken. The weight of the dead universe seemed to crush the breath from his lungs, as though he were being buried in a lightless grave.

"I know how I got here . . ." Bashir spoke, hoping to keep the human presence of the Kai near him for a while longer. "But what about you?"

She smiled. "I am only, as you might say, a little bit in this place. Though I exist in the universe of the living, the one from which you came, my meditations long ago brought me to this one, as well. On your world, as well as Bajor, the highest wisdom is to be as mindful of death as one is of life. These are not empty words; if you were to devote yourself to the raising of one's inner powers as I have, you would also be able to exist in both universes at once. Thus it is that the prophets see the future as clearly as the present, and the sages know that all things happen in timelessness as well as in time." Kai Opaka stretched her palm toward him, as though in blessing. "I saw that you had come to this place, by virtue of your concern for another. What you lack in wisdom—what you have not within you yet—is equaled by that sacrifice. I could not let you suffer alone."

A spark of hope moved inside Bashir. "Can you . . . can you take me back? To the living?"

"That is not within my abilities. But those who are more powerful than I am, those who were created of timelessness—the ones who brought you here—they can do that. And they will. You chose not to harm them, and they are grateful for that."

He closed his eyes, feeling the weariness drain away from him. "But when . . ."

I have already communicated with them. It is as much as done.

The Kai's voice hadn't spoken aloud, but inside him. As he opened his eyes, he turned toward the observation ports.

And saw the stars. And felt, resonating with his own pulse and breath, the living worlds turning beneath every sun. . . .

He looked over his shoulder and saw that Kai Opaka had gone. But he wasn't alone.

There was only one form lying on the command center's deck. And she was alive.

He stepped toward Kira and reached down, taking her by the arm and pulling her to her feet. She blinked in confusion, as though she were still mired in the troubled dreams into which she had fallen.

CHAPTER
17

"ARE YOU SURE that's all you require, Commander?" The Cardassian's face peered from the Ops screen. "I expected something rather more . . . *elaborate* from you."

Sisko gave a brief nod, a simulation of courtesy. "As I've tried to explain to you, Gul Tahgla, it's really a very simple matter. And while I admit a degree of embarrassment about the glitch that's interrupted our communications with our substation, I suppose I should also be grateful that your services are available to help us out."

Behind his chair, his chief officers stood and watched, listening to the interchange between their commander and his counterpart out in the Gamma Quadrant. A brief conference between him and the others had been enough to formulate their strategy. Now, all he had to do was get Gul Tahgla to fall for it.

"I'm not quite sure about this. . . ." Suspicion clouded Gul Tahgla's face. He studied the panel before him, drawing a finger along the words that one of his adjutants had written down for him. "Let me see if I have this correct. The text of the message you would like me to relay to your substation is 'That which would have been simultaneous will now be sequential.'" He glanced up. "And that's it?"

"That's all of it." Sisko smiled pleasantly. "I tried to be brief; I didn't want to put you and your crew to any more trouble than absolutely necessary."

"It sounds rather like a—what is that amusement of words?—a riddle." Gul Tahgla tilted his head, as though he could better puzzle out the meaning by viewing the message at a different angle. "Are you sure the ones aboard your substation—if there are any alive, of course—will understand such compression? Perhaps you would like to . . . *expand* on it just a bit?" He looked up, as though hoping for a clue.

"No, it's quite adequate the way it is." Sisko hoped it was. The wording was of his own devising, intended to be just enough to serve as a key for Kira and Bashir, so that they would be able to figure out the rest on their own. And at the same time, it had to remain impenetrable to Gul Tahgla, hiding the status of the substation. "My crew members will know what it means."

"Commander Sisko." The expression on Tahgla's face had hardened, his eyes narrowing. "I must tell you that I find this artful simplicity to be most dubious. I sense not just mockery here but a very real threat. The mistrust your request evokes is grave. My officers and I will have to study this intended message, to make certain it's harmless."

"Now that is disappointing. I expected better of you, Gul Tahgla. Are you telling me that a Cardassian *gul* can't make a decision on his own, over something as simple as this? You might want to be concerned about the damage that will be done to the reputation of yourself and all the Cardassian officer corps, when the story gets out that you were frightened by something that's hardly more than a fragment from a children's game. Entities across the known galaxies might speculate as to whether the warriors of the great Cardassian empire worry about their own shadows creeping up on them." Sisko could see that his comments were hitting home, from the smoldering look that creased Gul Tahgla's brow. "And then, there are the political repercussions to consider, when it's determined that my message was in fact harmless to Cardassian interests—and you personally refused to honor traditional standards of conduct between nonwarring parties. I'm sure many planets with whom you have alliances could begin to wonder what your empire's true relationship with them might be. That's the kind of suspicion that would set back your diplomatic efforts a great deal." Sisko shrugged. "Of course, you might not be concerned about what your superiors on the council would say about your placing them in such an awkward position . . . all over a simple little riddle . . ."

"Very well." Gul Tahgla's mouth twisted into a snarl. "Your message will be transmitted to your substation unit; we will continue to repeat until such time as you are satisfied that we have made every effort to accommodate you. But I warn you, Sisko: this changes nothing. I will sweep your abandoned unit out of the sector surrounding the wormhole's exit."

He nodded in his own mockery of civility. "Perhaps I will find the answer to your inane riddle in the pieces that are left when I'm done."

The screen went blank, the subspace link with the Cardassian vessel broken.

Sisko looked over his shoulder at his chief officers. "He bought it."

A fire burst the bounds of his heart, swarming upward into the chambers that had once held rational thought. That had all been torn away by the rage that both consumed and left him whole. Stronger and purer than before; that was what pain and anger had done for him. There had been weakness before in his physical body, the frail bone and flesh that held his spirit. But his own poisoned blood had been let, and now he felt himself glorified, a wrathful spirit of justice.

Hören moved through the corridors of the substation, the vibration of each step sending a jagged spear up into his shoulder. His broken arm dangled at his side, its angle twisted even sharper than at first. That was good; the crying of the nerves within kept him alert, his senses scanning at a fevered pitch across the darkness.

His other hand gripped the knife, tight enough that it had become an extension of his thought and will. Its glittering edge turned radiant inside his skull; he could picture the thin metal sinking through flesh as easily as through air itself. As though his prey were a ghost, a dead thing already. For so it had been ordained. His own voice howled wordlessly inside him, a prophecy that he carried in his fist. . . .

The gridded deck rose unevenly beneath him, and

he stumbled. He found himself on his knees and one hand, his knuckles scraped raw between the knife's handle and the floor. The darkness swam up toward his face, as though it were a pool that he could ease his burning face into and drink deep.

Part of him, the weak and diseased part, wanted to curl onto his side and find sleep, let dreams roll over him, let the darkness become an ocean swaying him in its slow tides. He could have wept in frustration, in the bitterness of knowing that the blood always returned, that he had to let more and more of it out. To sanctify himself.

"It's *her* fault," he whispered. It always had been. The fire had blossomed inside the temple; the lucky ones who had been confirmed in their holiness had lain on the blackened ground, alive just long enough to taste the sweetness of their perfected state. He should have been there with them; he would have been, if *she* hadn't cheated him of that moment of grace. A timeless moment, eternal, all weakness purged. Then, perhaps they would have forgiven, and blessed him.

He pushed himself up from the deck, sitting back on his haunches. His strength began to return as he concentrated on taking one breath after another. The pain from his broken arm dulled a fraction, as though it were a partner in his great task and had recognized how much farther they had to go.

Carefully, Hören got to his feet, resting his shoulder for a moment against the bulkhead. The strength grew in him, the purifying flames leaping even higher. He raised his good arm, looked at his haggard face in the knife blade above.

Soon. That was the vow he sealed upon his heart. It was time to bring everything to an end.

He stepped away from the bulkhead, moving on his ordained course. Toward her.

She had been so angry that she had almost torn his head off. When she regained full consciousness and understood that it wasn't a hallucination generated by fatigue, but the actual physical form of Julian Bashir standing in the substation's command center, she pulled her arm away as he was examining the blood-soaked dressing.

"I *ordered* you!" The words had snapped from Kira's mouth. "You were absolutely forbidden to activate any unbuffered engine and cause any further damage to the wormhole—"

"You know, I really expected a more cordial welcome than this. It wasn't easy getting here."

Bashir had had to show her, by a visual check through the observation ports and the readouts from the monitoring instruments, that the wormhole was still in existence. "This end of it, at least." He had tapped his finger against one of the gauges. "Until we get back on board the cargo shuttle and establish a subspace comm link with DS Nine, there's no telling what's going on back there."

She studied him with equal measures of puzzlement and mistrust. "So, exactly how *did* you get here?"

"Those minor details will be in my report." He smiled. "They have somewhat more to do with my area of expertise than yours, I'm afraid." He paused, listening to the substation's silence for a moment before turning back to her. "What about Hören? Is he still—"

Kira nodded. "He's still out there . . . somewhere." She gestured toward the command center's doorway.

"He could be just outside in the corridor, listening to us, for all we know."

"And he's still intent on killing you?"

"He's somewhat persistent," she said dryly. "Let's just say I've had a few encounters with him. That'll all be in *my* report."

"Then, what we need to do is transfer back to the cargo shuttle—right now. Where he can't get at either one of us." Bashir glanced at the doorway. "We can use the augmented personnel module—it can hold two people if necessary. It'll be tight, but then, we don't have far to go."

"Negative on that." She shook her head. "You can go back to the shuttle if you want. But I'm not leaving the substation. Not until he's taken care of."

"Are you joking?" Bashir stared at her. "Why take the risk?" He pointed to her bandaged arm and bloodstained uniform. "You've already barely survived your 'encounters' with this maniac. In the shuttle, we could just wait him out. Or at least, we'd have time to rest and think about what we're going to do." He tilted his head back, realization dawning on him. "Perhaps you don't want to leave the substation because you've become as obsessed as he is. Some of Hören's madness has rubbed off on you. So, now you're locked into this . . . this *dance* with him."

"It's not a matter of obsession." Kira's voice remained controlled. "I was sent out here to the Gamma Quadrant on a specific mission, to claim sovereignty over this sector surrounding the wormhole's exit. Before the Cardassians are able to. This substation has to represent the legal basis for that claim. If Gul Tahgla gets here and discovers there's no one aboard except some homicidal lunatic roaming the corridors with a knife, he'll be able to lock down a claim for Cardassian sovereignty even tighter." She pushed her disordered hair back from her brow. "There's too much at stake—not just for the Federation but for Bajor—for me to let that happen."

"The claim of sovereignty won't hold up if Gul Tahgla finds nothing but corpses here, yours included."

"All right, then." Kira shrugged. "As I said, I'm going to stay here and take care of Hören."

"Kill him, you mean."

"If I have to."

Bashir gazed up at the ceiling. The exasperation he felt over her stubbornness was made worse by his knowing that she was right.

"You're in charge, Major." He knew when he was beaten. "Except for one thing."

"What's that?"

"I intend to disobey any order you might give for me to return to the shuttle. Until we're done here. Between the two of us, we should be able to handle Hören."

One side of Kira's mouth lifted in a smile. At the same time, from the corner of his eye, Bashir saw a light appear on one of the command center's panels.

"We've got a transmission coming in." He studied the words scrolling on the comm link's readout. "It's from Gul Tahgla's vessel."

He switched the link onto the overhead speaker. A monotone Cardassian voice sounded.

"This message is relayed by us from the Deep Space Nine station, its point of origin. Your commander, Benjamin Sisko, wishes to advise you, verbatim quote: *That which would have been simultaneous will now be sequential.* End of transmission. Do you acknowledge?"

Bashir pressed another of the switches. "Receipt acknowledged." The lights on the panel died as the comm link was broken. "What the hell do you think that was supposed to mean?"

"If Sisko wanted us to hear, it has to mean something." Kira stood beside him. "Especially if he went to the effort of convincing Gul Tahgla to relay it to us." She turned toward Bashir. "My guess would be that it refers to some operating mode of the substation. Think—is there any onboard function that was originally designed to operate simultaneously?"

"Well, there are the standard life-support systems . . . but those are ongoing." He rubbed his chin. "The message seemed to indicate something that hasn't started up yet . . . something that would have to be triggered—" His eyes widened. "The autodestruct devices! Of course—the charges are set to explode all at the same time, when the fuse codes are programmed into them, so that the combined force would be enough to tear the substation apart."

"So if they went off in a delayed sequence instead . . ."

"It must have been something those Redemptorists wired in, when they were working to convert the quarantine module. If O'Brien were here, he could probably explain how they did it."

"What would the effect be?"

Bashir shrugged. "The damage would still be pretty severe. The interior of the substation would be essentially gutted, the atmospheric seals would be blown out. Structurally, it would remain intact; most of the explosive force would be directed inward, so the exterior would still be in decent enough shape."

"Total loss of life aboard?"

"Sure—for anybody who wasn't protected. The decompression alone would be sufficiently lethal."

"Then that's it." Kira squeezed her hand into a fist. "That's what Sisko wanted us to know. It's the perfect means of taking care of Hören."

"It's still chancy. He'd have to be lured to a sector of the substation that doesn't have any emergency life-support systems stocked in it. The only section like that is the anterior storage lockers." Bashir drew in a long breath through his teeth. "And that's the end of the explosives chain—that's exactly where the charges would start going off, once the codes had been given from here."

"Don't worry about it." Kira wiped her palms on the trousers of her uniform. "That's my job. . . ."

He saw her. In some ways, it was easier now that he wasn't relying on the doorway sensors and the tracking device. Hören could tell where she was, her movements through the substation's corridors, just by sniffing the trapped air. His senses had grown sharper, the purifying anger strengthening him.

A shadow in darkness, a footstep that rang upon metal . . . that was enough. His prey was moving toward the farther reaches of the substation, away from the command center. He had thought he would be able to trap her there, but she had bolted from that false security. Panic must have set in, a desperate hunt for some kind of hiding place. He had survived her trap, clever as it had been; perhaps she had realized at last that there would be no stopping him, that he would keep coming toward her, implacable. There would be no hiding places where he could not find her. And at the end, she would be caught in some corner, a narrow angle of bulkheads and ceiling. Then his shadow would fall upon her, a darkness broken only by the shining of justice in his upraised hand.

He moved through the corridors that had become as familiar to him as his own body. All around, he felt the sureness of time embrace him, the fulfillment of prophecy.

"Hören!"

Her shout rang through the dimly lit spaces, echoing from the banks of storage lockers surrounding her.

A silhouette, its shoulders made even more massive by the lowering of his head, appeared in the doorway. One arm dangled, twisted and useless, at the figure's side. The knife glittered in the other hand.

"I've been waiting for this, Kira." He stepped forward, a trace of light revealing the hollows of his face. "For centuries . . ."

"I know you have." She moved sideways, slowly, along the bulkhead behind her. Even in his madness, which had stripped away so much of him, there was still something of the Redemptorist leader remaining. His voice, the thundering pronouncements of blood and fire. She had counted on that. "It was ordained, wasn't it?"

"Now is not the time to mock me. You blaspheme in addition to all your other sins. Better that you should repent and seek forgiveness."

She glanced from the corner of her eye at the narrowing space to one side. "Would that change

265

anything?" There was another doorway leading out of the area, a few meters away; almost as close to her as Hören.

"Of course not." His eyes glinted like sparks of the same radiance that ran along the knife blade. "There are sins that lie upon your heart, that are beyond forgiving. They can only be purged, like a sickness in your veins." He raised the bright metal. "That is why you should welcome this release from your life of defilement."

She said nothing. For a moment, she braced her hands flat against the bulkhead. He had come near enough for her to smell the acrid sweat that had seeped through his skin.

Close enough to smell her own blood staining the blade . . .

Kira leapt shoulder-first as the knife swung toward her, ducking beneath its arc. Diving for the open doorway, she landed on her side, then reached up to hit the control panel. As Hören loomed in the shrinking gap, the thrust of her kick caught him in the abdomen, staggering him backward. The door's edge sealed shut.

"Bashir—" She slapped her comm badge. "Initiate explosives sequence *now!*"

His voice came through an overhead speaker. "Are you sure?"

"Goddamn it! Of course I'm sure—do it!" She scrambled to her feet and headed toward the passageway's end.

She heard the door sliding open behind her, and Hören's footsteps. As she glanced over her shoulder, another sound erupted, a deep rumble. The shock wave from the explosion hit, the corridor shaking on all sides, throwing her from her feet. She grabbed hold of a doorway frame and pulled herself upright, bracing herself against the bulkhead. Behind her, she saw Hören on his knees, raising himself with the knife still in his hand.

Another explosion; the air began to stream past her face. She pushed herself away from the door and ran, as the deck jarred and buckled beneath her.

He heard the sounds, the low bass notes vibrating through the substation's frame. Immediately, the alarms went off on the command center's panels, signaling the loss of perimeter integrity. Bashir punched the controls to dump the reserve oxygen storage and bring on-line the emergency atmospheric generators. His ears popped with the fall in pressure, partly muting the alarm sirens as he opened the doorway into the central corridor.

There was no time now to worry about Kira; he could only follow his part in what they had planned together. In a few minutes, he had reached the airlock and climbed into the augmented personnel module. The opening narrowed into a thin slit, then disappeared as the metal edges locked into each other.

With the maneuvering jets set at low thrust, Bashir inched the APM forward. The doorway to the interior of the substation was meters too small for the APM to pass through. He activated the fusion weld torch, the tip of the articulated metal arm turning into a glowing white point of energy. With the largest of the grappling arms, he grabbed hold of the doorway frame, bending it free as the torch cut through the structural member behind.

He could feel the heat through the segmented

windows; that and the seconds ticking past brought sweat trickling down into his eyes. The walls of the airlock shook as another explosion went off, closer this time. He pulled back on the grappling arm's control, the metal tearing like heavy paper.

The explosions, the blasts that had surged louder and louder, the impacts throwing her against the bulkheads, had confused her. She had had her route to the airlock figured out and memorized, but it had been knocked from her skull.

Kira stopped, her lungs straining in the thin atmosphere. The draft had grown stronger, rushing past her ears as more oxygen poured out from the substation's ruptured seals. The wailing alarm sirens seemed to come from kilometers away.

She looked toward the end of the corridor and saw a dead end. *No,* she told herself. *To the left at the last branch, not right . . . you're almost there. . . .*

Turning, she could see past the junction of the main corridor, to the airlock's doorway. Metal glowed and screeched, as the APM beyond battered its way through the jagged opening. Bashir's face was just visible inside the machine.

Go. . . .

She staggered toward the airlock. The deck rose up and twisted, slamming her shoulder against the bulkhead. She managed to keep her balance, but thought for a moment that the impact had blinded her. She couldn't see the airlock's opening anymore; a wave of darkness had risen above her.

Then she saw the light cut through, the gleam of metal. And knew that he had found her.

"Kira . . ."

Hören could manage no more than a ragged gasp, his own chest heaving as his arm grasped round her shoulders, drawing her to him. The knife came up under her jaw, forcing her head back.

"I've waited . . ." She could barely hear him through the roaring wind. "For so long . . ."

The sound of metal ripping apart, distant as another world; she looked past Hören and saw the APM burst into the passageway, the jagged tooth of the broken doorway frame scraping a line down the armored shape. The jets at the APM's base flared brighter as it moved through the clearance between the bulkheads.

Another explosion, from what seemed only a few meters away; the air was pulled from Kira's mouth as she fell. The blow had torn Hören's grasp away; he toppled beside her.

A shape loomed over her. The metal carapace of the APM split open, revealing Bashir at its controls. He reached down and grabbed the collar of her uniform, dragging her onto her feet and toward him. He shouted something, but she couldn't hear what words came from his mouth.

With his other hand, Bashir pushed against another control; the APM rolled a few degrees, enough to lift Kira and let her fall inside. She landed heavily against Bashir's chest.

"Now, we're getting out of here—" He punched one of the switches, and the opening's metal edges moved toward each other.

Weariness claimed her; she felt herself collapsing, only the confines of the narrow space keeping her upright. She twisted about, watching the gap slide shut. The opening suddenly seemed to disappear, filled by darkness. And a face with maddened eyes.

His face.

A hand reached through and caught the front of her uniform, gathering the torn fabric into its fist, dragging her toward him. The edges closed on Hören's wrist as she braced her hands against the metal.

Light flared from the end of the corridor, in sync with the force that surged through the substation's frame. A silent torrent pulled taut the muscles of Hören's face as the last of the oxygen rushed out, the tatters of cloth around his chest and arms streaming into ragged pennants.

A warning light blinked on the APM's panel, as its air supply was sucked keening through the broken seal of the opening. Bashir brought up the thrust of the forward maneuvering jets, backing the APM toward the airlock.

Hören's fist stayed locked upon Kira, the white-knuckled fingers curving into claws, the nails sinking through and into the palm. The streaming air drew the rivulets of blood along the tendons of his forearm.

She grabbed the inside brace of the opening, her fingers catching at a thin metal ridge. Gasping for breath, she added the last reserves of her strength to that of the machine.

Bone cracked and splintered through flesh. The metal edges ground through the last shreds of tissue. The opening sealed shut as a wet thing loosed its grasp and slid away.

She had only a last glimpse of Hören, his face contorted beyond rage. With his broken arm hooked around a jet nozzle, he clung to the exterior of the

APM, his bloodied stump raised to batter against one of the windows.

The last explosion hit. The corridor erupted around the machine. Bashir had already worked the APM through the torn entrance of the airlock; the impact of the explosion tumbled it through the chamber . . .

And out.

To silence.

They drifted, the substation slowly turning and growing smaller against the stars.

The curved space of the APM fit tightly around its two occupants. She couldn't have pressed any closer to Bashir if she'd wanted to.

"I know it will be difficult—" He didn't turn his face toward her, but kept watching as he maneuvered the APM toward the shuttle. "But if you try not to get too excited, I think we have just enough oxygen left to get there."

CHAPTER
18

A SUBSTANTIAL INCREASE in communications traffic was noted.

The pitch and volume of Gul Tahgla's shouted words alone would have required an expanded bandwidth. As his voice came out of the overhead speaker, Bashir wished that it would have been possible to view him, as well.

"What is the meaning of this—"

Kira handled the comm chores; it was obviously something she had been looking forward to. "I repeat: this is Gamma Quadrant Remote Station, advising that you have entered a sector under Federation control. Please observe all appropriate navigational procedures. I'm sure you're familiar with them."

"Impossible!" The Cardassian's voice went up another level. "You can make no claim of sovereignty here . . . your substation unit is out of commission. . . ."

"We seem to be doing all right." Kira leaned back in her chair. "As you can tell, the minor technical problems we were having with our communications systems have been repaired. I assure you that we have met all the requirements for establishing a claim to this sector. This end of the stable wormhole will be administered by Starfleet, for the shared benefit of all the developed worlds. You are certainly free, as are all other vessels, to make arrangements to travel through. And just to show there are no hard feelings—" She let a smile come into her voice. "We'll drop any investigation into certain misleading statements of purpose that were made by you prior to leaving DS Nine. After all, we can't really blame you for trying, can we?" The smile grew even more malicious.

"This will go to the tribunal!" Gul Tahgla sounded as if he were about to explode from sheer frustrated wrath. "This is an outrage! You have no right—"

She hit one of the comm panel switches, cutting him off.

"What do you think their chances are?" Bashir stood at the other side of the shuttle's pilot area, tinkering with the external sensor readouts.

"Legally?" Kira shrugged. "They could make a case, depending upon how much they find out about what we've done here. But politically . . ." She shook her head. "The Cardassians aren't too popular, even with their allies. Any vote would go against them, just so most of the world would still have the access to the wormhole that the Federation has guaranteed."

"I wish we could get a look at Gul Tahgla's vessel right now." He knew there was no way of accomplishing that, not without revealing their ruse. They had piloted the cargo shuttle in back of the empty substation, hiding themselves from view by the approaching Cardassians. The direction of their comm signal gave the indication that the substation was on-line and inhabited. "I bet it's really shaking—what with Gul Tahgla bouncing off the walls."

She turned her smile toward Bashir. "Maybe we should turn the comm link back on. So we could listen."

He had left the others behind, back on the DS9 station. This way, piloting the runabout with no other crew, he had a precious moment of time to himself. It was when he had been alone before that things had happened. Mysteries beyond all comprehension.

While still on DS9, he had used the station's subspace link to communicate to Kira and Bashir aboard the cargo shuttle. "I have some news for you," their commander had spoken from the Ops deck. "The wormhole's entrance has reappeared in this sector. Preliminary monitoring indicates that it has resumed its previous stability. A relief vessel will reach you shortly."

Kira had answered him. "That's what we were hoping for. About the wormhole, I mean."

"I'll expect a full report on my desk as soon as possible. From both you and Doctor Bashir." He had allowed himself to make one small comment of praise before breaking the link. "Good work, Major." He knew that was all that would be necessary.

Inside the wormhole, he cut the buffered impulse engines to minimum forward thrust. And waited.

A voice moved inside his head.

It is the one called Benjamin Sisko. We recognize you.

He spoke aloud. "I'm flattered."

The other one, to whom we showed ourselves . . . he exists somewhere else now?

"Yes. He and the one who was with him; they're both safe now."

That one was not of time as you are, Benjamin Sisko. Not as wise. But he tried not to harm us. For that, we have made this universe, our flesh, that which you may enter again.

He nodded. "I suspected as much. You still have my promise about that, about the engines being buffered. You won't be hurt again."

That is a thing of time. The voice spoke gently. *You do not know, and we do not know.* It slowly began to fade. *Go to the ones of your kind, who wait for you.*

For a moment longer, he sat in silence. Then he reached out and brought the engines to full power.

He had recognized the voice, a memory that the wormhole's inhabitants had taken and used as their mask.

His wife's voice . . .

Eyes closed, he laid his head back against the seat. He wished they had shown her to him, as well.

She had cleaned herself up and changed into a fresh uniform. Exhaustion rolled through her muscles. She'd have to do some thinking when she got back to her quarters. There would be time for that now. Time to let the blood slow within her veins, to sleep and let dreams come. Instead of memories. The sickness, the weight of guilt and the past, had been purged from that blood. The dead slept; even Hören. She would give herself that much, as well.

As Bashir fastened a new bandage on the wound below her rolled-up sleeve, Kira watched him.

"You know," she said, "when we get back to DS Nine—"

He looked up at her. "What?"

"We can have that drink together then."